BEER GOGGLES

PREVIOUS TITLES BY BRANDON WILKINSON

- Memoirs of the Messed Up Minds
- Me 1 Arthritis 0: A Young Man's Real Life Journey to Beating the Disease

BEER GOGGLES

Brandon Wilkinson

iUniverse, Inc.
New York   Bloomington

Beer Goggles

iUniverse books may be ordered through booksellers or by contacting:

iUniverse
1663 Liberty Drive
Bloomington, IN 47403
www.iuniverse.com
1-800-Authors (1-800-288-4677)

ISBN: 978-1-4401-2851-6 (sc)
ISBN: 978-1-4401-2850-9 (ebook)

Printed in the United States of America

iUniverse rev. date: 03/10/2009

Acknowledgments

Thanks to all my friends and family who have supported me throughout my writing days.

It must be noted that any antics in the story relating to Uddingston or any of the surrounding areas are purely fictional.

Thanks again to my editor Melina who provided an invaluable and extremely timely service.

Introduction

Beer Goggles is not a book for the easily offended, and does contain more than a light scattering of crude language as well as sexually explicit material. At the end of the day though, the content is not unlike many of the real life pub culture activities that go on in Scotland every day of the week, particularly with regard to the language and overindulgence in alcohol.

I had originally planned to write the dialogue using Scottish slang, but decided I wanted to appeal to readers in the United States – where I now reside – as well as those back in my homeland. There is still an element of language at times that Scottish readers will be more familiar with, but it has been kept to a minimum, and within the context it has been written should be understandable by all.

Enjoy the ride.

The Weekend Countdown

F ive minutes to five and Stevie's workweek was almost over. An itch of excitement was running through his entire body as he could almost smell and taste the hops of his first beer.

Everyone claimed he had a drinking problem, but he couldn't disagree more. He did go to the bar virtually every night, got drunk, but *he* had no problem with it at all.

Four minutes to five and his arrogant colleague, Josephine, with her thick glasses, long greasy brown hair, and pimply skin, approached him looking for some meaningful input on the customer satisfaction project they had been working on for the last couple of weeks.

"What's the main element you think we should focus on for this project review we have on Monday morning?" said Josephine with much enthusiasm.

"Well, on Monday morning we should decide what we are going to focus on. I'm not talking about it now. I've got a five o'clock appointment with John Smith," replied Stevie bluntly.

"Oh OK, well tell John I said hi. He's the tall fair haired guy in our commercialization department, right?"

"You *really* don't drink do you? I was referring to the beer. I have an appointment at the bar."

Realizing her naivety and determining she'd have more success squeezing blood from a stone, Josephine turned on her heels and scurried back to her desk, shaking her head in frustration.

Two minutes to five. Stevie began shutting down his computer and stared at Maggie's tits across the open plan office. They were bursting out of her low-cut top like a couple of oversized beige balloons, totally fake, but breasts were breasts and he loved all shapes and sizes.

Maggie caught his eye and Stevie gave her a nod and a smile, which was immediately reciprocated. She knew he was checking them out, but appeared glad of the attention from a young guy, and continued putting folders away in the tall metal filing cabinet, but consciously sticking out her prize-winning assets even further than usual.

Maggie was in her late forties and well past her prime, but there *was* an element of sexiness to her appearance, even if it was in a slutty sense of the word. She obviously modeled her fashion sense on Britney Spears or one of those other nasty pop queens. Her body was hot though, legs like chiseled concrete and an ass so perfectly formed that it appeared like she'd had a couple of implants down there also. Her face though was as rough as a raccoon's scrotum, darkly tanned with wrinkle lines, probably a result of her tanning bed addiction. She was dried up like a prune. Stevie was convinced that if her cheeks were exposed to the howling wind on a cold Scottish morning, you could've grated a block of cheese on the side of her face.

That being said, Stevie was a young, testosterone-fuelled horn-dog, and would've slept with Maggie without hesitation should she raise the green flag; obviously doggy-style, with her face jammed firmly into an unappreciative feathered pillow.

One minute to five. Stevie considered nipping to the bathroom to crack one off. All the thoughts of huge naked breasts and taking Maggie from behind had him pitching a small puppy tent in the crotch of his pressed black trousers, but he refrained. The magnetic pull of that first beer was winning the tug-of-war. He was craving alcohol *that* badly.

Five o'clock chimed like a starter's pistol and he took off like a greyhound without saying goodbye to a single colleague. He didn't care much for any of them anyway. Most were tea-totallers who disapproved of his antics, and in a way that offended him, as he didn't approve of their lifestyles either.

There was a bar next to the office, but drinking and driving was actually something he disagreed with; maybe one of the few alcohol related subjects he did have in common with his co-workers. He didn't see the point in popping in for just a couple in order to remain under the legal limit; in his mind that was like being hungry and ordering a single chicken wing. A couple of beers might have worked for some folks, but not for him. Those first few tastes just got his juices flowing and made him yearn for more. Once he started, he rarely knew when to stop.

He pushed the accelerator hard as he raced along adjacent to the motorway. Friday evening traffic was typically busy, and today was no exception. Stevie was on the ball though and had opted for the back roads to avoid the congestion. It was a gamble, as many others often had the same idea, but today it had been a stroke of genius. From his vantage point he could see the stationary lines of traffic on the motorway and even hear the impatient honking of horns. He was relieved of his decision to take this usually slower alternate route, but Friday traffic was known for being a bitch, and whereas this way would normally add fifteen minutes to the journey on a quiet day, at this moment in time would likely save him anywhere between thirty minutes to an hour depending on whether road works or a serious accident were the cause of the current congestion.

Stevie McDonald had always enjoyed a social drink. It was a popular form of interaction in Scottish society, and there was a time in his life when he went to the bar for a couple of pints in order to mingle amongst friends. These days however, he planned social activities as an excuse to have a drink, and even then he'd often go there alone and sit at the bar by himself and play "kill the keg" on his own.

He *used* to be a fit guy, a keen rugby and football player, but those days were gone and his gradually increasing gut was a more than accurate indicator of a change in lifestyle. He was around five feet eleven, but when asked, he'd always say six feet. With the exception of the ever growing beer belly, his overall build was fairly stocky and muscular. He took after his father with his square, chiseled jaw structure and always maintained his clean-shaven face and short brown hair. As for dress sense he always went for the well known fashionable brands. He was a bit of a ladies man and enjoyed the female attention he regularly received. A relationship in his eyes was anything that lasted more than a week, and something casual was usually defined as beginning at last call and ending after breakfast. In a way he was the envy of his friends as a result of the number of sexual encounters he'd racked up over the years, and had probably seen more ladies arses than a seat in the local doctor's waiting room.

His drinking had escalated into another dimension in the last twelve months, and his usual care and attention on the work front had been deteriorating at more or less the same rate.

It had been a little over a year since the death of his father, and not much more than two since the passing of his mother. She had been the tragic victim of a car accident on her way home from her religious weekend shopping escapades. Some idiot on their mobile phone had run a red light and ploughed directly into her driver side door and she was killed instantly. Stevie was virtually inconsolable, but nothing in comparison to his father's grief. His parents had been like two peas in a pod all their married life. They'd worked at the same factory for twenty years, ate lunch together every day, and even went to the bar at weekends together with their close group of friends. It was fortunate for the idiot driver that he wasn't wearing a seat belt and was also killed on impact. If he had lived to tell the tale it would've only been a matter of time before Stevie and his father took the law into their own hands.

Since that day, Stevie's father was like a lost soul, and Stevie tried hard to take her place as the element of stability in his life. His father had lost the will to live and Stevie moved back into his parent's house and made the nightly dinner as his father had essentially stopped feeding himself. He did the washing also, as his father's previous immaculate appearance was gradually being replaced by that of a homeless tramp. The social drinking increased in occurrence, and four months after the loss of his wife, it would've been easier to count the times when John McDonald wasn't actually drinking. Stevie was drinking more also, figuring it was better to go with his father to the pub and keep an eye on his fragile state of mind. This pattern continued on, and Stevie believed he was finally getting through to John that all was going to be fine and that time was indeed a great healer. That's what he had thought, until the day he returned home from work to find his father hanging by the neck from the living room ceiling.

Stevie became like a recluse after that day. He loved his father more than life itself and had viewed himself as the rock to get him back on the straight and narrow. He *really* had been proud of himself until the day of the suicide. He *really* thought he'd been a major force in his father's *recovery*. John McDonald hadn't even left a note for Stevie, which was the main reason for Stevie's hibernation and daily drinking, just like his father before him. A note could've really made all the difference. What had John been thinking? Stevie was now left to wonder, searching for answers as to why, and speculating whether he could've done anything to prevent the tragedy. Had his father been giving off signs that he was *that* unstable? Had Stevie just not been paying attention, too busy selfishly claiming benefit for the suspected turnaround in his father's spirits and neglecting to notice a down turn right under his very nose? Stevie could answer none of these questions and racked his mind every minute of the day attempting to find an answer. Even when he wanted the internal interrogation to go away it would not. In fact it came on stronger, bashing him in mentally, pushing for a solution. Alcohol was the only thing that offered a temporary reprieve.

Over time though, Stevie managed to turn it around *a little*. His drinking had become an addiction though, and although he was mentally more stable, he did occasionally search his mind for answers to the puzzle of his dad's death. But the worst part was the periodic nightmares that plagued him. He'd see his father beside him, and he'd press for answers, but none was ever given.

Dad, I Wasn't Ready

"Another Guinness please Sandra," shouted Stevie.

The bar was empty other than Sandra, the red-headed and freckly-faced bartender, Doris the cleaning lady, who was adding a few finishing touches around the picture frames with her favorite brown feather duster, and Stevie, who sat in the corner next to the log fire that was blazing up a storm; an instant antidote to his chilled fingers and toes.

"You're hitting it very early today," stated Sandra, but with a twinkle in her eyes that indicated she wasn't exactly surprised.

She was right though, it *was* only 11:15 am, and The Crown bar had only opened its doors to the public fifteen minutes earlier, and Stevie was already on his second pint.

It had been a rough night for Stevie. He'd been thinking about his father and was unable to get to sleep, tossing and turning until around 3:00 am, before the sheer physical and mental exhaustion had caused him to pass out. He'd bolted upright in his bed just after 7:15 am, dripping with cold sweat. There was a perfect tracing of his upper torso sketched onto the mattress cover. The only thing missing was the white police chalk outline. He felt like he *was* dead, or at least he wanted to be.

It had been a horrific nightmare, and had such intensity to it that it would've probably caused Freddie Kruger to shit his pants.

His father was beginning to frequently enter his dreams again. They seemed to come and go in phases, but this one had been extremely striking, with a realness to it that had the hairs on his arms and neck standing upright for minutes after he'd rationalized that it had all been in his imagination.

Stevie had begun pacing his living room, again questioning the reasons behind the suicide. The dream was obviously a dream, but it had felt *so* lifelike, and even as he strutted around the room peering out of the front window as the sun began to rise, there was a presence in the air, almost like John McDonald was *actually* there with him in some spiritual capacity. If only he could've been. There was so much left to say, so many remaining questions, and so much still to understand. Every day though the potential answers only complicated those from the previous day.

He needed a drink. Alcohol wasn't the answer, but it was *his* answer. It relaxed him, and enabled him to forget and put all his issues aside, even if only temporarily. It was hours until opening time, but it would be worth the wait.

"Same again Stevie?" inquired Sandra as she pinned her long red hair into a ponytail.

"Absolutely," said Stevie, walking over to the bar and placing his empty glass down.

"Fresh glass?"

"Nah, the same one is fine," said Stevie, giving Sandra a forced smile.

Sandra knew Stevie was still going through much emotional pain. She'd known him and his father for several years, serving them both together on literally hundreds of occasions. She had lost her own mother a few years back as a result of lung cancer, so she could relate to the passing of a loved one, but could only imagine the degree of pain Stevie was going through due to the unexpectedness of a suicide.

Sandra was a reasonably attractive woman. She would never win any beauty contests, but her bubbly personality made up for any shortcomings in that area. She was petite with large breasts, and carried a little extra weight in the hips and arse department, but overall she wore it well. She was in her late thirties, about ten years Stevie's senior, and was essentially a single mother of two young boys; her husband having ran-off with another woman year's back and nobody knew where the hell he was.

Stevie watched intensely as she poured the Guinness, his mouth watering as she filled it three quarters full and the settling process commenced.

"Why don't you sit at the bar and keep me company? Doris just left and it'll probably be a good half hour before anyone else shows up. You're the first customer I've had before midday on a Saturday for quite some time," said Sandra, genuinely hoping he'd take her up on the offer and relieve her current boredom.

"Sounds good," said Stevie, this time with a sincere smile. "The chill is out of my fingers and toes now anyway, so I don't need to be beside the fireplace. It might've been sunny out this morning, but that cold wind was a bitch to walk in on the way here."

Sandra finished topping up the pint as Stevie went back to the corner table by the blazing fire to pick-up his black leather jacket and returned to the bar. He hung the coat over the back of the chair and took a hefty gulp of his new beer.

"Someone's thirsty this morning," said Sandra.

"Well, it's Saturday, and I don't have anything else planned for the day," said Stevie, removing a pack of Marlboro Lights from the inside pocket of his jacket.

Sandra picked up her lighter and flicked on the flame.

"Cheers sweetheart," said Stevie, leaning forward and lighting the cigarette from her outstretched hand and taking an almighty drag. "You can't beat your first smoke of the morning," he said, as Sandra sparked one up also.

"That's true. It only gets better if the first one in the morning is right after having sex," replied Sandra, starting to giggle.

"Well it is still technically the morning and we've only just sparked these up," said Stevie with a wink.

"Are you suggesting what I think you are young Mr. McDonald?"

"I might be," replied Stevie nervously. "It didn't offend you did it?"

"Not at all, I was just wondering if you were joking or being serious."

"What if I said I was being serious?" said Stevie, wondering where the conversation was headed.

Sandra gave him a sultry look.

"Let's just say I'll be in the ladies bathroom for the next two minutes, so arrive at whatever conclusion you like," she said, immediately turning her back on him, lifted up the detachable part of the bar, and made her way through the wooden archway that led to the bathrooms.

Stevie was rooted to the spot, virtually in disbelief. He had originally been kidding, but had wanted to sleep with Sandra for a long time now. He was just surprised that she was up for it, but decided to move fast, so got up and made his way through the wooden archway, popping a stick of gum into his mouth as he went.

The door to the ladies room creaked loudly as Stevie gently tried to open it. It was just typical, the quieter he was trying to be the noisier he was being. Stevie stepped inside. The bathroom was small in size; floored with white tiles, white painted walls, and directly ahead were black sinks with silver taps. There was a lemon freshness smell in the air; no doubt a result of Doris's earlier cleaning.

"Is that you?"

It was Sandra's voice coming from one of the three cubicles on the right hand side of the room.

"Who else would it be?" said Stevie sounding confused.

"Just hurry up and get in here you stupid boy," said Sandra opening the cubicle door furthest to the right.

Stevie walked into the cubicle and locked the door behind him before turning to face Sandra, who was in the process of removing her tight black long-sleeved t-shirt. Exposed was a crisp looking white bra. Stevie stared, seemingly unable to take his eyes off her massive boobs.

"Just you stand there. I'm sure this bra can take itself off," said Sandra sarcastically, and seeming very eager to get the show on the road.

"Oh shit, I'm sorry sweetheart, I was just admiring your fine pair," said Stevie, arms now around Sandra's back and unclipping the bra strap.

"Well save the admiring for when you're looking at them from behind the bar. Now pull up my skirt," hastened Sandra, pulling down Stevie's fly and slipping out his penis.

He was solid as a rock already, and had been since the unexpected exchange at the bar. Sandra's red skirt was one of those long, tight ones that caused women to sort of walk from the knees down. Stevie pulled it up firmly and really had to work to get it over her child-bearing hips, but once it was over them they acted well to prevent it slipping back down.

He looked down in awe as Sandra wasn't wearing any panties. The carpet certainly did match the curtains, as a bright red bush like a privet hedge seemed to be draped around her vagina lips. Stevie liked the "au natural" look at times, but had to fight his laughter as he thought this must be what an axe wound looked like on an orangutan's back.

"Are you just going to stare at that as well?"

"Not at all, I'm dying to get in there," said Stevie, frantically pulling a condom from his wallet. He ripped open the square package and rolled it on with the ease at which he'd removed Sandra's bra. He was quite the expert when it came to rubbers and underwear.

They kissed passionately, Sandra leaning back on the side cubicle wall, right foot on top of the toilet seat like a pirate on a treasure chest. Stevie maneuvered himself with a dip of his knees and slipped a couple of fingers in between her blazing bush, before firmly slipping his erect penis into her. Sandra let out a huge groan as he pumped away vigorously. It was sliding in and out with ease, and although it wasn't the smallest cathedral his bishop had worked in, he *was* enjoying it. She was flowing like Niagara Falls and he could feel her juices beginning to run down his thighs. It was a massive turn-on.

"OH, OH, OH," yelped Sandra.

"Yeah sweetheart, can you feel it?" replied Stevie, chuffed to bits that he was getting such a positive reaction from an older woman.

"No Stevie, stop a minute, it's my right calf muscle, it's starting to cramp. We need to change positions."

Stevie seemed a little disappointed at not being the reason behind the loud cries, but turned her around for some doggie style. She was bent over at ninety degrees, hands placed on the top of the toilet cistern.

This was more like it he thought, as Sandra moaned loudly, telling him it was now going in really deep and to go harder and faster. He didn't need to be told twice and began to speed up his hip gyrations until his arse was going back and forth like a fiddler's elbow.

A bell sounded just as they simultaneously climaxed. It was a faint chime, but was enough to cause Sandra to bolt upright from her crouched position.

"Holy shit," she said, pulling away from Stevie so furiously that the condom came off and landed in the underpants around his ankles. "That was the service bell at the bar. Somebody is here!"

She frantically pulled her red skirt down and threw on her black shirt, pushing past Stevie and made her way out of the cubicle.

"Aren't you forgetting something?" said Stevie smugly.

"What?"

"Do you want me to keep your bra as a memento?"

"Shit, keep it, leave it in here, I really don't care right now."

Sandra made her way out the door in a hurry.

Stevie bent down and reached into his underwear, delicately removing the used condom with his thumb and index finger before rolling it up in some toilet paper and flushing it down the pan.

Sandra composed herself the best she could before making her way through the wooden archway and back into the bar area. The fair skin on her face was bright red from all the exertion, and not unlike a milk-bottle-white Scottish lass who'd just spent an afternoon sunbathing.

"Oh, you *are* here," said the elderly grey haired gentleman standing at the bar wearing a long coat and a tartan cap. "I was beginning to think it was self-service today," he said with a chuckle, and seeming very happy with his witty remark.

"Sorry about that Jack, I was just finishing up some cleaning in the ladies. It's hot work in there. I think I'm still a bit flushed," replied Sandra, touching both cheeks with her hands.

Jack initially seemed satisfied with the reply until he noticed the half-full pint of Guinness sitting on a beer mat and the leather jacket on the back of one of the chairs.

"Is there someone else here?"

"Yeah, young Stevie McDonald should be around somewhere. Not sure where he is at the moment, but he was sitting there when I popped through to the bathroom."

Technically it wasn't a complete lie, as Stevie had been sitting there when she left the bar area, but she knew he was probably still in the ladies room cleaning himself up.

Just at that moment Stevie came sauntering through, looking more than a little flush in the face himself.

"Hey Jack, how you doing?"

"Not bad son, how's yourself? Were you through there doing a bit of scrubbing yourself or maybe you were giving Sandra a hand cleaning out her pipes," said Jack, again ecstatic with his wit as he pointed at Stevie's red face.

"Cleaning out Sandra's pipes! Fucking hell Jack, take it easy mate. If you must know I was in the gents constipated. Not sure what I ate, but it wasn't breaking down too easily. Shit, I nearly gave myself a hernia and a burst blood vessel in my temple trying to squeeze it out. I nearly called the hospital to schedule a caesarian section, but fortunately the little bastard finally surrendered. Think my arse is still bleeding though. Christ, I took a look at the toilet paper after I wiped and it was like looking down at a miniature Japanese flag."

"Jesus Christ Stevie, too much information. Look I apologize for suggesting you and Sandra were at it, but I was just messing with you," replied Jack, genuinely feeling bad, and turning a little red-faced himself.

"I know you were Jack, no worries. And I apologize for being a little too graphic, but it was quite a strenuous ordeal for me in there," said Stevie, turning to an open-mouthed Sandra and flashing her discrete wink as Jack stood there not feeling quite so delighted with his humorous comments.

They all settled down and their faces returned to the usual paler than pale color. Jack was entertaining Stevie with stories of what the village used to be like back in the early fifties, detailing what bars were around then as well as telling him he was sitting in the same spot he was now, the very day the builders put in the wooden archway that led through to the toilets.

"The bar was still open while they were doing that work?" said Stevie, wondering if Jack was being sincere or just plain full of shit.

"Of course it was son. There were none of these safety rules and regulations in place back then. If the bartenders could pull a pint the place was open."

"What if you needed a piss?"

"Well, if you could get through to the bathroom if the workers were on a break or something, that's what you did. If you couldn't, you went outside and around the back of the building and went up against the wall and came back in and continued with your pint and conversation."

"What if you needed a shit while they were still working?"

"Well Stevie, you either went home, found another bar, or crapped your pants."

They both laughed emphatically, Jack again back on track at being delighted with his wit, before excusing himself to the bathroom.

Sandra scurried over to Stevie.

"I really thought we were busted there."

"I think he bought the constipation story," said Stevie.

"I think so, very creative."

"I have my moments."

"By the way, thanks for the sex, it's been a while and you really hit the spot."

"You weren't bad yourself sweetheart."

"Maybe we can do it again sometime, no strings attached of course. Although maybe we can wait until after I close up the next time or even in the comfort of a bed or something," said Sandra, gazing into his eyes.

"I'd like that," replied Stevie, simulating a kiss with his lips.

Just then Jack returned from his pee.

"Nice job washing down the ladies room Sandra," said Jack. "It smells really fresh in there, but I think you left your wash cloth behind," he laughed, swinging her white bra in the air.

The Quality Controller

Work for Stevie used to be about pride, responsibility, and ultimately doing the right thing. Now though, those values had become an afterthought, and his only concern was maintaining employment in order to pay the bills and finance his daily trips to the bar.

Customer service was his business. His title was Quality Control Manager at a Telecommunications call center operation. It was his job to ensure that the folks answering the phones were professional, looking out for the best interest of the paying consumers, and ultimately making sure they were providing the correct solutions to problems in a timely and efficient manner. He and his staff would randomly listen in to live calls and document any deficiencies in performance and turn them into corrective action plans. Many times an improvement in the training provided to staff was the root cause, other times it was a case of a firm verbal boot up the arse for the offending workers, telling them they were now being watched and to leave their personal problems and resulting bad attitudes at home in the future.

Rarely did Stevie write anyone up for attitude issues. He felt it would've been extremely hypocritical on his part to do so. His work ethic sucked right now, and the only difference between the customer service representatives and him was that the reps spoke *directly* to the customers.

Before the loss of his father, Stevie was known as a bit of a bastard, a real company man totally focused on improving the business. He'd even previously requested that every call center agent display a huge photograph of their partner and/or children directly in front of them on their desks. He then initiated the "let me hear you smile" program, citing that anytime they felt their attitude beginning to subside, they had to look directly at the family members staring back at them.

"These people who call us are essentially the ones paying your wages. If they are paying your wages, basically they are feeding your families. Think about that *every time* you look at their faces, and *let me hear you smile*, because I *will* be listening," he said firmly in a speech to the masses.

It had been a successful initiative, but was now losing a little momentum as a result of his fading motivation. He had to be careful. If worker performance started to significantly drop, then the buck would stop at him and he could not afford that to happen. He knew it as well, but his mind was so in the gutter right now that he didn't give a shit.

Four o'clock sounded and Stevie excused himself for the day.

"Sorry boss, I need to leave. I've got a doctor's appointment in forty minutes."

"And you're just remembering now," replied Rob Andrews sternly.

Rob was Stevie's manager, but truth be told he was afraid of his junior. Rob was about five feet five inches tall in his platform shoes, built like a golf club, and had less fat on him than a butcher's apron. He tried to be a tough guy; making up for the bullying during his school years, but it didn't fly with Stevie.

"You know boss, I did just remember. It's been such a busy day that it totally slipped my mind."

"Well get on your way, but I expect you to make up the hour sometime this week."

"Not a problem boss, I'll be here bright and early tomorrow."

There was no doctor's. There *was* a pub appointment though. One thing Stevie was was smart, and knew how to play the business game. He knew Rob was a pussy making up for schoolyard beatings, but made sure he addressed him as "boss" all the time. It gave Rob the feeling of being in control, even although he wasn't.

It was early and Stevie knew he'd likely skip the rush hour traffic, so he ploughed his way along the motorway at around ninety miles per hour, keeping an eye in the rear-view mirror for any cops sneaking up on him.

He arrived back at his second floor, one bedroom flat in record time, dropping his car off in the car park and began the short walk to The Crown. He'd contemplated taking a quick shower, but his earlier statement to Rob about it having been a hectic day was a complete smokescreen as he'd barely broken sweat.

The main street was bustling for a Wednesday. He passed the barbershop and gave Danny and Andy, the hairdressers, his customary wave before reaching the traffic lights at the village cross – as it was called. It was classed as the center of the "town" of Uddingston, but the word town was stretching the meaning a little and implied it was more substantial in size than it actually was.

He made a left turn at Newman's, the solicitors, followed by a sharp left into The Crown. The clock struck 4:39 pm and Stevie was impressed he was a minute early for his doctor's appointment.

The bar had a moderate scattering of the usual suspects and there was even an elderly guy sitting beside "Jack the Bra Hunter," who had a dog in toe. The little Scottish terrier was happily slurping on a little bowl of water that was crammed with ice cubes, as his master waffled away in conversation with Jack, probably more stories about the way things used to be.

Stevie gave Jack a nod before taking the same seat he'd occupied the previous weekend. He noticed Jack whispering into the ear of his old crony and they both looked up to give Stevie a stare. No doubt the story about him and Sandra was now making the rounds.

Sandra was part of the reason he was there. He didn't really fancy her or want anything of significance to evolve, but he *was* feeling horny and she was definitely a frisky one that he wanted to get into the bedroom in a relaxed setting to see how freaky she could really get. Maybe she'd even let him give her little red hedge a trim.

"Guinness Stevie?" said Sandra, appearing a little self-conscious, no doubt a result of Jack spreading the gossip.

"Yes please sweetheart. Are you getting off anytime soon?"

"I get off at five."

Stevie knew the shift change was coming, but acted as though he was surprised. He wanted to tell her that if she played her cards right she'd be getting off in an entirely different way by 5:15 pm if she wanted, but decided to play it cool.

"You fancy doing something when you're done?"

"I'd love to Stevie, but I need to pick the kids up from my father's tonight. It's his domino night at the miners club on a Wednesday so I can't even ask him to keep them longer. Friday would be good for me though if you want to grab a bite to eat or *something*," said Sandra with a wink.

"No worries sweetheart, I'll try and pop in on Friday then, but I'm not quite sure what's going on yet."

Stevie was genuinely disappointed as he was looking for some company, but knew he had no intention of popping in on Friday as he had a night out planned with the boys, but just incase that fell through he didn't tell Sandra the specifics in order to have some sex to fall back on.

It didn't solve his dilemma this evening though. He didn't want to go home alone and end up sitting around thinking about his dad. His friends weren't available until Friday, so he'd just have to slug it out on his own at the bar for a while, which was hardly a rare occurrence, but he was just feeling a little sorry for himself today.

Sandra's replacement for the evening was Stephanie, a woman possibly as old as the bar itself, and one who had probably done to Jack in the bathroom as Sandra had to Stevie. She had a heart of gold though, but was as friendly on the eye as a dash of Tabasco sauce.

Despite the unfortunate change in scenery, Stevie stuck it out for over a couple of hours, wolfing down the pints like a Greek marathon runner on cups of water. His head was spinning, but that wasn't an unusual scenario.

A younger crowd had assembled in the corner by the fireplace. They were obviously novices to a drinking session as they were already losing all inhibition after a couple of beers and were firing money into the jukebox like it was going out of fashion.

The bar began filling up as the Glasgow Rangers versus Hibernian match kicked off on the large screen in the opposite corner from the fireplace. Stevie had one eye on the game and the other on the younger crowd. There were six of them; four guys and two girls, and the little cute brunette was instantly grabbing his interest. When he heard the words "party back at my place" coming from one of the guys, more of his attention was on their proceedings than there was on the football.

Stevie approached the now vacant jukebox.

"Any of you guys got change for a ten?" said Stevie to the young group, holding out a ten pound note.

"Let me check for you mate," said the tallest guy of the bunch, reaching into the pocket of his jeans. "Here you go," he said, counting out a five and five ones, and they made the exchange.

"Thanks chief," replied Stevie. "You guys got any requests?"

"Anything by Coldplay would be good," said the little brunette's buddy, who resembled a younger and dumpier version of Rosanne Barr.

"Excellent choice, I like those guys. I'm pretty sure that lead singer guy is partial to a spliff or two, so that's good enough for me."

"You got any?" said young Rosanne in a lowered voice as she glanced warily around the bar.

"Got any what?" replied Stevie, acting dumb, but knowing precisely what she was asking.

"Any weed," she said, really whispering.

"Not on me right now, but I've got some at home."

Rosanne's eyes lit up, as did all her friends. The tall guy who'd given Stevie the change leaned over to him from his chair.

"Hey man, we're all heading back to my gaff for a bit of a party in a wee while. If you want to supply the gear you can drink as much as you like. My fridge is stacked with beer and I've even got a few unopened bottles of Smirnoff and Absolut. It's up to yourself chief, but you're more than welcome big man."

"Sounds like a plan mate. Where do you live?"

"Over in Hamilton. We can get a couple of taxis."

"Alright man, sounds good. Let me nip back to my flat and I'll grab the gear. I should be back in about ten minutes."

And with that Stevie went back to the bar, chugged his beer down and went on the short walk to get his bag of grass.

His head was really spinning on the way back to The Crown and he started to question what he was doing. He didn't even know these people and was carrying enough weed to potentially get into *a lot* of trouble, but the prospect of more socializing to keep his mind off everything, more *free* drink, and possibly getting a little action with the young brunette caused all the doubts to be flushed from his mind.

He opened the door to the bar and felt the heat from inside rush past him. It felt good and was a welcome reprieve from the chilling wind. He shouted over to Stephanie for a pint of Guinness before glancing over to the eager-looking twenty year olds.

The tall guy gave him a nod, which Stevie reciprocated, signaling he had the drugs. They all looked back at him, smiles of excitement gracing their youthful features.

Stevie supped down about half of his pint and ventured back over to the young crew.

"Just let me know when you want me to call a couple of taxis," said Stevie to the tall and slim guy.

"Already taken care of mate. They should be here in about ten minutes."

"No worries chief. I'll finish up my pint and we can get this party on the road."

Two taxis pulled up outside the bar as they all waited by the grey stone steps in the cold, yet fresh, Scottish air. Both cars were on the rundown side; one a blue Ford Sierra, probably a 2001 model, and the other a white Vauxhall Vectra, an 04 or 05, but obviously hadn't seen a wash in six months and had a significant dent in the bodywork around the back right wheel arch that made it look in even worse shape than the Sierra. Around the dent, some smart arse kid or some unemployed adult with nothing better to do with his life must've taken a permanent black marker pen and circled the damage, sketching in an arrow pointing to it and writing the word "OUCH" beside it. It was actually very comical, but was surprising the car driver hadn't made any attempt to remove it; well, surprising until Stevie climbed into the back seat.

He opened the door beside the damage and stepped in, feeling a solid metal object crush under his shoe. It was an empty can of Coke and was surrounded with a variety of food wrappers and what appeared to be paper used to roll-up fish suppers. The smell inside the vehicle was as close to fresh as the floor was tidy. The ringleader of the young group was sitting up front with the driver and two of the other guys were in the back with Stevie. He'd been hoping to be the meat in a two girl sandwich, but wasn't exactly surprised they'd been ushered into the Sierra with the least popular guy of the bunch.

"Can we smoke in here?" said the young ringleader to the little fat driver.

"No, no smoking in the car mate, sorry. I smoke myself, but I need to think about all the other passengers I have. I don't want to stink up the place with the smell of cigarettes."

"Fair enough," was the young guy's reply.

The irony was incredible. For one, the inside of the car resembled a litter dumping ground. Secondly, deodorant was obviously not high on the driver's priority list; the pungent smell of his body odor was like a mix of lumpy milk and an athlete's running shoe. Thirdly, a burning Marlboro Light would've been as effective as a Glade air freshener in the current environment. The stench really was potent, and Stevie gave a look to the other guys in the back with him – whose names he'd already long forgotten – but it was as though it didn't bother them.

The journey was thankfully a fairly short one and Stevie closed off his nose and breathed through his mouth, slightly paranoid that the fustiness from the interior would taint his breath for the remainder of the night as a result.

There was virtually no words spoken during the ride; the only interruption to the silence being the occasional interaction between the middle-aged plump driver and the dispatch controller via his little walkie-talkie.

The housing estate they pulled into was as rough as a badger's arse; graffiti-covered walls, an array of shady-looking characters walking around, and every other terraced home had at least one boarded up window. Stevie was too buzzed to worry about the potentially dangerous surroundings, but was feeling a little sorry for the folks living in such an environment, particularly the kids.

The unemployment rate of the area pulled the percentage of the town up considerably. There was no doubt there were the folks content to laze around most of the day, smoking pot to pass the time and picking up the weekly government check and supplementing their income via petty crime when required. That was true of many, but there was no doubt there were honest living people visiting the job center on a daily basis, trying their hearts out to land whatever menial task they could in order to put food on the table. It *was* the kids that suffered. What chance did they have in life growing up in such a way? Either they would fall into the lay about mode or end up forced to leave school at the earliest possible age in order to bring in some dough and contribute to the monthly rent and grocery bills. It was a reality check for Stevie and he'd never felt as fortunate.

The taxi pulled over at a corner house of a terraced row with no boarded windows, which was at least a good beginning. To the left of the house was a separate wooden garage that looked as though it had been there so long that they'd built the houses around it. A four foot high metal grated fence surrounded the perimeter of the row of homes and was lined on the inside with a thick green hedge that was finely trimmed no more than three inches above the top of the fence. The surprise for Stevie was the pristine nature of the street in comparison to the others they'd seen on the ride since entering the community. He'd almost started to make the comment about what a shithole the estate was but managed to bite his lip just in time, realizing that *at least* one of the strangers in the car lived there, and that he wasn't sitting beside his friends like he usually was when they ventured out of the local village for the night.

"OK boys, let's get this party started," said the leader in the front beside the driver, opening his door and stepping out without even an offer of some cash to put towards the fare.

Stevie figured it must've been his place and as he *was* supplying the beverages for the night it was a reasonable action to take.

"I'll get this guys," said Stevie to the two in the back with him as they both reached into their pockets.

"Cheers Big Man," replied the kid directly beside him with the short dark hair and acne scars.

Stevie wasn't necessarily much bigger than any of them but it was recognition of his seniority in years. Even though he was supplying the dope he felt it was appropriate to pay. When he met the kids in The Crown he noticed the two remaining in the car with him looked a little on the scruffy and neglected side. Now he figured they probably lived around these parts also and likely in one of the grubbier streets so weren't exactly rolling in money. He handed the driver the cash that included a healthy tip, and hoped the burly, smelly guy would put it towards a stick of deodorant and a little Christmas tree cut-out air freshener to hang from his rear-view mirror. He could only hope for future passengers but wasn't too optimistic.

They entered the house, Stevie following last, and they made a sharp right turn in to a square-shaped cozy living room. It was anything but modern-looking; thick shag-pile red carpet with a yellow floral arrangement entwined, plain yellow wallpaper on each wall, and a brown sofa arrangement consisting of a three-seater and two armchairs, looking as though they'd been sat in since the early seventies.

"Make yourself comfortable chief and roll a couple of fat ones," said the leader of the gang as he handed Stevie a can of Tennent's lager.

Stevie had never asked, but it was obvious the guy was the home owner.

"No worries mate, you keep the lager flowing and I'll keep the joints coming."

The leader flashed Stevie a wink and made his way back to the kitchen. Stevie sat in one of the armchairs situated directly ahead of a light brown cabinet with a glass front that contained a collection of tiny porcelain animal figures on various shelves. He began using the arm of the seat to lay down his cigarette skins until the acne-scarred kid pulled over a little knee-high glass table to assist with the assembly.

"Thanks young man," said Stevie to the kid, who was looking eager for a puff.

Stevie populated the table with his papers and a small, clear Ziploc bag containing a mix of grass and a resin cube. He took out two cigarette papers, glued them together flat with his saliva like he was licking the back of a stamp, and rolled the middle of them around a cigarette from his Marlboro box, forming a momentary u-shape before gravity flattening it out ever so slightly. Next he busted up the cigarette, spilling the tobacco into his open palm before spreading it out along the length of the two thin papers. Taking the cube of hash in between the thumb and index finger of his left hand and sparking on his lighter with his right, he began burning the corner of the resin until it started to smoke. He blew on it a little and then crumbled off the edge, trailing an even proportion of the black granules across the top of the tobacco line in the cigarette papers. He put the remainder of the cube back into his clear bag and started to roll the papers into a fine cylindrical shape. Stevie glanced up briefly and there were now many eyes watching him, most of them fixed on the ever evolving joint like they were tigers staring down a gazelle. Unfazed, he went back to work, forming a picture perfect spliff looking not unlike one of the flawlessly formed Marlboro's in his packet. Stevie had a talent for rolling smokes, and there were very few people, probably in the entire country that were any better than him. If it ever became an Olympic event he would definitely be a gold medal contender. On the off chance dope was ever legalized it might've been in the interest of the Scottish Parliament to pursue it as an event as the current ones weren't exactly piling up the medals.

Next he tore off about a centimeter worth of cardboard from the top of his cigarette pack and formed that into a tiny cylinder and pushed it into one end of the joint, tucking in the slight overlap of the Rizla paper to act as a filter. He sparked the other end with his lighter and took a hefty drag, holding the smoke in his lungs before exhaling a thick cloud out into the living room.

"Here you go chief, grab yourself some of this," he said to the acne-scarred kid, holding out the joint in his direction.

The young man was on it in a flash with a huge smile on his face, showing his wonky nicotine-stained teeth. Meticulous dental care was obviously not high up on his family's priority list and Stevie felt even sorrier for him than he had before.

"Cheers Big Man," replied the kid. "Fuck dude, you'll need to teach me how to roll like this. This one is tight," he said, examining it closely. "I can usually get one going but it ends up looking like a wind sock and if I'm fucked up it's so baggy that half the gear ends up on the floor," he said, pointing to a burn mark on the carpet, obviously an unfortunate incident from a previous party.

The kid took a puff and handed it back.

"That's some good shit Big Man," he said in a slightly higher pitch than before.

"Yeah it's some of that good Moroccan shit. Half a joint of it is usually enough to fuck you up pretty good. Listen, take this one back and share it with your buddies and I'll put another few together."

"Seriously?"

"Absolutely, I'm a guest here tonight. You guys batter in and have some fun."

"Cheers Big Man, you're the best."

"What's your name again? I know you guys told me already but I've got a memory like a sieve."

"The name's Thomas," he replied, shaking Stevie's hand. "What's your name again chief? My memory is probably even worse than yours."

"Stevie."

"You're a good man Stevie," said Thomas before disappearing through to the kitchen with the cigarette.

More bodies filtered into the house, most hanging around the living room and helping themselves to vodka and a few went through to the kitchen to announce their arrival. Stevie focused on his rolling process until five joints were spread out on the small glass table. He picked himself off the chair and lifted the smokes and half-empty beer and quickly scanned the characters in the room before heading through to the kitchen.

The guys from The Crown sat at a round wooden table playing poker; the leader of the gang dealing out the cards. The theme of the kitchen was just as old-fashioned as the living room. The cooker in the far corner was white, except for a few gravy stains around one of the rings. Slightly up from that separated by a set of built in drawers was a small, white stubby-looking fridge.

Stevie sat one of the joints down in front of the leader.

"Knock yourself out chief," said Stevie, nodding at the roll-up and giving him a smile.

"Cheers partner. You want in on the game?"

"Maybe later mate. Think I'm just going to throw a few beers back, smoke one of these and chill out for a while."

"No worries man. Just help yourself to the cans in the fridge. There's vodka and whiskey out in the living room as well."

"Thanks bud, I might just do that."

The two girls from The Crown were sitting on top of the kitchen counter tops watching the card game like a couple of cheerleaders. They stared at Stevie with puppy dog eyes as he sparked up one of his joints and took a drag.

"Here you go ladies. Get one of these down you," he said, handing them one of his spares.

"Thanks Stevie," said the young cute one, eagerly taking the cigarette as her little dumpy friend magically produced her lighter.

"You're very welcome girls."

He was pleasantly surprised she'd remembered his name. Maybe she fancied him but he couldn't be sure. It was a lot easier for them to remember one name rather than a bunch that he had tried – and failed – to enter into his memory bank.

He wandered back into the living room and the party was in full swing. Techno tunes blared from the cheap-looking stereo system in the corner beside an oak cabinet with an array of alcohol bottles and glasses on top. The place was virtually a sausage festival; about twenty in the room, four of them female, three hand in hand with their apparent boyfriends and the other was a tall, long haired bleached blonde girl with a pointed nose, who had less body fat on her than Calista Flockhart. From across the room she seemed anything but appealing, but in the current situation it was a toss up between her and the cutie on the kitchen counter.

Half the room was in the middle of the floor dancing around as though they had claustrophobic, epileptic ferrets stuffed into their underwear. The three couples were squeezed onto the three-seater like sardines in a tin; two side by side and the other with the girl perched on her man's lap.

The girl with the pointed nose looked a little lost. She was glancing aimlessly around the room as her right foot tapped furiously to the music, occasionally sipping on what appeared to be a glass of vodka and coke; her nose almost dunking itself into the liquid every time she took a swig.

Stevie walked over to where Pointy Nose was, dragging on his joint, and stood next to her. She really was tall, eye to eye level with him, but as he peeked down he noticed the five inch platform heels she was sporting. She was dressed like a hooker; short white mini-skirt and a black off-the-shoulder top. A more conservative outfit would have done her some justice, but her current attire only exposed and emphasized her thin chicken legs and boney shoulders.

"I'd ask you to dance but The Prodigy isn't really my thing. I'm more of a rock guy myself," said Stevie as he stood shoulder to shoulder with her, both of them facing the enthusiastic ravers.

"Yeah, me too. I like Nickelback and maybe some Franz Ferdinand, but I hate this shit. I still find myself tapping along to the beats but I really don't like it."

"Smoke?" said Stevie handing the joint towards her.

"Sure," she replied, her skinny fingers taking it from him and putting it to her lips.

Her lips were full and plump, and delightfully surprising considering the rest of her. There was probably more bulk on them than any other part of her body and were striking enough to neutralize out her nose and deem her overall face reasonably attractive. They *screamed* blow job and were covered in a fine film of gloss that gleamed seductively every time she looked in his direction.

She handed back the joint to him.

"Thanks, that's some good stuff."

"You're welcome. What's your name?"

"Nilda."

"Nice to meet you Nilda, I'm Stevie."

"Nice to meet you Stevie," she replied, extending her dainty hand for a shake.

Her hand felt tiny in his palm and he resisted applying any pressure in order to save a trip to the emergency room. Stevie was such a dog. His first thought after the hand shake with her minuscule fingers was that his cock would appear monstrous if she ever grabbed hold of it.

Stevie took another puff of his joint and handed it back to Nilda.

"That's an unusual name you have," said Stevie. "I've never heard it before."

"Yeah, my mum and dad were a couple of real hippies back in the day and wanted to go for something unusual. It's Italian in origin. They went backpacking across Europe many moons ago and it was the name of the daughter of an old couple from Napoli. They stayed at their bed and breakfast place and said they fell in love with the name back then, and here I am."

"I like it," smiled Stevie.

"Thanks," replied Nilda, blushing a little.

"You having fun?" he asked.

"I'm having more fun now that I've found some decent weed."

"Well don't go too crazy on that stuff. It'll fuck you up pretty quickly."

"I was planning on getting fucked up tonight anyway; if it's not with dope it's going to be alcohol."

"Fair enough, just don't pass out on me before I get a chance to dance with you. Maybe they'll put on some better music later."

"I know when to stop."

"So is that a yes to a dance later?"

"If they put on some better music I'll dance with you," she said, exposing a smile.

She had a slight space between her two front teeth but they were extremely white and a serious contrast to the other hillbillies in the house.

"Sounds good. I might even change the music myself so that can happen."

"Good luck with that. Half these idiots would probably stick a knife in you if you mess around with their techno."

"You might have a good point," replied Stevie, checking out the ravers on the floor, their arms flapping around like a fat kid in a lake who couldn't swim.

"Yeah, they're really into this shit. They're here most weekends popping ecstasy and dancing enough to take the tread off their shoes."

"Why don't they just go to a club?"

"Most of them have no money. By the time they get their drugs there's not a lot left over to feed themselves never mind anything else."

"So, what do you do for a living Nilda?" said Stevie, eager to change the flow of conversation.

"I'm a dental technician."

It certainly explained the pearly white teeth.

"That's pretty cool."

"It's not bad. It pays like shit which means I still need to live with my parents, but it's a safe enough job and there are some decent benefits. It's boring at times though and really disgusting. All I do is help with x-rays, hand the dentist his instruments, and use the little Hoover to suck out the excess saliva when the patients have their mouths open. A lot of the folks have some really skanky teeth and a few guys who come in from time to time have breath bad enough to knockout a dog."

"Sounds awesome!"

"Yeah, but as I said it's secure and they're helping me pay for the course I'm taking. I'm studying to be a hygienist."

"That's great. I really admire people who try to better themselves," he said genuinely.

"Thanks Stevie, that's really nice of you," she replied, looking sweetly into his eyes.

She appeared to enjoy the confirmation from a third party that the route she was taking was a positive measure.

"Can I get you a refill on your drink? Vodka and coke, right?"

"That's right, but I'll come over there with you, I could use a brief change of scenery."

"After you sweetheart," he said, ushering her in the direction of the alcohol bottles.

Nilda made her way gingerly across the room in her platform shoes. Stevie discreetly checked out her arse but there was no evidence of a wiggle even though her short white skirt was super tight. She wasn't too bad though, and after talking to her and establishing she was fairly bright, she had only elevated herself on the attractiveness scale.

Stevie swiveled open the red cap of a bottle of Smirnoff and began pouring it into Nilda's empty glass.

"That's plenty," she said, but Stevie continued for a second or so before stopping.

"Sorry, I've always got a heavy hand when it comes to pouring drinks. I just feel the bars screw us over with their inflated prices and fifth of a gill measures, so when I get a chance to do a free pour I usually get more than generous."

"Oh is that what it is. Here was me hoping you were trying to get me drunk."

"You were hoping?"

Nilda's cheeks turned bright red.

"Well it's not too often I get much attention from boys. Look, I find you attractive and most of the time I'm too shy to say or do anything unless I'm at least tipsy. Oh my God, you weren't hitting on me were you?" said Nilda, now appearing horrified.

"No I was totally hitting on you. You got me," replied Stevie, making sure not to hurt any feelings.

He was also delighted that she'd essentially saved him doing any work in order to score with her.

"Well that's a relief," she said, taking a nervous gulp on her vodka and coke, her nose this time touching the top of the liquid in the overflowing glass.

"I'm just glad you find *me* appealing," lied Stevie.

"You're hot," she said, wiping the end of her beak.

"You're pretty hot yourself," replied Stevie, putting on a performance that Tom Hanks would've been proud of.

"Do you wanna take these drinks outside and we can talk for a while without this ghastly music, and maybe we can smoke another one of those joints?" she asked hopefully.

"Works for me."

They took their drinks and made their way towards the front door, slipping unnoticed past the ecstasy-laced dancers, being careful not to receive a smack in the mouth as their arms flailed around in multiple directions.

A few more people were climbing out of a cab as they got outside, so Nilda quickly made a sharp turn right after descending the cold stone steps, leading Stevie up a dark pathway between the side of the house and the hickory old wooden garage.

"I figured it would be more private back here."

She took a seat on the steps leading to the back door after giving the top one a quick wipe with her hand in order to minimize any stains on her short white skirt.

"It's very peaceful tonight," said Stevie, parking a squat next to her and looking up at the full moon.

The only sound to speak of was the presence of the bass coming from the stereo. Even the vibration from the techno tunes had followed them and could be felt under their backsides as they sat there gazing at the sky.

"Yeah, it makes a pleasant change to all the rain we usually get."

The night was clear, but warm it wasn't. A chilly breeze was rushing through the channel between house and garage, but fortunately the back wall where they sat was offering some reprieve.

"There's something about a full moon that relaxes me," said Stevie genuinely, although it could've easily been taken as a cheesy, almost fabricated romantic line attempting to accelerate the process of removing her panties.

"They say it brings out all the crazy people, but I don't believe it. I live around here and there isn't one every night, but there always seems to be crazy people roaming around."

"Is it really that bad here?"

"Probably worse. The people who live here don't mess with each other very much, but there's a lot of domestic violence, a lot of rival gangs from other areas come by and start fights and break windows, and the police are always around. A lot of the guys around here don't work and either push drugs, steal cars, or rob houses. There's always someone being taken away in the back of a squad car. You'll be alright though even though you're not from around here if you're buddies with Mad Dog. You're not from around here are you?"

"No, I'm from Uddingston."

"I was pretty sure I hadn't seen you before."

"I'm not really buddies with Mad Dog. I assume you're talking about the guy who owns the house?"

"Yeah that's him."

"I just met him tonight at a bar from my part of town. They knew I had some gear and asked me if I wanted to come over. I wasn't doing anything else so decided to say what the hell."

"Well I'm glad you did," she said, looking longingly into his eyes.

"Why do they call him Mad Dog?"

"Not totally sure, but probably because he's mad and a bit of a dog. He's done time for stabbing a guy once and he's always got the cops watching him. He's also a bit of a ladies man or so he thinks. Most of the people here look up to him because he's a nutcase and makes them feel safe when he's around, and they enjoy the fact he owns his own house and gives them somewhere to hangout. I grew up with him."

"The inside of his house is a bit old fashioned. I mean it's nice enough, but just wasn't what I was expecting."

"It's his but he inherited it. His mother and father died of a drug overdose when he was five and he was raised here with his grandparents. His grandfather died of a heart attack about two years ago and his grandmother passed away from cancer around six months ago. I don't think he's quite ready to change any of the house yet. He really loved his grandparents."

"Shit, that's tragic."

The story forced Stevie into a flashback of his own mother and father and how much he loved them. His eyes began filling up but he fought hard to prevent any tears streaming down his face.

"You don't need to get upset about it, he's doing fine now."

He wanted to tell her that his emotions hadn't been triggered by the news of Mad Dog's past, but he refused to taint his night by putting his nightmares at the forefront of his thoughts. Spilling his own tragedies with Nilda would've probably guaranteed a sympathy screw but he didn't want to talk about it, and in particular, share such intimate details with someone he barely knew, so decided to lie.

"I know, but I just hate hearing stories like that."

"I know, we don't know how lucky we are."

He resisted temptation to contradict her statement.

"Are you cold?" asked Stevie.

"A little bit. Do I look cold?"

"Not for nothing, but I could probably hang a wet duffle coat on either of your nipples right now."

"Oh my God," she said, grasping both of her A-cup breasts.

"If Stevie Wonder could run his fingers over those right now it would probably be Braille for go inside and have a warm mug of tea."

Nilda doubled over with laughter.

"You're a trip Stevie. Actually it's Braille for come over here and warm me up."

Stevie needed no more of an invitation. He sat his beer and joint on the step below and took her in his arms, pulling her in close and planting his lips firmly on her. His right hand instinctively grasped her left breast, squeezing what there was, but focusing primarily on her bullet for a nipple. She groaned as he tasted her alcohol-tainted tongue buried deep inside his mouth. Her kissing ability was exceptional and her full lips were a delight. His only concern was for the left side of his face as her sharp nose was jammed into him and he hoped and prayed it wasn't going to leave a permanent mark.

Stevie pulled away from her.

"You feel warm now but your nipples are still like a couple of football studs."

"You've such a way with words Stevie. I *am* feeling warmer now but my nipples are still like that for a different reason."

"So you're saying I'm turning you on?"

"No, I just grunt and groan like that when I'm having a bad time!"

"I'm having a good time myself if you couldn't tell," replied Stevie, nodding his head down towards the bulge in the front of his jeans.

"Well hello there," she said, rubbing her hand over his protruding package.

"See I told you I was having a good time. I find nipples and dicks extremely amusing. Why in the world can't a man's cock behave like a woman's nipple? When you guys are cold they get bigger. When you're aroused they get bigger. When I'm aroused my penis gets bigger. When I'm cold, the little man's like a bear going into hibernation, which is a lot in this country. Maybe it wouldn't be as bad if we lived in Florida or something."

"You really have a weird way of looking at things," she replied, laughing, but increasing the intensity of her hand on his groin.

"If you keep rubbing like that I'm going to take this to a whole new level."

She continued to rub.

"OK young lady, I'm being serious. I'm going to take you right here and now if you keep that up."

"You talking about the rubbing or just your penis in general?"

"Both actually."

"OK I'll behave *for now*."

Stevie had mixed emotions about her comment, but wasn't too keen on throwing her down on the back lawn and having his way with her. Someone could appear at any moment and he didn't fancy the ridicule. It would've been worse for her though as she was from around these parts and would've only got a name for herself as being a slag. Perhaps she already did have the title but he hoped not. He *was* losing any inhibition that may have existed though. He was extremely buzzed from the drink and was becoming sleepier and mellower with every puff of his dope.

They shared the remainder of the joint, kissing occasionally, but the fondling had subsided for now.

"Ready for a refill?" said Nilda, shaking her empty glass at him.

"Yeah, let's head back in."

They made their way back up the path between the house and garage, the breeze blowing furiously into their faces. Nilda was now very unsteady on her feet, and the cause was more than her awkward footwear.

"Easy there," said Stevie, steadying her as she stumbled against the wooden garage.

"I'm OK," she replied. "I think between the smoke and standing up too quickly there I got a little light headed."

"No more weed for you."

"You're such a party pooper."

"I have plans for you and I'd rather you were awake when I get a chance to do something about them."

"Well if you put it like that I suppose I'll agree."

He was advising her to take it easy, but he should've been having the same chat with himself. He was in a strange place, fooling around with a girl he knew almost nothing about, and he'd already had a bunch of beers over the course of the night as well as two full joints of potent hashish. His head was feeling light and a tingle was beginning to flow through his entire body, but as usual he didn't know his limits.

The ravers were still in full swing. It was remarkable how much energy they had, but speed and coke were probably the root cause of their staying power. Two gnarly looking guys were dead to the world in both armchairs, and the three couples on the sofa were all involved in their own passionate make-out session; the girl on her man's knee appearing as though she was actually trying to climb inside his mouth.

"Pour me a vodka and coke and I'll be back in a second. I'm just going to check in with Mad Dog and the boys."

"OK but don't be long. I might run off with someone," said Nilda, winking at him with one of her glazed and bloodshot eyes.

The poker game was still in full flow, but each of them looked as though they'd been awake for two days straight. Thomas was drifting in an out of consciousness. When he was awake he had a slow blink going and would burst into laughter for no apparent reason. All the others were on par with Thomas and it was no wonder. On top of the resin they'd been passing around, they were doing shots of Jagermeister. They'd made the chugging of the German firewater part of the Texas hold'em game. Everyone but the winner of each hand had to pound down a shot. Even the two young girls were involved. They had to pick one of the players to root for. If their player had to drink then they had to also. The cute little one was virtually dead to the world. She and her chubby friend were still perched on the counter-top, but the little fox was slouched against Chunky like a drunk against a toilet wall. Chunky wasn't far behind either. It was a shame, but it was obvious to Stevie that if he was going to get his hands on any action it was now destined to be with Nilda. She was pickled herself, but in comparison to any other option she was as sober as a judge.

"You winning chief?" said Stevie to Mad Dog.

"I've no fucking idea man. I've tried to count these chips three times already and I'm still fucking lost."

"As long as you're having fun mate."

"Having a tear chief. Here, take one of these," said Mad Dog, pouring Stevie a Jager and handing him the shot glass.

Stevie didn't particularly want or need any more alcohol, but he didn't want to be perceived as a lightweight, so toasted Mad Dog's glass and threw back the dark liquid in one. He hated Jagermeister, and he could feel the burn all the way from his throat down to his stomach. The Germans, for humorous purposes – which wasn't too often – would refer to it as "liver glue." In Stevie's mind it wasn't quite as bad as straight tequila, but the semi-sweetness of it added a sickly quality that just turned him off. It was potent though. Anything originally marketed as a medicinal product or used during World War II as a field anesthetic usually was. It was also commonly used in small dabs around the home as an insect trap; flies and other insects being drawn to it. Stevie had heard of this use but had never tried it. He giggled as he finished the shot, wondering if any flies back at his flat tomorrow were going to be *doubly* excited when they picked up on the scent of it when he went for a shit. For them was it like adding a delicious peppercorn sauce to an already perfectly cooked sirloin?

A second shot and Stevie's head was really beginning to spin, but he still believed he was one of the most sober people in the house. The boys at the table, with the exception of Mad Dog, were all but dead to the world. Stevie thought about calling a taxi and getting out of there with Nilda and heading back to his flat, but he knew it was only going to be nothing more than a one night event, so didn't want her knowing where he lived as previous experience told him that could potentially lead to unwanted problems. Her place wasn't an option either. She lived with her parents and he wasn't risking any issues on that front. Who knew how crazy her mother and father may be. That just left bailing out on his own and sleeping by himself. It would've been the smart option, but as usual his head upstairs wasn't the one doing the thinking for him. He thought fast. Maybe he could just bang her up against the back wall of the house, but she was fairly plastered and he was pretty much in the same boat. It would've been a disaster, both of them likely losing balance and landing on the ground. Most of the people in the house were either in a semi-conscious state, busy dancing their arses off, or locked in an embrace on the sofa. Therefore he figured the best option was to take her upstairs and give her a quickie in one of the bedrooms and be back downstairs before anyone was even aware. He considered asking Mad Dog if it was OK if he used one of the bedrooms for a little bit because if he was a bit of a dog as Nilda had said, he would've probably given it his blessing and told him to "give her one from me" followed by a wink and a pat on the back. However, the house was only a two bedroom and as his grandparents hadn't passed away all that long ago there was a possibility that he would've objected to anything going on in their old bedroom as well as not consenting to any action going on in his room. There was always the bathroom, but there was even more of a chance of interruption there. The amount of alcohol being consumed was likely having those able to walk pissing like horses.

"Here man, smoke the last of these joints I rolled," said Stevie, handing Mad Dog his remaining roll-up.

"You sure?"

"Absolutely mate. I'm fucked up already and don't need any more, and it looks like everyone else is done as well. It's just my way of saying thanks for inviting me over and supplying me with drink. You didn't need to do that."

Stevie could be such a manipulative prick; all sincere and appreciative, creating this Santa Claus persona and handing out gifts of cannabis resin. He figured it wouldn't be long before Mad Dog was passed out in his chair like the rest of them, giving him easily half an hour of uninterrupted time in one of the bedrooms to slip Nilda a length.

"It was no problem man. Anyone supplying some good gear at any of my parties is always welcome back."

Mad Dog lit the cigarette, taking a humongous drag on it that surprised – yet pleased – Stevie as he watched the orange glow work its way back towards Mad Dog's face, burning away enough of the Rizla paper that you would've sworn the joint had already been passed around the room. Mad Dog finally pulled it away from his mouth and inhaled the smoke into his lungs, holding it there for a couple of seconds before exhaling enough of a cloud to fog up the entire kitchen.

"Holy shit," was all he could mutter as he slouched further into the wooden chair.

"Yeah, it's some potent stuff."

"It's super man."

Ironically, one person not resembling Superman was now Mad Dog. The intense hit was having an instantaneous effect, and Stevie could tell his entire vision was seeing nothing but white stars.

"Can I get you anything?" said Stevie, virtually certain of the response that was coming.

"Nah dude, I'm just gonna chill here for a wee bit," replied Mad Dog, shakily setting the joint down in the black Guinness ashtray on the table that looked remarkably like the ones used throughout The Crown.

Stevie's work was done. Mad Dog slipped into unconsciousness before his very eyes and he was now the only fully functioning person in the room. He took a quick hit of the burning joint and picked up the ashtray, holding it above his head and peering at the base. The white sticker on the bottom read "PROPERTY OF THE CROWN BAR" in black marker pen. He wasn't surprised. All the folks in the house would've probably stolen anything unless it was nailed down, and even then they'd probably find a way. He wasn't really sure why the folks at the bar put in the effort of labeling them. They obviously were frequently stolen, but a name tag on the bottom was hardly a huge deterrent. He placed the stolen item back on the table and put the remainder of the cigarette in its original position and went back through to the living room to find Nilda and his vodka and coke.

There were a few less dancers now, but a few more incapacitated bodies. There was no sign of Nilda though. He gave a quick glance around the floor on the off-chance the impact of the alcohol and drugs had just bubbled over, rendering her immobile, but she was nowhere to be seen. Stevie was beginning to dance, but it was a result of his bladder bulging like an overinflated balloon rather than the current techno tune.

He went out into the small hallway beside the front door, which was slightly ajar. He peeked outside, but the only sign of life was a scrawny-looking stray cat clawing away at a dead sparrow. He closed the door and headed up the red and yellow floral carpeted stairs. The bathroom door immediately at the top was open and the light was on, but there was no sign of life there either. He locked the door behind himself and wrestled furiously to get his dick out of his pants. He was so backed up he felt as though his back teeth were floating, and let out of huge sigh as his thick urine flow bombarded the clear water in the bowl below.

The interior of the bathroom was even more old-fashioned than the living room. It reminded him of his grandparents toilet when he used to visit them on weekends as a young boy. The toilet seat had the same knitted wool cover, fitting around it perfectly, but this one was red, probably to match the carpet and his grandparents had been pink. Stevie had never understood the concept of this. It may have been insulation on the backside to combat the generally cold seat, but even though it was *initially* more pleasant, the wool, long-term, created more of an irritation and you ended up with an itchy arse for the rest of the day or night, walking around scratching yourself like you had fleas or an unfortunate sexually transmitted disease.

He was *so* glad that only a number one was required. There was plenty of toilet paper, but on closer examination it was the cheapest sort you could find. The texture was smooth and shiny and took him back to his primary school days and the economical, low-cost rolls they used to stock their bathrooms with. It was the type of paper that belonged in the bottom of a baking tin or for some kid in elementary art class to use for tracing a picture in a magazine. It could be rendered useless for cleaning your arse crack. It was more likely to spread any remaining feces further around rather than absorb them into the pores like a proper roll of paper was supposed to.

On top of the cistern was a photograph frame – also coated in a little red woolen sweater – containing a picture of two old people, obviously Mad Dog's grandparents. He could understand Mad Dog's motives behind leaving the house unchanged for now considering his grandmother's passing had been fairly recent, but to have the constant reminder of both of them glaring back at him as he exposed himself and took a piss puzzled Stevie. By all means keep the photograph as a memory, but put it on your bedside table or something, not create a visual of the good old days while you stood there with your dick cupped in your palm.

The white ceramic bathtub was surrounded by small glass bowls of potpourri and a variety of red and yellow soaps molded into shapes of fruits and seashells, and a bunch of red and yellow artificial roses were perched in the corner against the tiled wall, blocking any vision of the hot water tap.

Stevie gave his penis the customary three shakes and flipped it back into the comfort of his jeans, washed his hands briefly, shook them rapidly, and wiped any water remains on the back of his jeans. He didn't know where half the gypsies occupying the house had been, so resisted any temptation to opt for the towel hanging through the clear plastic hoop attached to the door.

He opened the bathroom door resigned to the fact he was going to call a cab, but suddenly let out a screech that almost caused loss of control of all bodily functions.

"AAARRGH."

Standing immediately outside the door was Nilda, her nose virtually touching his even though their feet were almost a yard apart.

"Holy shit, you nearly caused me to crap my pants," said Stevie, heart pounding at a hundred miles an hour.

"I was in the bedroom. I figured you'd come looking for me and I saw you going into the toilet. I was hoping to catch you before you put the little guy back in your pants."

"Well he only just went back in there. It's easy enough for me to pull him back out."

"I wouldn't want to put you to all that effort," replied Nilda, her eyelids blinking slowly like Thomas before her, as she unzipped Stevie's fly and dug her hand inside.

She rummaged around like an uncoordinated magician looking for a rabbit in a top-hat. Five seconds or so elapsed before the situation became awkward. She wasn't grasping the fact that he wasn't going commando, and didn't realize his boxer shorts had buttons and were the barrier between her hand and the desired prize.

"Let me help you with that," said Stevie, in a tone more of an order than a supportive suggestion.

He unbuttoned his boxers - which he figured was the root cause of her problem – and exposed himself.

"Wow, that's the biggest one I've seen in a while."

Her comment pleased and humored him at the same time. It was always nice for a guy to hear compliments on the size of his manhood, but it wasn't so much that he *was* actually that big. All her fumbling around inside his jeans, even although it wasn't skin on skin contact, had caused him to realize that the inevitable was about to happen, so he was already semi-aroused before he pulled it out, but she never needed to know that.

"Well either that's true or you just haven't seen one in a while."

"Well you might have a point with that."

Stevie sulked inside. He'd been hoping her response had been no, I've been with a different guy every night for the last six months and I can definitely confirm you have a whopper. He was such a dreamer at times, but a smile returned to his face as she dropped to her knees and swallowed him like a sword at a circus display. She attempted to mutter something as he was engulfed in her mouth but it was completely illegible, so Stevie just groaned with satisfaction as a method of response. Her head bobbed back and forth, slurping and grunting in the process. Her technique was exceptional and one of the best he'd ever experienced. She was all mouth and no hands, which were grasping firmly on each of his buttocks. Stevie was beginning to sway around a little, but Nilda continued on unfazed. The effects from the drugs and alcohol were kicking into overdrive and he needed to lie down. The hallway at the top of the stairs was beginning to spin and he worried he was going to collapse.

"Let's continue this in one of the bedrooms," said Stevie, eagerly trying to focus his vision and keep his head under control.

Nilda clambered to her feet, stumbling slightly, and had saliva running down onto her chin.

"We can go in this one," she said, pointing to the furthest of the two doors. "The other one is Mad Dog's room."

They both staggered across the hallway and through the bedroom door. It was virtually pitch black, but there was just enough light from the outside street lamps slipping through the horizontal blinds to enable them to identify the outline of a large double bed. Both of them collapsed onto the top of the quilt like a couple of rag dolls. Stevie let out a yelp as he landed on the mattress face first, too drunk to remember that his erect penis was still sticking out the front of his jeans. It jammed hard into the bed like someone ramming an umbrella pole into a white sand beach.

"You need me to kiss that better for you?" slurred Nilda.

"That would be nice."

Nilda took direction well and immediately went back to work on him. He lay there, hands behind his head as she straddled his shins, back arched towards him as her head moved up and down in rhythm with the muffled beats from the living room. Stevie was in heaven, but he was becoming drowsy, and felt his eyes beginning to close. He knew if his top eyelashes made contact with his bottom ones it was goodnight Vienna. His plan was to do the dirty deed and then call a taxi. There was plenty of time to sleep things off in the comfort of his own bed, so he needed to keep active in order to prevent from passing out.

She looked up at him as her tongue ran laps around the head of his penis.

"Come up here," he asked, and she duly obliged.

They kissed briefly before he flipped her onto her back and pulled off her top, kissing her neck and rubbing her nipples that were virtually poking through her bra. He nibbled his way south, sliding off the white mini-skirt and her tiny pink thong. The crotch of her panties was already soaked through and her scent was divine, much to his relief. He buried his face between her moist legs and flicked his tongue rapidly on her pulsating clitoris. She squirmed like an eel, panting and groaning, and intermittently muttering the word fuck. Her fingers rummaged through his hair and pulled his head further and further into her wetness.

"Oh my God, I want you inside me," she urged.

Stevie wanted the same and needed no further encouragement. He fumbled around, pulling his wallet from his jeans and taking out one of his ribbed condoms, tearing off the corner of the square-shaped wrapper with his teeth, and carefully removed the rubber. The last thing he wanted was to drop it on the bed cover or floor and have it pick up any grit or other unwanted particles. He wanted her badly, so left on his shoes and pulled his jeans and boxer's down to his ankles before skillfully rolling on the contraceptive.

"OK it's on," he said, sounding rather pleased with the achievement.

Nilda grabbed hold of it and guided him inside her. It was initially a little tight, but a light push from his hips and he slipped all the way in and up to his balls.

"Oh my God Stevie, give it to me."

This was no time for gentle loving. That was something he reserved for women he truly had feelings for. This would be fast and furious with zero cuddling afterwards.

He did *start* slowly though, on the off chance his gun was going to fire before he wanted to pull the trigger. His control was good though, and after a few medium strokes to put him at ease and get into a rhythm, he picked up the pace, following her moans and dirty verbal instructions.

"Oh yes Stevie, give it to me, give it to me harder."

He was working up quite a sweat and certainly keeping active, but his head was still swirling.

"Take me from behind," panted Nilda.

They both clambered up from their traditional missionary position, Nilda taking two attempts at forming an all-fours posture; first time losing balance, with her head falling erratically into the soft feather pillow.

"You alright sweetheart?" said Stevie, as worried about his own drunkenness as he was hers.

"I'm trashed, but I still know what I'm doing," replied Nilda, but not too convincingly.

Stevie shakily positioned himself behind her like a quarterback ready to receive a snap, and slipped himself inside her again. He felt it going in extremely deep this time, almost feeling each side of her bony pelvis.

"Jesus Christ," was her only words.

Needing no further input, Stevie began moving back and forth on her like an out of control cuckoo clock, each movement forward trying to bury himself even further.

"Oh yeah Stevie. Pull my hair and spank my arse," she said with venom.

Stevie was completely taken aback with the aggressive nature of her demands, but after a brief pause to digest the order, he put in every ounce of force he had, almost losing balance himself as he leaned to the left, but straightened himself out as he smacked her on the arse with his right hand.

"Oh yeah, that's what I'm talking about."

He was shocked by her transformation into such a masochistic state. Prior to any sexual interaction he would've almost guessed the opposite, picturing her more of the type to lie there like a sack of potatoes, but he couldn't have been further from the truth.

"Do you like me slapping that arse?"

"I'd love it more if you were pulling my hair at the same time."

This girl was a maniac, but Stevie adhered, virtually pile-driving her through the headboard, smacking her butt cheek and tugging on the back of her hair. He visualized himself as jockey Frankie Dettori on a champion racehorse, battling for the finish line.

And it's Stevie on the outside...

The pace was frenetic, and on top of the room spinning out of control, his knees were hurting and his hand was stinging. He couldn't imagine how Nilda was enjoying herself. The room may have been dark but he could still see his bright red handprint on her right cheek. It *looked* painful and was glowing like a lava lamp. His hair was as wet as Nilda's vagina and the sweat was pouring down his forehead into his eyes, and adding to his overall discomfort.

Less than five minutes had passed in the doggie position, but he was virtually ready to pop. It was nothing to be ashamed of, as a journeyman porn star would've struggled to continue much longer at such an astounding pace.

"I want you to cum Stevie. I want you to cum inside me," she said in an exhausted yet seductive tone as she turned and looked back at him.

Stevie couldn't have objected even if he'd wanted to, and instantaneously ejaculated, given a few extra thrusts to expel every last drop and letting out a creepy-sounding echoing groan not unlike Chewbacca in the early Star Wars films. He was now a broken man and they both collapsed in a heap on top of the quilt.

"WHAT THE FUCK IS THIS SHITE?"

The screaming words rang in Stevie's head as he wearily opened his eyes. Daylight filled the room, snapping him immediately into full consciousness. Nilda was awakened also, lying there on her back, private parts on display for all to see. Stevie was naked other than his shoes, socks, as well as jeans and underwear, which were doing nothing to cover him up other than double as a pair of ankle-warmers. He couldn't believe he had passed out and it was now morning.

"I SAID WHAT THE FUCK IS THIS SHITE?"

Stevie looked up and focused. The yelling was from Mad Dog, who was standing beside the bed glaring down at them.

"Hey man. Look I'm sorry about this. I didn't mean to disrespect you by using your grandparents bed," said Stevie, genuinely apologetic.

"I couldn't give a rat's arse about that pish. Nilda, you're a bitch. You told me yesterday there was a chance that we'd get back together. Three fucking years we were seeing each other and you do this to me. In my own house!" said Mad Dog, his eyes visually tearing up.

"That was yesterday," replied Nilda, getting up off the bed and pulling on her pink underwear. "But I was thinking about it last night and all the crap you've put me through. All the cheating and treating me like shit. You don't deserve another chance. Anyway, I'm with Stevie now so get over it."

Stevie couldn't believe his ears. She was with him now. What was she on? She'd told him she'd grown up with Mad Dog, which was more than a little white lie since they'd been long-term boyfriend and girlfriend.

"OK, let's settle down a minute," said Stevie, getting off the bed and fastening his trousers. "Mate, I had no idea you guys used to be together, and as far as me and her now being an item, that's utter bollocks."

Nilda had a sulk on her face and looked hurt by his words.

"Well maybe not right now, but maybe if we go out a few times or something then perhaps we *can* be together. Stevie, you make me feel like a better person and the sex was the best I've ever had."

The veins on Mad Dog's temples were starting to pulsate and his face was turning redder by the second. What was this crazy bitch thinking? Why would she basically tell her long-term ex that he was inferior in bed to the guy now standing in from of him? Stevie's uneasiness magnified as one of Mad Dog's buddies – whose name eluded him – entered the bedroom, no doubt alarmed by the earlier shouting. Closely behind this short, stocky guy was Thomas; the geeky, acne-ridden young man who was looking petrified. Stevie's senses were now on full alert. There was only one door out of the room and there were now three guys between him and an escape.

"You're a slag Nilda, a complete slag. You soil my grandparents sheets with your filthy juices and then tell me to my face that I suck in bed."

"Easy mate, no need to talk to her like that," said Stevie, as the hairs on his arms popped to attention.

"You keep the fuck out of this. This is between me and her."

"Oh grow up Mad Dog. Just get over it. I'm done with you and your little dick," interjected Nilda.

Without a further word, Mad Dog delivered a slap to the side of Nilda's face; the sound echoing like a gunshot in a canyon, and she dropped to the floor. Stevie didn't know what his next move should be, but it suddenly became crystal clear. Stevie *partly* felt the slap was justified as she had belittled the guy's penis size in the presence of a relative stranger, but he couldn't sit back and watch such physical abuse. Hitting a female was a big no-no that his father had instilled in him. His dad and his deep-toned voice flashed into his mind.

You stand up for this girl son. She might be a nutcase, but no woman deserves that.

His respect for his father was second to none and he would *not* question his judgment. Without hesitation he hit Mad Dog squarely on the jaw with a right hook as Mad Dog was staring down at a helpless Nilda. It only rocked him, so he followed it up with a right cross to the nose. Mad Dog fell on top of Nilda, blood spurting from his nostrils. It all seemed like it was moving in slow motion, but before Stevie knew it, a body was clinging to his back and punches were raining down on top of his skull. He spun around, the body still hanging from him. It was Mad Dog's stocky friend. A now more terrified Thomas was standing frozen to the spot by the door, obviously unsure what his next move should be. Stevie quickly bent his head towards the floor, flipping the stocky young guy over and he sailed onto the carpet, landing with a thud on his back. Stevie kicked him in the face and then stamped on Mad Dog's head as he was attempting to get back to his feet. Enough was enough, so he made his way in the direction of the door. Thomas was there looking nervous, but he had formed a karate stance.

"Thomas, don't even think about it. I like you chief, so don't act the hard man. I didn't do anything wrong, so please just let me past and don't get yourself hurt," pleaded Stevie.

Thomas did as requested, perhaps to maintain his looks; although the ugly stick had already paid him a visit on more than one occasion and a beating may not have been doing him a disservice. He dropped his hands and Stevie bolted past him, fleeing down the stairs like an escaped prisoner and out of the front door. He ran and ran, not completely sure where he was going, but the farther from the place he got, the better he felt inside.

The few people he passed in the streets glared at him like he was a mental patient. Initially he hadn't realized as he'd been so caught up in the moment, but he was shirtless. There had been no time to ensure he was completely dressed. There was no point in carefully pulling on his t-shirt if it could've meant the difference between getting out of there or taking a knife in the back.

He wanted to stop running as he was seriously out of breath and wasn't exactly in the best of shape. If a bar-rat was the equivalent of a gym fiend he would've been tearing along unfazed, but it wasn't even close. He pulled up suddenly, bending over and holding his side. A group of young kids looked skeptically at him. He could see them, wondering why they were out this early in the morning. He had no idea what time it actually was but the dew-covered grass told him it was earlier than he had been up on a morning for some time. The kids sent obscene heckles in his direction but they were drowned out by the ever increasing noise from a siren. He was now panting, snot dripping onto his upper lip, but managed to raise his head as the white car with the red stripe in the middle pulled up next to him, blue light flashing as the kids scarpered in a variety of directions. Stevie wanted to join them in their pursuits but was too out of breath to even give it serious consideration.

There were two cops in the car as it screeched to a halt beside him. Both climbed slowly out of the car, walking towards him like John Wayne leaving his horse behind.

"Am I glad to see you guys," said Stevie, puffing and panting as he looked them in the eyes.

"Do you have any idea why we pulled you over sir?" said the younger of the two policemen.

"I don't suppose it has anything to do with me running around like a madman through this neighborhood without wearing a shirt on a cold morning."

"And we have a winner," said the middle-aged man in the tone of a game show host.

Stevie hated cops. He respected what they had to do and that they had to put up with complete scumbags a lot of the time, but he detested why they had to be condescending smartarses *all* the time, treating everyone immediately as though they were a criminal. You would've thought the law was guilty until proven innocent. This seemed to be one of those times. The younger officer, around Stevie's age and height piped up.

"Training for a marathon are we?" was his input, and the pair of them chuckled heartily, more than the line deserved.

"And we have a winner," was Stevie's reply.

Stevie laughed, as did the younger officer, but his grin abruptly changed to a straight face after a scowl from his partner.

"OK, enough of the smart talk. What's your hurry and why *aren't* you wearing a shirt? Also, why are you covered in bite marks?" said the senior of the two.

Stevie had been all set to come clean on the sequence of events until the final question. The perplexed look on his face transformed to horror as he peered at his chest. Sure enough, there were many bite marks circling a six inch diameter around both nipples. He had no recollection of any of them, which he couldn't believe considering that pain must've been involved. They must've been from Nilda, hadn't they? There was no other explanation. They must've had sex again. There was no way she just decided to start munching on him like a vampire while he was snoring. He hated these blackout occurrences. The loss of control scared him. Immediate panic mode set in and he quickly reached into his pocket which promptly put both officers on high alert.

"Keep your hands where we can see them," said the older of the two.

"Sorry, I just wanted to check my wallet."

"OK, but take it out nice and slowly. We need to see some I.D anyway," replied the younger guy.

Stevie gently removed the wallet from his jeans, opened it up and handed over his driver's license. While they scanned over it, looking at the photograph, then at Stevie, then back at the photograph, he opened up the small pouch at the front where he kept his two condom stash. It was empty, so he breathed a huge sigh of relief. He didn't recollect using the second one, but it was more than likely he had. His heart rate calmed down as a result. He had no idea who Nilda had slept with over the course of her sexually active days or whether she was always as careful as he was, and he didn't need the additional risk of impregnating a crazy girl who he barely knew.

"I'll be back in a couple of minutes," said the older officer. "I just need to run your license. It's just procedure so you can take it easy for now."

He headed back to the car and Stevie stood there with the younger partner in an awkward silence, but he was relaxed by the fact he knew his record was clean.

The couple of minutes passed by and the senior officer returned with a disappointed look on his face.

"You'll be pleased to hear your record is clean."

"I knew that already. It may not seem like it right now, but I'm just a run of the mill law abiding citizen."

"Well that remains to be seen. You can begin *right now* by telling us what you've been up to and why you are running around this place half naked," said the younger guy.

"OK, I was invited to a party by some guys I met in my local bar in Uddingston last night. I caught a cab back to their place with them and got a little drunk to say the least. I hooked up with a girl who gave me the impression she was single. We ended up sleeping together and passing out on the bed afterwards. The guy whose house it was woke us up just a short while ago. Turns out he had a history with the girl and went a little nuts. He smacked her across the face and she hit the floor. Now, you might have a problem with what I'm about to say, but I was brought up to believe that hitting a woman is cowardly and just plain unacceptable. Anyway, I kicked the shit out of him. One of his buddies decided to have a go at me. It wasn't even a fair shot as he jumped me from behind, but I beat the crap out of him as well. At that point I wasn't about to hang around and just bolted. As you can see I didn't pussy around to get fully dressed. I just wanted to get as far away from there as possible, and here I am talking to you guys now."

"Did anyone get seriously hurt?"

"I don't think so."

"You don't think so or you don't know?"

"OK, I don't know."

The younger cop was doing all the talking while the other scribbled feverishly in his little notebook.

"So it's possible if those guys are alright they could've given the young girl a further beating?"

"It's possible I suppose."

The young policeman was a slick questioner and it seemed like he could've given the finest of lawyers a run for their money.

"OK, if that's the case we'll need to investigate. Get in the back of the car and take us to this place."

"Oh come on guys, I'm sure all is well. I just want to get home."

"It's not a request sir."

At that moment Stevie realized he still had his Ziploc bag of drugs in his pocket. He'd been fortunate they hadn't decided to search him already so quickly changed his tune.

"No problem, I'm sorry. It was just quite a stressful situation for me and I'm eager to get home and forget it ever happened."

"I understand, but you need to understand we are just doing our job. If we ignored every assault story and suspicious circumstance we stumbled across, don't you think that would be neglect on our part?"

"Fair enough."

Stevie was ushered into the back of the Ford Mondeo cop car and played navigator.

"Take the next right and it's the first house on the left, the one on the corner."

"Well surprise, surprise," said the younger cop who was sitting in the front passenger seat. "You should've told us it was Mad Dog's place; James 'Mad Dog' McFadden, a serious pain in our arseholes."

"I take it you know him?"

"You could say that," said the older cop. "We're out here about once a week for some reason or another. Can I assume the girl in question was Nilda?"

Stevie could hardly believe what he was hearing, but was relieved that the cops were probably coming around to believing his sequence of events.

"So you know her as well?"

"Very well. A little too well. I think her and Mad Dog have been on and off for a long time. She's called us before about him abusing her."

"Unbelievable," was all Stevie could manage to say.

They pulled up to the house and turned off the engine. Whoever was inside obviously heard someone arriving as one of the horizontal blind slats in the front window slowly moved up.

"Can I stay here?" inquired Stevie.

"Absolutely not, we need to make sure all is good and verify your story. Don't you think it would be a good idea if you were there to hear what they have to say?"

"Yeah, I suppose you're right, again."

"Don't worry; nobody's going to pull any crap while we're here."

They opened the front gate and proceeded up the path, Stevie following at the back. He glanced around the street as they approached the door as he hadn't had time during his fleeting departure to catch much of it earlier. The neighborhood looked even worse in the daylight, but Mad Dog's place was pristine in comparison to the rest. It was like a diamond stuck in a pile of dog shit.

The senior officer thumped on the wooden door with three rhythmical knocks. It opened almost before the officer's hand reached his side. Mad Dog stood there with a red left jaw and some dried blood remains on his upper lip.

"Officers Henderson and McMichael, what brings you here on this lovely morning?"

"Cut the crap Mad Dog, you know why we're here," said the older of the two, nodding his head backwards to Stevie behind them. "We picked this young man up running half naked through the neighborhood. He tells us there was a bit of a skirmish here this morning. We're just here to check that out and make sure everything is OK."

"Everything is grand chief, so don't worry about it. Thanks for asking anyway and have a nice day."

Mad Dog began closing the door, but the middle-aged officer was having none of it and jammed his black leather shoe in the way, preventing the door from shutting tight. Mad Dog opened it again.

"Not so fast son, you know it doesn't work that easily."

"Oh come on guys, everything is fine."

"Give Nilda a shout; we'd like to get a look at her."

"NILDA, THE COPS WANT TO SPEAK TO YOU," he screamed in the direction of the living room.

They stood there in silence awaiting her arrival; Stevie and Mad Dog exchanging a few deliberate glances. Nilda appeared looking none the worse for wear and Mad Dog put his arm around her as they stood in the doorway.

"You OK young lady?" asked the senior cop.

"Never been better," she replied, planting a kiss on Mad Dog's left cheek as she stared into the eyes of the officers with enough intensity and conviction to detach a retina, but didn't even acknowledge Stevie's presence.

It was as though he didn't even exist, as though no physical encounter had ever taken place, and as though her relationship with Mad Dog had never skipped a beat. She was a strange one, that was for sure, but he glowed inside, thankful he hadn't taken a shine to her for anything more than a cheap thrill and it appeared she was now in the same mind-frame, so the chances of being a crazy stalker were diminished significantly. Mad Dog was a nut, but on closer inspection it was beginning to seem that Nilda was the royal flush to his full house in the barmy army stakes.

"Never been better, eh," said the older officer. "Somehow I don't believe that, but if that's how you say you are, then we'll take your word for it."

"Honestly, everything is fine."

"OK then, but one last thing. Give your other mate a shout; the one involved in the earlier incident.

"HEY VILLAIN, COPS WANT A WORD," he hollered, again in the direction of the living room.

Stevie could barely keep the smirk off his face and was dying to say something. Mad Dog and Villain; what were these kids thinking about with these nicknames? You would've thought they were tough as nails gangsters or something that could actually pull off such titles without a flinch, but they were low-life nobodies. No doubt their bottom-of-the-barrel intellect levels had them figuring they were cool, rather than the idiots they actually were.

They waited patiently on Villain's arrival, and Stevie pondered again. Why were the cops waiting outside the house anyway? Anytime they'd arrived at a rowdy party he'd been attending they'd always come in for a nosey around. He was confused.

"Alright?" said Villain, appearing beside Mad Dog like his little lap dog and squeezing Nilda out of the way and behind his stocky physique.

Villain had the beginning of a shiner around his left eye. Stevie had kicked him pretty good, and although it was currently red and swollen, there was little doubt it would transform, chameleon-like, to purple by early evening, black and blue the following morning, followed by a jaundice yellow within a couple of days.

"We're alright young man; looks like we're a little more alright than you are for that matter."

"Oh this," replied Villain, bringing his hand up to touch his bruised eye. "Nah, this is just a wee graze."

The senior officer sighed and shrugged his shoulders as he glanced at his younger counterpart.

"OK, let's get this sorted out. We've established everyone involved is not seriously injured. Do *any* of you wish to press charges on anybody?"

There was a brief pause before a muttering of "no" was heard from all four of them.

"Good," said the youthful cop. "That'll save Officer McMichael and me a lot of unnecessary paperwork."

"Can I go now?" inquired Villain.

"You all can. Have a nice day," said the young cop.

Villain disappeared back into the living room, closely followed by Nilda, after she planted another kiss on Mad Dog's cheek.

"Hang on a minute guys," said Mad Dog, before disappearing up the stairs.

He returned in less than ten seconds carrying Stevie's t-shirt.

"Here man, here's your shirt," he said, stepping down two of the grey stone steps and placing it in Stevie's outstretched hand.

"Cheers," replied Stevie.

"Look man I'm sorry about this morning," said Mad Dog, lowering his head and looking towards his shoes. "I was out of order and deserved what you gave me. I had a word with her after you left and she told me everything. She said you had no idea me and her had been seeing each other for a while. She said she just did it to get back at me. Don't get me wrong, I don't like it, but I've fucked around on her a few times and I guess it was payback. Listen, I would've done exactly the same if I'd been in your shoes, so no hard feelings, eh?" he said, extending his hand out for a shake which Stevie duly accepted.

"It's all good chief."

"Still, I hope I don't see you around here again."

"I hope so too."

"OK, now these two lovebirds have kissed and made up, let's get out of here," said Officer McMichael to Officer Henderson.

Mad Dog closed the door and went back about his business and the three of them headed back to the car.

"Can you guys maybe give me a lift to a taxi rank or something?" asked Stevie, looking desperate.

"Yeah come on. I think we can even manage to take you home, you've had a rough morning," said McMichael.

"Thanks guys."

Off they sped in the Ford Mondeo and Stevie breathed a sigh of relief as they exited the crummy estate and back onto the main roads.

"One question for you guys. Why did you wait outside that house and not go in for a look? That's always been the case with what limited experience I have in the matter."

"Well it's simple really. Yes, we usually go inside. However, we've been in that house on many a weekend morning and it's always the same situation; comatosed bodies all over the place, people nursing sore faces and bloody noses, and a smell of weed that a sniffer dog could pick up on from half a mile away. They're a troubled bunch of kids, but for most part they keep their shit confined to the neighborhood. If we go in there and find a bunch of drugs we'll need to take action. Most of them have alcoholic or abusive parents and don't work themselves. We figure life has dealt them tough enough cards without rubbing salt in their wounds even further with a drugs charge. It wouldn't change them anyway, and as long as nobody is getting seriously hurt we cut them some slack."

"That's nice, as well as making a lot of sense," replied Stevie, hoping they'd feel the same way if they stumbled across the contents of his pockets.

He was tired and dozed most of the journey to his place. It had been a blessing in disguise being stopped by the cops. If it hadn't occurred he would've been none the wiser of the sequence of events that took place after he'd left and would've had no opportunity to bury the hatchet with Mad Dog. Instead he would've been watching his back every time he went for a drink at The Crown as they knew where to find him.

"If you could drop me just here on the right that would be great," asked Stevie politely as they drew level with his block of flats.

He was really looking forward to collapsing in his own bed.

"Let's hope this is the last we see of you," said young officer Henderson.

"You've got my word on it."

The older cop turned around from his position at the steering wheel and gave Stevie a sinister look.

"Just one more thing young man; please don't carry any more weed around with you in future. You might be immune to the smell of it, but the whole car reeks of it right now."

"Thanks officers," he replied, leaving the car at top speed with his cheeks burning cherry red.

He was an extremely lucky man.

Big G and the Boys

Stevie *was* killing himself, slowly, but killing himself nevertheless and the boys knew it.

"It's not the going out at night drinking that worries me," said Gordon. "It's the morning and daytime stuff that's the problem. Fuck, we all like a few shandies a couple of times a week, but if you're pouring whiskey into your coffee in the morning, you've got issues. He thinks I don't know about that, but I was over at his place the other week to drop off some holiday brochures and he'd just finished a cup of Joe. He went for a piss and I was helping myself to a brew and thought I could smell booze. He'd left a little of his coffee in the mug in the sink. I lifted it and took a sniff. It nearly knocked me the fuck out.

Colin and Sean shook their heads in disbelief. They knew his drinking had accelerated a lot since the suicide of his father, but every day was way too much, and if he was kicking off his morning coffee as a caffeine and Scotch cocktail, then he certainly had a major problem.

"If the booze doesn't kill him directly it's going to do it indirectly," said Sean. "If his liver doesn't shut shop then he's going to end up beaten to death or something. When he blacks out he has no idea what he's doing. I love him to death, but who the hell decides to go out on their own and hook up with a group of young kids you don't know and go back to their place in one of the dodgiest areas of Hamilton? He was lucky he got out of there in one piece. I don't know exactly what he did, and he doesn't remember everything either, but we could've been sitting here today talking about what a great guy and friend he *had* been, rather than how we can intervene and get him back on the straight and narrow."

"We need to figure out a way to convince him to at least slow down," said Colin. "I mean, we all enjoy a social drink, let's be honest, but the last thing I think about when I wake up in the morning is firing some whiskey into my coffee. Shit, he's probably over the legal limit when he's driving to work every day."

The three friends sat and pondered in the comfort of Colin's living room. It was a modern two bedroom semi-detached about three miles from Uddingston cross. Nothing was out of place and it was finely furnished; an extreme contrast to Stevie's messy flat. So tastefully decorated, it was usually the first thing women commented on when they walked into the place.

The four of them had been friends since they were young kids, and had such a strong bond together that would never be broken, no matter what the circumstances were.

Gordon, or Big G as he was referred to, was a tower of a man. He was pushing six feet five inches with a slim but toned build to him as a result of his passion for martial arts. He enjoyed a beer as much as anyone, but had the self-control that Stevie lacked, and knew the meaning of moderation.

He was a year older than the other boys and was like the big brother that Stevie never had. The times Stevie became a little unnecessarily boisterous in public, Big G could just draw him a certain look that translated into "shut the fuck up or I'll smack you around the ear." It worked every time as well, no questions asked. Gordon was the sensible one and policed Stevie as well as he could.

Sean was of a similar mould to Gordon in terms of knowing his limits. He was around five feet nine with short thinning fair hair. He was a bit of a fitness freak as well, but was more of a requirement than a passion. He was a physical education teacher at Uddingston Grammar School; the very place they'd all attended as young guys. On their nights out drinking he preserved a slower pace than the rest of them as he was paranoid of making a fool of himself and word spreading like wild fire across the small town. He had a reputation to maintain and didn't want the chance of any mischief spreading to his colleagues and certainly not amongst his students.

On occasions where they decided to take their weekend adventures into Glasgow city centre, Sean was like a kid in a candy shop and really let what hair that he had down, as he was far enough away from the village gossip to be comfortable that nothing would come back to bite him in the arse.

Colin on the other hand was as close in behavior to Stevie as any of them. He was a tough-looking guy, but his bark was louder than his bite. His firm stare and short brown number one buzz cut gave him a convict appearance at times and any head shot photographs of him shouted out police line-up. He was around Sean's height and had a small beer gut, but like his house, his appearance was always immaculate, dressing in the best of gear. Stevie and Colin were both ladies men, and looking clean and smart was everything. Colin had a one night stand count that would be impressive to most, but Stevie was still in a league of his own in terms of total headcount.

"OK guys, I have an idea," said Gordon with a huge smile.

Sean and Colin looked extremely intrigued.

Beer Goggles

Gordon had been giving significant thought to their dilemma. Finding a way to convince Stevie to change his ways would be no easy feat, but he'd informed Sean and Colin of his plan and they were *almost* as excited as he was.

Big G was an electronics whiz. He worked for a mobile phone manufacturing company as an electrical engineer, and was responsible for their product camera designs. His plan was this, design a miniature video camera that could be attached to the frame of a pair of glasses. The aim was to convince Stevie to wear the fake lens glasses and have the video camera record his every move when he went out drinking. That way if he had one of his usual blackouts, the glasses would continue to record his antics and if he was at a loss as to what occurred during the night, he could remove the tiny memory chip, hook it up to his computer and replay the events as seen through his very own eyes.

Two weeks passed and Gordon's design was going well. The nice part was that he could mix in some work on the camera design during regular business hours and remain unseen. The parts he was using were similar in nature to those he handled every day, so nobody had reason to question what he was doing.

The development continued for another week before the camera was ready for testing. Gordon purchased a pair of stylish-looking black framed glasses, as he knew if there was any hope of Stevie putting them on in public they would have to appear trendy or it would be a lost cause.

Gordon wore them on the drive home from work and removed the miniature memory stick. He downloaded the taped material to his laptop and waited eagerly for the media player to pop-up. The hairs on his arms stood on end as he watched the footage. It was a complete success; the picture resolution was immaculate and the audio almost as good.

The camera was encased in a tiny black housing to match the frames and was positioned on the top right corner where the join of the frame met the plain glass lens. He placed an identical housing on the left hand side to maintain the symmetry and give the impression it was all part of their design.

Gordon christened them "Beer Goggles," and the only remaining part of the plan was having Stevie agree that it was a good idea and for his best interest; an exercise Gordon knew was going to require as much effort as the entire design of the goggles themselves.

"So what's the big occasion?" asked Stevie, looking at them all suspiciously as they sat in Gordon's flat.

Gordon had invited him over, telling him it was a surprise, but it was extremely important. Stevie had been on his own at the bar for a couple of hours when Gordon had reached him on his mobile. He'd been planning on an afternoon rendezvous with Sandra when the call came in and had reluctantly agreed to meet with the guys as a result.

"We've got something to show you," replied Gordon, looking rather pleased with himself, but Colin and Sean looked on anxiously.

"Well I hope it's good. I was about to get my leg over with that barmaid Sandra when you called."

"I think it's great chief, but whether you'll feel the same remains to be seen. Take a seat and I'll explain everything."

Stevie was completely confused with their demeanors but complied nevertheless, and took a seat on one of Gordon's white suede armchairs.

Gordon's place was a couple of miles from Stevie's and was located in the small village by the name of Bothwell; directly in between Hamilton and Uddingston. His place was a one bedroom also, but considerably smaller than Stevie's, which was really saying something. However, Bothwell was renowned as one of the most up market locations in the county; home of many a rich football player and local television personality. Therefore, even such a small residence as Gordon's still commanded a purchase price roughly equal to the GNP of a small African nation. You were paying for location rather than square footage. It suited Gordon. He enjoyed the prestige of the place, its fine restaurants and upscale wine bars. Throw in his designer dress sense and expensive haircuts and they made it all fit like a glove and he couldn't have been happier.

"What's with the poofy-looking glasses?" asked Stevie, giving Gordon a puzzled stare and furrowing his brow.

Gordon was wearing the beer goggles as it was all part of his plan, but the fact Stevie had referred to them as being gay wasn't exactly the start the boys had been hoping for.

"They're anything but faggy-looking chief. Do you know nothing about fashion?"

"Well if they're your idea of fashion then no, I don't"

"Just watch for a second," replied Gordon, removing the glasses.

He flicked open the tiny compartment hosting the camera on the top right hand corner of the black frame and removed the chip, before loading it into a USB stick he'd designed, and plugged it into his laptop that was situated on the wood paneled floor beside his large screen TV. As the computer booted up he ran a cable from it to the television. He wanted the effect of it all to be as large as possible. The media player finally opened and the footage he'd recorded was blown-up on the screen.

"What the fuck!" exclaimed Stevie, startled as he appeared on the television.

He was baffled as he watched himself say 'what's with the poofy-looking glasses?'

"How the hell did you do that?"

"It's the glasses," replied Gordon. "I designed them at the office. They record as though it's through the eyes of whoever is wearing them. They pick up on sound as well. I'm really pleased with them and never expected them to work this good."

"That's excellent," replied Stevie, seemingly genuinely impressed with the work.

Colin and Sean looked on from their position on the matching white suede sofa, appearing a little more relaxed that Stevie was digging the piece of electronic genius.

"Cheers mate," said Gordon, smiling and enjoying the moment of sharing the accomplishment.

"One question though chief. It's great and all and you're a real smart bastard, but couldn't you have shared with me another time? What was the urgency?"

"OK Stevie, it's time for us to come clean. We're worried about you."

"You're worried about *me*. Worried about what? And what does all this have to do with being worried about me?"

Sean decided to join in with the proceedings.

"Look mate, we know things have been rough for you with your dad and everything, but we think you are drinking way too much. If you keep it up at this rate you're gonna need a new liver before you're thirty-five. We know you're pouring booze into your morning coffee, you're at the bar virtually every day and not just for a few, and there are probably a couple of times per week when you don't remember half the night or how you got home. It's more than just the health concerns as well. You get a bit crazy when you blackout and you're gonna end up getting into big trouble or even worse. I mean, come on, just last week you ended up at a strange house for a party and could've ended up stabbed or even worse. I know if it was me and I was asked to go back to a party at a guy's house by the name of Mad Dog, I know what my answer would've been."

"I didn't know that was his name before I went."

"That's not the point Stevie. All I'm trying to say is that the drink ends up putting you in situations you should avoid. What about a month ago when we left you in The Crown and you told us you were going home after one more beer. You woke up in some woman's house and her husband showed up unexpectedly, and then you had to hide under the bed for an hour until he left the house to catch a tee-off time. You still don't know her name, how or where you met her, or how you actually ended up back in her bed. The guy could've fucking shot you if he'd found you there so I hope you understand where we are coming from," said Sean, his frustration evident for all to see.

"Stevie, that's exactly why I designed these," said Gordon, holding the glasses towards him. "If you wear them and have one of your drunken blackouts you'll be able to watch the events of the night again, essentially through your own eyes, and see any of the shit you didn't remember. Maybe if you see for yourself what you're getting into it might give you the kick up the arse you need to cut back on the drink. We all like a beer, but you get greedy and take it to a whole new level. We're not asking you to quit, just give them a try, see for yourself what's going on and hopefully you'll realize you need to make some changes in your life."

"Guys you're right. I know what you are saying, and believe me, I appreciate your concern and it's great to have such good friends around me. I know I have to change and I'm really going to make a conscious effort to work on it. Big Man, I'm sure you went to a lot of effort to make the camera glasses, but I don't want to walk around wearing those things."

"We called them beer goggles," replied a deflated-looking Gordon.

Stevie chuckled.

"Well the name is better than they look, that's for sure," said Stevie. "Listen; let me try on my own for a while. If things get to the point where they're clearly not working, I'll let you know and I promise I'll give them a shot."

"Well I suppose that's better than nothing," said Colin, finally joining the conversation.

"Look, I'm gonna get out of here and try and get Sandra before she finishes her shift. I love you guys; I want you to know that."

"Well that didn't go exactly as I had planned," said Gordon after Stevie had left the house.

"Give him some time to think about it," replied Colin. "He's a proud guy who doesn't like to admit defeat. Trust me, if he encounters another incident or two that freaks him out, he'll be back begging you for the beer goggles."

"I really hope you're right," said Gordon, not looking completely convinced.

The Graveyard Shift

"I love you Dad. I'll always love you. I know you had your reasons for ending your life, but I just wish you'd confided in me. I'm a closed shop myself, and hate sharing my thoughts and feelings publicly, but *we* could've talked, kept our discussions as a secret between you and I. We could've grieved together, drank together, cried together, and just been there for each other in times of need. I'll never hold it against you Dad, but you've left me lonely and empty, wondering why and whether there was anything I could've done. I miss you my friend."

His dad's gravestone lit up as a hint of sunlight peeked its warm head around an angry grey cloud. Stevie felt easy about talking out loud here, even though he was alone. Addressing the stone was like they were together again as he knew he was only six feet away from him.

It was a little freaky how the weather seemed to change during his weekly visit. Even on the dark and overcast afternoons there always felt like a bright interlude after he delivered his words for the day. Was this a sign? Was he somehow looking over him? Maybe he was, maybe he wasn't, but it made Stevie feel a little better inside.

The bar was always his first port of call on the way home from the cemetery. The walk there was around fifteen minutes or so, but he'd *never* remember any of it as he was so caught up in the thought of his father and all the good times they'd spent together over the years. He'd arrive at the bar without any recollection of the scenery that had passed along the way.

It had been over a year now since his passing, but mentally Stevie was getting worse. He'd hoped by now that the good days would be outweighing the bad, but the opposite was occurring. It was hard for him to focus during many points of the day and his pining for alcohol was becoming worse and worse, and more of a way of life rather than a recreational activity. He was in a rut, and the longer time passed, the deeper into the hole he was falling. He needed to escape; he needed a getaway, a change of scenery to leave all of it behind him for even a short period of time. He wished he could pack in his job and backpack across Europe or something, but he had bills to pay and couldn't afford such a luxury. His annual holiday with the boys was still over a month away, but it was at least something he could look forward to. He wanted to fast forward his life to the Ibiza departure date but knew he was being ridiculous. Hopefully he could manage to keep his shit together until that day.

Miss Rub and Chug

"*Just leave me here son, I don't want to be saved. I can't go on. It's nothing personal against you, but life has just lost its meaning and every minute without your mother is just killing me anyway.*"

He was just hanging there in the darkened room, kitchen chair on its side directly below his swinging feet, and the thick rope around his neck digging in deeper and deeper as his white face turned red and then made its way to deep purple. He couldn't leave him there. He couldn't stand there and watch him suffer, but he was in shock, and all feeling in his limbs had gone, rendering him immobile. Deep purple was quickly becoming blue and the choking sounds were diminishing at about the same pace as Stevie's heart rate was accelerating.

Finally he managed to move his lead feet in his father's direction and stretched out his loving arms towards him.

"*GET OUT OF HERE,*" *he shouted in a high pitched tone as his eyelids began to close.*

Stevie screamed, again bolting upright in his bed; an all too familiar event these days.

As usual his sheets were soaked in sweat and his heart pounded like a drum, but he was comforted by the fact it had all been a dream. Nevertheless, the vision of his choking father was still eating away at his mind. He needed to get up and out of the house.

It was another cold morning as he stood at the bus stop; breath showing in the air like a chain smoker on a winter morning. The streets were surprisingly busy for such a chilly day; mainly women wrapped up tightly in their woolen clothing and many of them dragging complaining young children along, no doubt pissed off they'd been forced to tag along with the weekend shopping and not situated cozily at home together with their PlayStation. You had to love Scotland. It was only September, but still cold enough to freeze the balls off a brass monkey.

It was likely Stevie's imagination, but buses to him always seemed to take longer to appear when weather conditions were less than favorable. The elderly woman beside him was obviously on the same page.

"They need to put on extra buses on days like these. My arthritis doesn't take kindly to this weather," she said, obviously aiming her words in his direction.

"I'm with you there. I can hardly feel my fingers and toes."

The desperate look in her eyes indicated she was praying the big red vehicle would immediately come hurdling around the corner, but nobody in the sky appeared to be listening.

The wind was howling up the high street and he was glad the old dear had a tight grasp on her heavily loaded shopping bags.

She was a frail-looking old soul, slightly hunched and around four feet eleven, limbs like twigs, and a little woolen stitched hat sitting on her head like a thimble on a sewer's thumb. The weight in her grocery bags seemed like the only thing preventing the gusting breeze sending her airborne.

Stevie's teeth were chattering together in a consistent rhythm as the forty four bus finally appeared. He carefully helped his old lady friend up the step and then searched helplessly for change in his jean pocket with his chilled fingers. He questioned why he'd never invested in a pair of gloves.

He sat down well away from the old dear. She was a nice woman, but he couldn't bring himself to endure a journey of complaints until the center of town.

He gazed out the grubby window, unable to see any sign of a reflection. The folks in the street seemed in despair with their weather-beaten features, and the naked tree branches looked helpless and defenseless against the very wind that had already stripped them bare.

The journey was a familiar one for him, one he made around once per month. He owned his own car, but enjoyed using public transport when visiting the city as parking was a bitch.

Even though he was a regular visitor of Maria's, he always felt a sense of guilt as he made his way there. It *was* a massage parlor with a twist, but he was a single man, so wasn't exactly doing anything he shouldn't have, other than the fact the business they operated wasn't exactly above board; although the cops tended to leave the place to its own devices, probably a result of many of the clientele being members of the force and several of them also being attached.

The brakes on the rickety old bus squeaked to a halt and he jumped off after giving the old lady a wave goodbye. The stop was a mere fifty yards from the parlor door, which was more than a blessing on a day like this.

It *was* a massage parlor, but to the naked eye it was just another door to an apartment building. There was no sign, no advertising in the local newspaper, not a sign of any evidence. He'd only found out about the place via a friend of a friend; a guy who used to be a door-to-door salesman, selling any old junk he could get his hands on. He was a short little bald fellow, which was the main reason the madam of the house had let him in, figuring there was no way in hell he was affiliated with the police department.

Stevie pressed the intercom button and waited eagerly for a reply.

"Can I help you?"

"It's Stevie here to see Maria."

No further words were spoken before the buzzer sounded and he pushed open the heavy wooden door and made his way upstairs.

It was a typically old Glasgow sandstone building; dull hallway with grey stone stairs and slowly dripping exposed water pipes. It wasn't exactly the definition of cozy and clean. The place needed a good sweep and a few lights to assist navigation, but it was just like the other buildings in the neighborhood and blended in well as just being another normal residence.

Madam Mary – as the other girls called her - was there to greet him at the door; the owner of the establishment. She was a plump woman in her early forties with bleached blonde short permed hair; a looker in her day no doubt, but was now focusing on the business side of operations rather than the happy endings. Her build looked designed to iron out any knot in your back, but Stevie was certain there were very few clients making the visit specifically for the massage. Rumor was that back in her prime Madam Mary's oral technique was so intense she could've sucked a tomato through a tennis racket, bringing the meaning of happy ending into another dimension.

Very few women intimidated Stevie, but Madam Mary was one of them. She always gave him a warm welcome as he arrived, but she always followed it by glaring at his flesh up and down with a sordid, almost sinister look that had an element of Grace Jones mixed with Hannibal Lecter running through her pupils.

She ushered him into the second room on the left as they made their way up the warm hallway. The interior was a stark contrast to the dull and drab staircase of the tenement building, with a thick shag pile black carpet and bright red painted walls that were decorated with black and white framed pictures of her "girls" at regimented intervals.

"Enjoy. Maria will be with you in a few minutes," she said, with a smirk on her face that was extremely difficult to interpret. What was going through her mind?

He started to undress, and the sweet smell of the burning incense had a clearing effect on the nose and added to the relaxation. There was the usual soft instrumental music playing; *Enya* or something, and combined with the dim lighting, the sweet incense, and the scattering of flickering candles, was counteracting his excitement of knowing the glorious Maria would be laying her hands – and hopefully mouth – on him in a matter of seconds.

He neatly folded his clothes and sat them on the brown leather chair in the corner, then clambered onto the huge massage table and slipped under the pristine white sheet, face down, and eagerly waited on her arrival. The temperature in the converted bedroom was chillier than the perception the surroundings gave off, and he could feel his dick shriveling up by the second.

Stevie glanced around and made eye contact with Maria as she entered the dimly lit room and smiled. She was dressed in her usual hip hugging blue jeans and black bikini top. Stevie instantly broke-out in goose bumps across his entire body and was more than happy he was lying there in a face down position.

"Hello Stevie," she said in her low husky voice as she gently ran her long finger nails over the length of his back.

"Hi Maria; nice to see you again."

He peaked up at her and watched as she removed the bikini top and exposed a tanned set of double D's; obviously a couple of plastic efforts, but extremely pleasing to the eye and groin nevertheless.

"Any special requests today?" she asked as she squeezed some massage oil into her right palm.

"No, just the usual will be fine."

The usual implied the following order of activities:

1) Back and neck deep tissue massage.
2) Chest rub and light face massage.
3) Oiled up breasts used to massage genitals.
4) Heavily lubricated hand job.
5) Deep throat blow job until climax.

Stevie had been tempted to ask for more in terms of "special requests," but knew Maria did not do full service. He was more than happy though just lying there and putting in no effort. It was a pleasant change from the usual sexual encounter and a luxury he enjoyed once in a while.

Maria rubbed her hands swiftly together before applying them to his back. The friction warmed up the oil considerably and he let out an involuntary groan of relief as she worked her fingers deep into his back muscles.

The back and neck rub lasted about fifteen minutes of the hour session and she gave him two gentle smacks on his arse cheek which signaled it was time to roll-over onto his back. Stevie quickly obliged as he knew it was getting closer to the real fun.

"I guess you *are* happy to see me," laughed Maria; Stevie lying there naked with his one-eyed-willy winking at the ceiling.

"You just have that magic touch Maria; I can't help myself," replied Stevie, fighting through the moderate embarrassment.

The chest and light face rub were next. The face part was delightfully soothing but the chest rub was something he wasn't so fond of. The deep pressure applied snagged the occasional hair and caused a *voluntary* groan, but he figured Maria thought it was yet another pleasure noise as she continued on unfazed.

Finally the torture ended and Maria lubed up her fake breasts. There was so much blood flowing to Stevie's member that he was beginning to feel light headed, but extremely delighted he was perched in a horizontal position. She straddled him, leaning over and grasping each side of his penis with her plastic bags of fun and moved up and down slowly in a rhythmical motion while looking up at him and staring deep into his eyes. The eye contact only magnified the eroticism of the entire situation and he searched the depths of his mind in an attempt to curtail the excitement. Fly fishing on a tranquil lake was first to mind, relaxing him slightly and prolonging the inevitable. Next topic was dairy farming in the Scottish borders, but he quickly switched subject matter as the sudden visual of milking a cow focused in on the udders, and before he knew it he was back picturing Maria's erect nipples.

Eventually he settled on the visualization of laying back in a warm Jacuzzi, with the beat of the bubbles on his undercarriage being the mental substitute for what was actually occurring.

Maria removed her breasts from him and climbed off the table from her straddled position. Stevie knew what was coming next and closed his eyes, listening to the sound of her palms rubbing together at super fast speed, heating up some new oil. He gulped on his Adam's apple as he felt her warm lubricated hand grasp hold of him and he knew the finish line was in sight and that no amount of invented visual distraction was going to prolong activities more than a few minutes. His toes curled as he felt her hot saliva engulf every inch of him; her soft wet tongue wriggling around his shaft like a terrified eel in a fisherman's net. He clenched as hard as he could as her head picked up the pace, trying to hold off for a few more seconds before detonation, but his contracting thigh muscles were beginning to shake and virtually beg for leniency. He was tempted to just ejaculate without saying a word, but on their first ever meeting, Maria had set one of the ground rules of letting her know in advance as squirting in her mouth was *not* on the menu.

"I'm gonna cum," said Stevie, digging his nails into the sides of his legs and throwing his head back.

As soon as he felt her mouth pull away from him he unclenched his thigh muscles and instantly erupted like Mount Vesuvius; his entire body bursting into a spasm equivalent to an epileptic fit.

"Wow!" said Maria. "Can I assume it's been a while since you emptied the tank?"

"Not really. As I said, you just have that effect on me."

Maria left the room briefly and returned with two warm white washcloths.

"Here, you might need both of these," said Maria with a smile.

She wasn't joking either. His stomach resembled a glazed donut, his belly button was full and running over, and he even had a rogue hot droplet tentatively balancing on his chin, slowly contemplating whether to make its way down his neck.

"I'll be waiting outside when you're done Stevie."

"Thanks again Maria, I had a wonderful time as usual."

Stevie wiped himself down using both towels as recommended and slipped back into his clothes. As stated, Maria was waiting outside, back in her black bikini top, and Madam Mary was by her side with the same smirk on her face as before. Stevie wondered what her deal was, but she was the head of the house so she could do or say as she pleased.

"Thanks again Maria," said Stevie, reaching into his back pocket and handing her an envelope marked "gift."

"Thank you Stevie, please *cum* again," quipped Maria, and Madam Mary's smirk turned to laughter.

"Oh, I'll be back."

Maria escorted him to the door, kissed him on the cheek, and he made his way back for the return bus journey home.

The Big Reveal

The next few weeks for Stevie did nothing to improve his mental state of mind. His vivid nightmares of his father's suicide were on the rise. Sleep was becoming a luxury and his drinking only increased. It was a Catch 22 situation. If he didn't drink he got no sleep. If he did get trashed he got plenty of coma-like sleep, but the intensity of the dreams magnified ten-fold and continued to terrorize him throughout the day and ate into his already lackluster work days.

Today was one of those traumatized days, but fortunately it wasn't another work day. He'd planned on spending this Sunday afternoon in front of the television with a six pack and a pile of unhealthy food, but his mind was working overtime and he had to find something more interesting to occupy his head.

He called Sean, but no answer. He called Gordon, but no answer either. He called Colin and was ready to hang-up when a tired sounding voice said hello.

"Did I wake you up mate?"

"Do I sound like I've been up for hours dip shit?"

"Well I have chief, so get your shit together."

"*You've* been up for hours. That'll be a first for a Sunday morning."

"Yeah man, I'm still having those fucked up dreams about my dad. Listen, I need to get the hell out of the house for a bit to take my mind off things. Are you up for doing something?"

"Sure, I'm up for doing something. What did you have in mind?"

"I was thinking we could head into town and have a couple of drinks and a few games of pool at *Hot Pockets* on Hope Street."

"I'm good with that."

"Well I'll meet you at the train station. It's quarter to ten now, can you be there in an hour? The train is at five to eleven."

"Yeah I can do that. I just need a quick shower, shit, and a shave."

"Alright buddy, see you then."

"Later mate."

It was a fresh morning as Stevie made his way down the main street in the direction of the station. The sun was out but the wind was as crisp as ever. The street was quiet as a result of most of the shops being closed for the day. The few folks that were around were either buying their morning newspapers and heading to the bars for opening time, or making their way towards the church that was located around the corner from The Crown. Church was something that Stevie had been forced to attend as a young boy, but he figured there was now a probable chance he'd spontaneously combust if he tried to enter such a holy place given his current lifestyle.

McAlpine's, the bakers, was one of the few places open in addition to the newsagents. He could smell the freshly made pies and sausage rolls from more than twenty-five yards away as he approached. For once he was early for his planned meeting time with Colin, and hadn't eaten yet, so decided that the left turn into the shop was the sensible option and would prevent kicking off the drinking binge on an empty stomach.

"One meat pie and one chicken and mushroom pie please sweetheart."

"You got it Stevie," replied Betty, the elderly shop assistant.

The smell of the place was verging on orgasmic and not surprisingly so. On a mid-week lunch hour the place was usually queued out of the door and into the street. They were famous for their puff pastry pies filled with chicken and mushrooms and their secret white creamy sauce. The store was a little gold mine and the only feature lacking was a small restaurant area in the back of the store that would've only added to their overall success.

Betty wrapped both pies separately and placed them in a brown paper bag. She'd been working there ever since Stevie could remember. She used to serve him his lunch during school two days a week when his father threw him some extra pocket money on a Tuesday and Thursday to break-up the monotony of Mum's homemade sandwiches.

"Have a good day Stevie."

"Thanks Betty; you take it easy."

Betty was an absolute diamond. She put up with the crap customers used to give her about having to wait so long in line with the skill of a seasoned negotiator. It was never her fault the popularity of the place resulted in significant wait times; she wasn't responsible for staffing levels. She would just look back at the offending customer, wearing her not so fashionable hair net and blue apron, and apologize with a concerned tone and a smile, occasionally offering a free donut to keep the flapping business-types somewhat more content. She deserved a medal considering the minimum wage she was probably making.

On this day though things at the bakers were slow, and as usual, Betty still showed all the courtesy that would've been given to a member of the Royal Family.

Stevie marched down the main street, taking a couple of bites out of his meat pie. Seeing Betty only flooded back the memories of his father giving him lunch money as a young boy. He searched for anything to keep his mind occupied on other things. His mind worked in strange ways at times and he created a game that even kids would've thought was dumb.

He figured the meat pie would take twelve bites to finish, but the chicken and mushroom would be around fifteen, giving a total of twenty-seven bites to leave him with an empty brown bag. However, he'd already taken two bites from the meat pie, which left twenty-five. He simulated a bite of the pie, carefully looking around to see if anyone was watching as he didn't want to appear as a complete nutcase by being seen biting into a tasty piece of fresh air. He walked as he pretended to chew and worked out it would take seven steps between biting, chewing, swallowing, and then onto the next bite. He began further calculation. Twenty-five bites to finish both pies. Each of his steps covered approximately one yard, so he would advance about seven yards per bite, multiplied by twenty-five meant he would be walking one hundred and seventy-five yards before he was finished with the food. He still had about five hundred yards to go before reaching the train station, but figured he would be just about finished with his food by the time he got to Mario's, the pizza place, just before Station Road.

He ate and walked, making sure he adhered to a bite every seven steps. He focused on the task at hand, fighting off all thoughts about how crazy he was being.

The remainder of the meat pie was devoured in the planned ten bites, although the final piece was considerably larger than the previous nine, but he was determined to stick to the plan so gobbled it down and chomped at an accelerated rate. He was robot-like as he marched down the main street, staring directly ahead, ignoring all passers-by and concentrating on his chewing and mathematical calculations.

He almost raised his arms in jubilation like the winner of a sprint race as he pushed the final chunk of chicken and mushroom pie into his mouth. To his left at that moment was Mario's place just as he'd envisioned. He was such a dork, but at least it had kept his mind occupied and off the subject of his father.

He arrived at the station, breaking wind twice and burping as a result of his full belly, before entering the door of the ticket office. It was a rundown looking place; peeling grey paint and in need of a serious sweep. He purchased a single ticket to the city center from the sour-faced rail worker and headed out track-side. A return ticket was cheaper than two singles but there was always a chance of hooking up with a girl or taking a taxi home, so he decided against that option.

A few minutes later, as he stood there in a trance, his mind replaying old footage of Ally McCoist scoring against Celtic – again as a way of keeping depressing thoughts out of his head – he received a tap on the shoulder.

"Alright ya drunken bum,"

Stevie turned to see Colin standing there in his blue jeans and a brown duffle-style jacket, and gave him a friendly hug.

"How you doing mate?"

"Not bad Stevie. I'm glad you called. Going out for a few is certainly going to beat the boredom of staring at the four walls."

"Yeah, I hear you. I'm really trying to put all this stuff with my dad behind me, but I'm struggling big time."

"Well, a few pints and some games of pool will have your mind off it in no time."

Colin was lying. He wasn't overly enthused about spending the afternoon on the sauce as he knew it would probably make its way into the night as well, but he knew when Stevie called that regardless of whether he agreed to going out for the day, Stevie would've gone out somewhere on his own anyway, so he wanted to try and keep an eye on his troubled friend.

The train made its way along past Newton station and then stopped at Cambuslang. A bunch of poor-looking souls climbed aboard and sat in the general vicinity of them. There were a group of teenage boys, around fifteen or sixteen years old, who all looked as though they'd been dodging a bar of soap for around a week. All of them were obviously intoxicated from some liquid or other substance as they were giggling and messing around at the silliest of things and their eyes looked as though they were painted on.

A young mother and her two kids sat down opposite them.

"Sit down and behave. I won't tell you again," she said to both kids.

"But I'm hungry Mum," said the elder of the two.

"I know son, and I'm sorry, but we'll get some chips or something when we get into town."

"OK Mum."

Stevie may have had problems but there were so many people out there that looked as though they were really hurting and as though every day was a game of survival rather than something that could be savored. The young mother was perhaps in her early twenties, but her face looked weather-beaten and fatigued. She was either a single mother or was with a guy who left the kids, cooking, and cleaning all to her while he drank away the welfare money. The kids looked about five and eight years old. The older kid looked cleaner and tidier than the younger one. The baby of the two was wearing little black jeans that were frayed and washed-out looking, and his jacket was in a similar vain. Stevie figured it was a result of the family not being able to afford brand new stuff for the both of them; the little fella getting the shitty end of the stick by receiving all the hand-me-downs from his older brother. The mother and both kids had greasy skin and hair, almost matted into thick strands. They needed some good nutritious food, fresh vegetables, and pure fruit juices, not oily chips like their mum had just promised. It was like a disease all across Scotland as thousands pushed batter-covered sausages and greasy chips into their mouths every day of the week. Whether it was convenience or a more economical option was debatable, but heart disease and child obesity was an ever increasing problem. Stevie felt lucky but depressed as he watched those less fortunate than himself. He definitely needed a drink now.

Hot Pockets, as usual, was fairly busy. It was located at the top end of Hope Street, no more than a stone throw from Stevie's massage hangout. The place was huge; formerly a nightclub by the name of Alexander's. It was an American themed sports bar with over fifty large screen TV's spaced out throughout the premises, as well as twenty pool tables located in the back quarters. It still had all the original club features; upper deck balcony overlooking the old dance floor area that was now the 8-ball arena, and the previous DJ booth was still an active element; resident mixer AJ McLaughlin spinning tunes during times when football games weren't being broadcast.

Only English Premiership football games were ever shown, but their play was attractive and entertaining enough to attract many neutral supporters. Scottish games used to be the main feature of a weekend afternoon until all the trouble had broken out. A Rangers and Celtic showing resulted in the death of one guy and the serious injury of seven others. The tension had been building up throughout the afternoon in a close fought match; both sets of supporters represented on opposite ends of the circular bar. The game at Parkhead was decided by a single goal from an Ugo Ehiogu overhead kick that took the spoils for Rangers. When the full-time whistle blew all hell broke loose. All injuries were a result of stab wounds. The poor kid who was killed had been celebrating a little too emphatically in the minds of the Celtic hooligans and his chest was bombarded many times by more than one blade. The worst of it was that the kid wasn't even an old-firm supporter at all. He was a season ticket holder at Partick Thistle, but just happened to have Ehiogu starting in his fantasy football team. The consequence of the scuffle and the severity of it all was a permanent ban on the broadcast of all Scottish games, which was a positive move on behalf of the bar.

"Guinness?" asked Colin.

"Absolutely mate," replied Stevie, licking his lips.

They sat at the bar and Stevie surveyed the clientele while Colin flagged down one of the female bartenders. All the staff – with the exception of the security – was female and clad in tight fitting black shorts combined with Stars and Stripes t-shirts. Stevie found this slightly ironic. It might've been the colors of the American flag, but red white and blue in Glasgow was most closely associated with everything Rangers football club.

It was just pushing midday, but the seating around the bar was virtually fully occupied. It was approaching kick-off of the Merseyside derby match between Everton and Liverpool, but all drinks were half-price during matches, and there was nothing like cheap alcohol to bring Scottish punters crawling out of the woodwork.

"Here you go chief, get that down you," said Colin, sitting a pint of black velvet down in front of Stevie.

"Cheers buddy," replied Stevie, clinking his glass against Colin's pint of Tennents Lager.

"Should we have a few and watch some of the game before playing some pool?"

"Yeah, I'm in the mood for a few beers before I kick your arse on the table," said Stevie, flashing him a wink.

"A pound a frame?" was Colin's reply, and they shook hands on the bet.

Glasgow folks were a real mixed bunch of people. There were the rich, the middle of the road, and a "healthy" scattering of the poor. Many Edinburgh people – particularly the avid football fans – referred to them as the soap dodgers, and there were certainly a few of them on site in the bar to back up this definition. Two middle-aged gentlemen were sitting beside the boys who looked as though they'd spent the early hours of the morning on the streets begging for money. There was a damp, musty smell to them and they both appeared like they hadn't seen a bathtub or a razor in over a week. Combined with the fact they were counting out the cost of each round of drinks with spare change on the wooden bar top only added to the perception.

Stevie leaned in towards Colin.

"If two seats anywhere else around the bar become open, let's move. I don't want any chicks potentially coming up to us and thinking it's me who smells like a sack of shite."

Colin sniffed the air and virtually gagged.

"Absolutely mate. I don't need anyone thinking that either, but if they smell something and look at us, you're probably going to be the one automatically labeled with the stinky bastard tag."

"Fuck you."

"You know I'm joking with you chief. Hey, grab your drink. Looks like there's two chicks over there that are leaving."

Stevie couldn't get off his barstool quickly enough, but the smelly guys were too busy counting their coins to realize why their current neighbors were moving.

"Sweet, but it had to be two women that are leaving didn't it. There's hardly any in here as it is right now. The place is like a fucking gay bar."

Colin just laughed as they made their way around the circular bar.

"You leaving ladies?" asked Colin.

The question had an obvious answer as they were already off their stools and throwing their handbags over their shoulders, but he was just being courteous.

"Yes we are," replied the cuter of the two, which wasn't saying a lot as neither were contenders for a full page spread in Maxim magazine.

"That's a shame," said Stevie, flashing them his infamous smile.

He was without doubt a dog of a man and would've probably slipped his penis through a hairy donut if he knew it would get him off.

"Well we're not leaving completely, just going over to play the slot machines for a while," said the other girl.

"Cool, maybe we'll see you later for a drink then," replied Stevie, still grinning from ear to ear.

"Maybe you will," she replied, both of them blushing slightly, but loving the unfamiliar attention.

Off they trotted down the set of three stairs and away from the official bar area, looking back for a sneaky glance as they headed in the direction of the gambling machines located towards the back of the place, just before the mass of pool tables.

"You are unbelievable," said Colin, shaking his head.

"What?"

"They were a couple of old boilers mate. I was half expecting one of them to start shouting 'the bells, the bells,' or something."

"Now you've taken that too far. None of them had a hunch on her back."

"That's about all that was missing," replied Colin.

"A hunch on the back wouldn't be all that bad. It would certainly prevent us having to put in a lot of effort."

"What the hell are you talking about?"

"Think about it. You get them into bed, missionary position obviously, knees in the air. Reach your hands under the back of their thighs and lift them up in the air a bit and quickly pull your hands away. It would set them in motion as their legs came back down, causing them to swing forward a little. As they swing back they'll hit the hunch and it'll automatically set them into motion not unlike a rocking chair. You can just lie there, propping yourself up on your hands a little and let their momentum move their private parts subtly up and down your shaft. Everyone's a winner."

"Stevie, you actually have something wrong with you. Why would you even think up something like that? You say I took things too far, you just sent that entire concept into another stratosphere."

Stevie howled with laughter and Colin tried to refrain, but it was a lost cause.

"I'm just messing around. You've gotta have a laugh. I know I do or I'd go absolutely insane. Anyway, let me buy you another few beers and maybe those chicks will look a bit better to you by then."

Colin's comment about the ladies being a couple of old boilers was a little on the harsh side. They weren't that old, maybe late thirties, but their looks weren't an immediate reminder of Quasi Modo. That *was* taking things too far. A fitness club was obviously not a regular hangout for them though as they both had a slight podge to their midsections as well as a little extra flab visible on their triceps area. Facially they were reasonably disguised; heavily caked in make-up, with bright red lipstick carefully applied. Both were decked out in tight blue jeans that were more than amply stacked in the rear end. Both their arses as they'd walked away from the bar area had looked as though they were chewing a stick of Wrigley's, jiggling furiously with each step, creating the impression they could blow a bubble at any moment. Neither of them had any real advantage over the other. If it came to a choice it would've been whether you had a preference for short blonde or long dark curly hair.

The boys chatted and knocked back beer after beer as they watched a closely fought battle between Liverpool and Everton on one of the large flat screens littered around the walls; the reds scoring a late injury-time header to take the spoils two goals to one.

"Right, you ready for a spanking then?" asked Colin.

"Well as long as you're talking about pool, then yes," replied Stevie.

They grabbed another two pints and made their way towards the pool area. A few more people had entered the bar since their arrival, giving it more of an atmosphere as a constant muttering from the crowd could be continuously heard, but disappointingly for the boys all the additions were male.

"You winning ladies?" said Stevie as they passed the two girls from earlier as they sat in a couple of high-back seats, glued to the spinning reels of the fruit machine.

The question snapped both of them out of their trance and back to the land of the living. They both turned and smiled after realizing who was talking to them.

"We're up about twenty pounds," said the one with the long dark curly hair.

"Nice one. I was going to buy you both a drink later as well, but it sounds like the beers might be on you guys."

Stevie really knew how to work on women he'd never met before. He always played the quick-witted smart arse with a twinkle in his eye that lower-class Glasgow girls seemed to respond well to for some reason.

"I wouldn't bet on that if I were you," said the dark haired woman, flirting back and giving him a run for his money.

"Alright, I'll buy the drinks then. I'm Stevie by the way and this is Colin. What's your names?"

"I'm Fiona and this is Hazel," said the one with the dark hair.

"Nice to meet you ladies. Listen, we'll catch up with you in a little bit. I'm just going to quickly show my friend here how the game of pool is supposed to be played."

The poolroom had more atmosphere to it than the bar area. The sounds of breaking balls, laughter, and the periodic cries of jubilation provided a warmer, cozier feel. The tables were American-style nine footers with intense blue felt that was only magnified by the large rectangular lights hovering above each of them.

"Let's grab that one in the back corner," said Colin, pointing towards the far right of the room. "I think the closer I am to the toilets the better. It's about time to break the seal, so I'm probably going to need to piss once per game after that."

Around ten of the twenty tables were occupied and everyone was intermittently dispersed throughout, creating the perception that the place was busier than it actually was.

"Rack them up and I'll be back in a minute," said Colin, putting his pint down on the thin wooden shelf that lined the walls of the entire room.

The area was dark other than the twenty spotlights and the red neon signs above both bathroom doors set against the back wall. Rather than the traditional "Men" and "Women" wording, each neon sign was a series of thin hand-crafted glass tubes sculpting the shape of a stick man and the same for the ladies other than the addition of a triangle representing a skirt, and two individual glass pipes attached and pointing downwards from the circular head, acting as long hair.

Stevie threw a pound coin into the money slot and the balls shuffled their way down the little ramp and into the square-shaped opening at the end of the table. He made his way to the nearest cue rack attached to the wall; each of the sticks perched there like a formation of army cadets. He inspected a few of them, examining the tips and rolling a few of them on the surface of the table in any attempt to isolate one without even the slightest of warping, and gain an instant advantage over Colin before their game had even commenced.

Colin emerged from the bathroom holding his nose.

"That place fucking stinks in there. I don't know who's in one of the stalls, but from the grunts and groans that are coming from him, it sounds like an extra hot vindaloo was on his menu last night and is burning as much on the way out as it did on the way in."

"Well I'm alright for now but I know how that feels after a curry night."

"Right, enough of the shit talk," said Colin, chuckling slightly after realizing the pun. "You ready for an arse kicking?" he said, changing topic as he grabbed a cue from the rack and briskly chalked the tip.

"Oh I'm ready for you chief. A pound a frame and I'll even let you break first."

They shook hands and the game began.

About forty-five minutes into the match and two more pints from the waitress and they were tied up at three games a piece.

"OK, first to five wins," said Stevie, preparing to break off rack seven.

"Sounds good to me."

"So who's winning?"

They both turned to find the two girls from earlier standing next to them.

"How you doing ladies? Fiona and Hazel, right?" replied Stevie, squinting his face slightly, but he knew very well he had their names correct.

"Well remembered, we obviously made an impression on you," said Fiona with the dark hair.

"Absolutely," said Stevie, lying through his teeth. "Our game is all tied up at three each, first to five wins."

"Would you mind if we watched," asked Hazel.

"Not at all," was Stevie's response, raising his hand to signal the waitress who was cleaning up some glasses in the opposite corner.

She caught his eye and smiled, scurrying over happily in their direction, no doubt in prospect of adding to her current collection of tips.

"Hi sweetheart, could I have another two pints and whatever the ladies here are having."

"Certainly," said the petite blonde twenty-something with her elevated breasts almost pushing their way through the cotton material of her Stars and Stripes top.

"I'll have a Bloody Mary and she'll have a Pina Colada," said Fiona enthusiastically.

"I see you are ladies with expensive tastes," replied Stevie, now wishing he hadn't made the offer.

"Just ladies with class," said Hazel.

Colin gave Stevie a glance, raising his eyebrows as if to say "they wish."

The cute little waitress returned, balancing the four drinks carefully on her black tray and placed them one by one on the shelf.

"That'll be thirteen fifty," she said.

"Here, keep the change," said Stevie, handing her a twenty.

"Thank you very much," she replied, eyes beaming and teeth shining.

It was likely the best tip she'd received all afternoon, and although Stevie wasn't necessarily in the habit of displaying such generosity – unless to his friends – he had learned over the years that acting a little flashy and creating the perception of having a lot of money in front of women whom he had just met only seemed to increase the chances of them ending up in bed with him.

"That was very nice of you," said Fiona, now looking even more intrigued than she did before.

"It's only money ladies. You can't take it with you, can you?"

"That's very true," replied Fiona, giving him a discrete wink, but Colin captured all of it and was cringing at the mere thought of leaving with either of these growlers.

"Alright rich boy, let's get this game over with," said Colin, attempting to put an immediate halt to the obvious flirting.

The next two games were close fought, with Colin sinking a tricky black ball down the cushion in the eighth to tie it up at four a piece, much to the delight of Hazel who had obviously signed herself up as his lone cheerleader.

Fiona had latched onto Stevie which suited him perfectly. There wasn't much to choose between them in the looks department, but she was without doubt the feistiest of the two and he assumed this would translate into being more adventurous in the sack should the opportunity arise, which was looking likelier with each ball that dropped into a pocket.

"Best of luck to you mate," said Stevie, both of them shaking hands before Colin broke the final rack.

Off the break he made a stripe in the side pocket and then ran three more balls before missing a simple cut in the top left corner.

"Shit," said Colin.

"Unlucky!" was Stevie's reply as he got set to work on the open solids that were now looking extremely inviting.

He surveyed the situation carefully and chalked his stick. He was just about ready to take his stance when out of the corner of his eye he saw her walking towards the bathrooms.

Maria, his periodic "masseuse" was strutting elegantly down the center of the room in a tight black, long-sleeved top and hip hugging blue jeans. Just like Hazel and Fiona, her jeans were tightly packed, but in an athletic and sexy way rather then looking like they were a size or two too small. She was the last person he'd expected to see, but figured she'd probably been working the morning and decided to drop in for a drink on her way home or something. Her eyes didn't stray from the direction of the bathroom doors and he refrained from calling her. For one, he didn't want to potentially ruin the current female choices, even if a possible encounter with Maria was obviously *way* more mouthwatering. He was all about keeping his options open. Secondly, the boys were unaware of his monthly trips to the parlor. He figured some things were better left untold. It might've been an uncomfortable introduction for Maria anyway, even if Colin and the boys were aware. Stevie respected that she might be keen on remaining anonymous and didn't want to put her in an awkward position, even if he openly lied about how they knew each other.

He decided to wait on her to return from the bathroom and make an excuse to leave for a few minutes and follow her to at least say a brief hello. That *was* the plan until he saw her walk straight into the gents. At that moment there was no way he could concentrate on shooting pool. The ladies' and men's rooms were clearly labeled with their respective neon stick pictures and should've been a dead giveaway, so he concluded she must've been a little intoxicated.

"Hold the fort here for a second mate; I really need to pee badly. I'll be back in a second to wipe the floor with you," he said, leaning his cue against the wall and virtually running to the toilet.

He pushed the door open and was immediately faced with a white tiled wall, obviously used as a privacy screen to prevent anyone peeking in the door for a perverted look. He turned to the right, then a quick left u-turn into the brightly lit square-shaped room, lined with four stalls on the left, sinks and mirrors at the back, and a long stainless steel trough on the right hand wall. After no more than a single step, he instantly froze to the spot. His plan of making fun of her for walking into the wrong toilet and then suggesting they went somewhere for a drink backfired like a rusty old car with a mal-adjusted carburetor.

Maria was standing near the far end of the trough, slightly turned away from him, but he could still see a stream of urine flowing in a *horizontal* direction. Stevie was silent and she hadn't noticed his presence. His emotions were a mix of surprise and confusion, but immediately escalated to horror and panic as he glanced at the row of mirrors on the back wall and saw the reflection of her shaking a few remaining drips from her penis! Maria was a man. It all started to make sense as thoughts flashed through his disturbed mind. Her deep husky voice, as well as Madam Mary's smug grins each time he left her establishment.

Before he or she could zip up his or her jeans, Stevie turned and fled. He'd been tempted to deliver a beating, but didn't need to cause a potential scene under such circumstances and risk the possibility of having to explain the reason behind his actions.

He wandered in a daze back to the pool table, trying in vain to repress the visuals of Maria's mouth engulfing his penis. Saliva gargled in his throat, and he swallowed furiously to prevent vomiting right there and then for all to see.

"You feeling alright mate? You're looking as white as a sheet," asked Colin in a concerned voice.

"I'm good chief. I think the smell in there just got to me a little bit."

"I told you the place was stinking," replied Colin, glancing to Hazel and Fiona, only to see them both turning up their noses at the mere thought of the interior of the gents.

Stevie was anything but fine. His skin crawled as he realized he'd essentially been involved in many a homosexual act over the previous few months. He had nothing against gay people, but knew he was a devout heterosexual and the entire deceit of it all was making his blood boil, but there was no way he could *ever* tell *anyone* about his current predicament.

The bathroom door opened and Maria appeared. Stevie turned his back to avoid any possibility of eye contact and the chick with a dick made her way back in the direction of the bar.

"Dude, I think that a chick was just in there using our bathroom," said Colin, eyes popping out of his head as he traced Maria's arse until it was out of sight.

"Really, I never saw that. Anyway, let's get this game finished," said Stevie, wanting to concentrate on anything other than Maria.

Colin easily won the final game. Stevie was so preoccupied with the demons in his head that he couldn't even make the easiest of shots. His mind was in turmoil and he needed a distraction, and one that called out he was a flaming straight guy. Without any indication of his intent he walked straight up to Fiona and planted his lips on her. She let out a surprised squeak and her arms briefly flapped around, but she quickly accepted the advance, throwing her arms behind his back and pulling him close. The closed mouth kiss turned into a deep open-mouthed French version. Colin and Hazel looked awkwardly at each other.

She gave him a suggestive glance, but he was having none of it. He had standards. She was a nice enough girl but just not his type. He'd never be like Stevie. There was no way he could live his life where the phrase "any port in a storm" was the motto of every day.

Finally Stevie surfaced for air and Fiona stood there with a huge grin lining her chops, exposing her set of nicotine-stained wonky teeth.

"That was a little unexpected," she said, wiping away a dribble of their saliva mixture from the right hand corner of her mouth. "I haven't been kissed like that in quite some time."

There's a surprise, thought Colin.

"I'm a spontaneous guy," said Stevie in a suave sounding tone.

"I'm glad you are and I hope there's plenty more where that came from."

"You can put money on that," he replied, flashing his trusty wink.

Colin stood there with a look of alarm on his face, wishing he was being spit roasted over a cannibal's fire, just anywhere other than where he was now. Stevie though, was content in his mind that the kiss had somewhat neutralized the effects of the Maria situation.

"Would you guys like to join us at the bar for a few more drinks?" asked Hazel.

"Sounds good to me," said Stevie.

Colin prayed for the fire alarm to sound.

They gathered up their near empty glasses and headed to the bar, the girls in front and the boys close behind; Colin cringing with every step they made as he watched the flabby jiggle of the ladies plump behinds and thighs.

As they climbed the short set of stairs to the circular bar, Stevie again stopped dead in his tracks. Sitting towards the far left of the bar was Maria *and* Madam Mary. There was no way he could risk any form of interaction as he wasn't sure he'd be able to keep his emotions in check and avoid confrontation, and there was no way he was going to risk Colin finding out his secret. Even if he sat there avoiding eye contact he knew that Madam Mary could potentially jeopardize things. He didn't trust her smugness, and any suggestive comments from her would only lead to an inquisition from Colin.

"Hey ladies," said Stevie. "Do you fancy a change of scenery? I was thinking we could head off somewhere else. I hear Rab Ha's down in the Merchant city has some great drink specials around this time in the afternoon."

"We can't right now. A couple of our girlfriends are meeting us here at 3 o'clock. Wait with us till they get here and we can all go," said Fiona.

"No worries. We're just going to pop across the street for a bag of chips or something. I haven't eaten much today and if I'm going to be drinking a lot more I'd like to line my stomach a little," replied Colin, eager to beat Stevie in response, completely unaware that he didn't want to hang around either.

"Can you not just have something to eat here?" replied Hazel with a puzzled look.

It was a fair point. The place did a roaring trade on burgers, hot dogs, and Buffalo chicken wings.

"We'll be back shortly. I just fancy some good old-fashioned Scottish fish and chips, not any of the American-style shite they serve here."

"Fair enough, but don't be too long," said Fiona, literally undressing Stevie with her eyes.

"Sounds good, see you in about twenty minutes," replied Stevie, eager to get the hell out of the place, at least temporarily.

A cool breeze hit them as they walked out onto the busy pavement. Hope Street was bustling with shoppers and people out for lunch or afternoon drinks. An elderly homeless man sat in the doorway between *Hot Pockets* and the shoe shop next door, legs crossed, filthy cap turned upside down in his outstretched dirty hands, and a rectangular brown cardboard sign by his feet with the words "YOU DONT LUKE THIS BAD WHEN U HAVE A LOT OF MUNNY." The boys looked sympathetically at him then at each other and dug deep into their pockets, depositing about three pounds of change into the empty cap, taking care not to touch the sides of it.

"God bless you boys," he said from the opening of his thick bushy beard.

"No worries man, take it easy," replied Colin.

Stevie walked to the edge of the pavement, checking for an opening in the flow of cars.

"Where you going?" said Colin.

"Thought we were heading across the street for fish and chips?"

"That was just an excuse to get away from those piglets. Let's go somewhere else or head back to Uddingston."

Stevie thought for a second. The original plan in his head was to eat then head back to *Hot Pockets* in the hope Maria and Madam Mary would be gone already and he could then bag Fiona the sure thing, even if she was a bit rough around the edges. Chances were though that Maria and her evil boss would still be there, so leaving and trying for something better elsewhere was the sensible option and the one sure way he could leave the demons behind.

"Sounds good," said Stevie. "Fancy just getting the train back and going to The Crown?"

"Yeah, let's go."

"Tell you one thing though Colin, I'm going to get really fucked up when we get there."

Colin just laughed.

"Now there's something I wasn't expecting to hear!"

Gimme the Damn Glasses

It was Monday morning and Stevie awoke with a pounding head as usual. He pressed his tongue against the roof of his mouth; it felt as dry as sandpaper. He was still half asleep and his vision was a little blurred, but he could tell he was at least in his own place as he peered over to his bedside table to see the pleasant sight of his alarm clock and dark blue bottle of Davidoff Cool Water staring back at him. There was *no way* he was making it into work so decided a sick day was the logical option.

He racked his brain, searching frantically for the sequence of events from the night before, but beyond ten o'clock at The Crown was a huge void that would likely never be anything but a gap in his time on the planet. He remembered Colin leaving to head home, but very little else.

The bed covers stirred ever so slightly, together with a short groaning noise. He wasn't alone. She was wrapped up snugly facing away from him, red hair being the only visible part of her. He'd remembered flirting with Sandra at the bar as she poured

115

pint after pint, but he hadn't remembered coming home with her never mind being involved in any sexual acts, but he knew they must've, as his penis felt raw and ached, almost throbbing with a heartbeat all of its own.

Stevie slipped his naked body quietly out of bed and staggered his way to the kitchen. He opened the fridge and the internal light startled his eyes. His head was spinning and his vision filled with white stars as the dizziness magnified. He reached quickly for a bottle of ice cold water and gulped down every last drop with the intensity of a desert nomad, before switching on the kettle and making his way back through to the bathroom.

The taste in his mouth even disgusted him. He gargled hard with some mouthwash and jumped into the shower for a quick rinse. The warm jet felt invigorating and gradually revived some life back into his hungover body.

The whistle from the kettle increased with intensity and he wrapped a thick white bath towel around his waist like a long skirt and headed back through, dripping water onto the carpet as he went, before reaching the tiled floor of the kitchen. He poured two mugs of coffee and added milk to both after briefly giving the open-topped milk carton a quick sniff test. The milk was surprisingly fresh. He then reached for the half empty bottle of Johnnie Walker black label and dunked a generous measure into his own mug; he was a great believer in hair of the dog. He tip-toed his way back through to the bedroom as deliberately as a trained tightrope walker, trying hard not to spill any of the piping hot coffee in both his hands, and also to prevent the towel from slipping off. The multi-tasking proved too much, and the towel slipped to the floor, much to his amusement. He laughed as he stepped over it. Sandra had seen him full flesh several times now and he wondered why he'd even bothered with it in the first place.

He entered the bedroom with the contents of the mugs still intact. Sandra was lying in the exact same position as he'd left her.

"OK sleepy head, time to wake up. Get this coffee down you and you'll be as good as new."

She awakened and turned her head wearily towards him. Stevie let out a shriek, dropping one mug on the floor, and although still holding the other, most of the coffee hit the carpet with the exception of a few hot splashes that landed on his flaccid penis, causing him to let out another yelp. It *wasn't* Sandra. She had the same colour of hair, but that's where the similarity ended. He had no idea who it was and in his mind they had never met before.

"Jesus Christ Stevie, I might not be the most attractive woman in the world first thing in the morning but surely I'm not that scary."

The boys couldn't contain their laughter as they all sat in The Crown over an evening pint. They howled as Stevie replayed the story of the mystery red-head to them, so much so that Colin and Sean almost fell off their stools.

"So where did you meet her?" asked Gordon, grinning from ear to ear.

"*Apparently* outside the bar last night. Supposedly we ended up at a couple of other bars for a few drinks before heading back to my place."

"And you remember none of this," said Gordon shaking his head, Colin and Sean still rolling around in stitches.

"Not a fucking thing mate."

"So did she tell you what bars you went to?" inquired Gordon.

"No, I didn't get that far. She was that pissed off that I couldn't remember any of the night *or her name* that she just pulled her clothes on and bolted out the door. Can't say I'm too disappointed. She had a face like a bulldog licking piss off a thorn bush."

"Was she at least a good ride?" said Sean, finally pulling himself together.

"What part of I don't remember anything did you miss? She was disgusting. In a sober state I wouldn't have ridden her into battle. In saying that though, she did have a weird-looking face; long like a horse. She was a sour faced cow as well. If I hadn't been so shocked with her being there I wouldn't have asked her why the long face. Seriously though, if you'd seen her you wouldn't have known whether to shout 'giddy up' or feed her a carrot."

"Anyway Stevie, did you just ask us all to come here to tell us your news?" asked Gordon, knowing there was more to come.

"Not exactly. I was thinking about those glasses with the camera. You might be right lads; I need to sort my shit out. I can't keep doing a bunch of shit and waking up without the foggiest of where I've been or what or *who* I've done. So just gimme the damn things and I'll start wearing them. I need to know what's going on. I wish I could just stop the booze but I know that isn't going to happen over night."

The three of them looked genuinely impressed with Stevie's revelation.

"Well, this really is a surprise, but a fine one at that. Let's have a toast. To the beer goggles," said Gordon lifting his glass.

"Beer goggles," they all said, clanking their glasses together.

Things Done and Not Remembered

Stevie was sticking to Gordon's request and persisting with the glasses. One morning he woke-up with a pounding headache and little to no recollection of his evening antics, so decided to download all the recordings he'd taken from the previous week, and watch intently from his armchair while sipping on a whiskey-laced coffee.

The film was a bizarre look at his lifestyle. It was as though he and his armchair were located inside his own head as he watched his life, his *history* of events that played as real-time to him. Over that one week period he realized he needed to change. He wasn't a young kid anymore, but his behavior suggested otherwise. An array of events was uncovered that even he found disturbing:

1) Drinking Games and Diced Carrots

It had been a midweek night at The Crown on his own that had originally been planned as a couple of after work beers before heading home. Surprisingly enough a couple ended up multiplied by six.

Stevie forwarded the film to around his eleventh beer as he'd remembered up until around that point. The video stream was as though a Parkinson's sufferer was at the controls; Stevie's drunkenness causing his head to sway all over the place, and he chuckled to himself as he watched the proceedings, saying the words "stupid alcoholic prick" out loud as he did so.

Old Jack - who'd discovered Sandra's bra in the bathroom – sent a whiskey shot over to him via Sandra. Stevie watched the screen as he raised his glass in salute at the kind gesture. Jack toasted back to him with his own shot glass and Stevie downed it immediately; the glasses capturing the flowing whiskey as it accelerated into his mouth. He did not remember anything about whiskey, but it certainly explained the intense headache that morning as well as the sour taste in his mouth when he awoke.

Being a typical Scotsman Stevie bought Jack a shot also, and the tennis match with the whiskey was no short-term affair as it extended on in duration, shot for shot returned and the match reached an intense tie-breaker; Stevie winning 7-6 as Jack lay slumped in defeat cuddling the bar in unconsciousness.

Stevie sighed as he watched all this. His liver was really taking a beating and Jack would probably have been as well to put his name on the transplant list ASAP considering his age and the punishment he'd given it over the years.

Before staggering through the wooden archway to the bathroom, Stevie checked on Jack at the bar, who let out a groan when asked how he was doing. He was at least alive so Stevie continued on his way to drain off some fluids.

The film on screen again swayed from side to side as he stood at the urinal, looking down at his flaccid penis, attempting to get all of his piss into the half-circle-shaped white urinal, but the floor was receiving more than a light sprinkle. He zipped up his fly, dribbling a few late drips onto his jeans as he carelessly did so. He meandered his way back through to the bar completely oblivious of the small wet patches on his leg. Three of them remained in the bar: Sandra, Jack, and himself.

"Do you want me to give you a hand getting him out of here?" slurred Stevie to Sandra as he shakily pointed to Jack.

"No it's OK Stevie. Just you get yourself home to bed. While you were in the bathroom I called his wife to come get him. I think I woke her up and she sounded pissed off, but he can't stay here all night. Between her and I we'll be able to get him into her car."

Stevie's short walk home took double the time it would've in a sober state. His weaving all over the pavement was causing him to cover at least twice as much ground as necessary. His stumbling progressed but it wasn't long before the pathway to his front door was finally in view on the other side of the road. His vision moved to his feet as he watched as he shakily but deliberately placed his right foot onto the road. Out of nowhere he heard a wailing car horn and instantly flashing before his eyes, a red van whizzed past no more than six inches from him. He sat horrified in his armchair, glued to the screen as he fell backwards onto the pavement, his beer goggles now capturing nothing more than the star-filled sky. His heart pounded as he realized it could've genuinely been the moment he joined his father in the afterlife, and could hardly comprehend how he had no recollection of such a potentially life ending event. The glasses were beginning to put into perspective how bad things had become and delivering the message that Gordon and the boys were hoping they would send.

He watched as he clambered back to his feet, this time looking right then left before he crossed the street. There were a couple of his neighbors watching from their front windows, no doubt appalled by the state he was in. Stevie paused the footage and took a large gulp of his coffee before pressing play again. He was beginning to cringe and hoped those who'd been watching him were only alerted to their windows shortly after the sound of the car horn, and prayed they hadn't seen him fall over, but he knew that was extremely unlikely. What occurred next shocked him every bit as much as the near death experience.

Stumbling up the hedge-lined pathway to the front door he watched as he bent over the shrubbery and let loose with some uncontrollable vomiting. The sight of the puke landing on top of the green leaves was disgusting and almost resulted in an encore as he dry heaved in the comfort of his armchair as mouthful after mouthful decorated the hedge in orange chunks.

Eventually the spewing was over and he staggered backwards, glancing up at the on-looking neighbors and flashed them a one fingered salute before finally making it to the main door, taking four attempts to get his key in the lock.

2) <u>Don't Mind the Yellow Stains</u>

On another evening with the boys at a local bar by the name of Angels, he discovered yet another alarming situation. It wasn't a place they frequented that often but it was renowned for the loose women that often occupied the lounge later in the evening. The name of the place was ironic to say the least; there was nothing angelic about the little tarts who dressed like hookers and flaunted any finely formed body part they possessed.

Angels was split into two rooms; the bar area which was scantily clad with your basic tables and chairs and very little character, and the lounge which had a warmer feel to it due to the dimmer lighting, brighter summer colors on the walls, and seating comfortable enough not to result in a numb arse after sitting for more than twenty minutes.

On weekends the bar area closed at midnight and the lounge kept going until two. After the bar closed down, the lounge transformed into more of a cruise ship style disco with a dance floor in the far corner roughly twice the size of a pool table. There was a late night DJ, "Randy Andy" spinning tracks from the eighties and nineties interspersed with the occasional current chart hit. Randy Andy was actually a full-time insurance salesman who DJ'd at weekends and believed he'd missed his calling as a radio personality. He was however, no better than an American Idol try-out with the singing ability of a cat being dragged through a grinder. Instances when he played old Run DMC hip hop tracks he insisted on interrupting the tune by screaming into his microphone "wave your hands in the air like you just don't care" to the few drunken fools that were "shaking their thang," and this summed up his creativity as well as credibility.

It had been a heavy drinking night and each of the boys had exceeded their tolerable limit and each were suffering from slow blink syndrome as they fought the urge to fall asleep right there at their table.

Sean and Gordon were ready to be poured into a taxi and Colin and Stevie were right there with them. Stevie however, was attempting to convince Colin that a trip through to the lounge was the way the night should progress, but fortunately Colin had enough sense to decline and indeed convince Stevie to follow suit and head home.

Stevie watched intently from his armchair. The footage he was looking at was new to him. He'd remembered up until Colin had wiped the floor with him at darts and they'd thrown a couple of pounds in the jukebox to play "Gimme Shelter" and "Honky Tonk Woman" by the *Rolling Stones*, but the discussion on calling a cab was now fresh news to him.

He watched on screen as he excused himself to the bathroom, stumbling through the toilet door situated between the bar and lounge and taking solitary position at the small stainless steel trough-like urinal that was about equivalent in length to a three-seater sofa. He looked down; glasses filming his feeble attempts at pulling his dick out of his jeans, giggling as the phrase "third time lucky" finally found a true meaning. It must've been warm in the bar as his cock flopped out like he was half aroused. Perhaps he'd been thinking about naked girls or something, but unfortunately the glasses only captured vision and sound and not thoughts. Nevertheless he was more than content with the inches on display and again giggled before taking another mouthful of whiskey-laced coffee.

He watched attentively as he peed. Strangely he kept looking at his watch, so figured he must've been struggling with impaired vision, unable to clearly read the dial. His head moved ninety degrees to the right and the glasses caught sight of a guy in his early twenties who'd just taken position next to him. He spat a mouthful of coffee back into his mug as the guy's penis was on display and he was a little disturbed as to why he'd held his gaze for so long, but figured it was due to the fact the dick on display was a silver medal compared to his gold, or so he made himself believe.

Alarm bells struck. Again he looked at his watch, seemingly as capable as Stevie Wonder at reading the time, but on this occasion turning his *entire body* ninety degrees and asking the young fellow next to him if he had the correct time, and as a result, spraying the tails of the lad's trousers and brown suede shoes with his bright yellow stream. The look on the young man's face was initially priceless, like he'd been pissing in the Rockies and a black bear had appeared before him, but the shock quickly turned to rage.

"WHAT THE FUCK ARE YOU DOING?" screamed the guy, seemingly dying to launch an attack, but his own urine stream was still flowing and he appeared reluctant to cause further damage to his trousers and shoes.

"Easy tiger," said the familiar voice in the background.

It was Colin, grabbing Stevie by the shoulders and escorting him from the bathroom and leading him straight out of the front door into the street where Gordon and Sean were already sitting in a taxi.

3) Beer Spill and Barred

Stevie made himself another cup of coffee and sat back down on his armchair, putting the laptop on his thighs and hit the play button.

On this night in question it was another return visit to Angels bar and lounge. He'd been drinking with the boys back at The Crown, and again, he was the only one of the four without the common sense to call it a night. It was as though the more he drank the more he craved and he'd do anything in his power to get what he wanted.

From his living room he watched his vision as he told the boys he was going to walk home, but as soon as they got into the taxi outside the bar and were out of sight, he turned and headed in the opposite direction from his flat and staggered his way down the Main Street towards Angels.

He shook his head as he stretched back in his armchair, tracking his meandering walk down the road. Why did he do these things he wondered? Was he really that dependant on alcohol? He knew what was likely on his mind though in addition to the beer; picking up a girl, but three Viagra pills and a condom fitted with a splint would've been the only thing to keep him rigid in his current condition, even if he was lucky enough to score.

The doorman, Ronnie, at Angels gave him a cagey look up and down at the entrance door to the lounge, but let him pass even though he could tell Stevie was plastered. It wasn't really a surprise though as most of the young clientele were usually walking around with double vision around this time.

This footage was like a new day for Stevie as he watched. It concerned him how many times his drinking resulted in a complete blackout. He hadn't even remembered leaving The Crown, and he certainly didn't remember how crowded Angels lounge had been which was something in itself as he was being bounced around like a pinball as he made his way through the masses of people towards the bar.

As he neared the horizon that was the bar he saw his body jolt forwards and he crashed violently into a large man who was no stranger to a game of rugby, just as he was about to take a sip from his pint of lager. Stevie wasn't sure if he'd been bumped by someone or whether his drunken legs had just given out on him, but half of the gentleman's beer ended up covering the front of his white shirt.

"YOU FUCKING PRICK," yelled the giant of a man.

"Shit, sorry mate, someone pushed into me," said Stevie.

At home Stevie was cringing as he watched, and literally wanted to pull a cushion over his face so he didn't have to witness what was going to occur next, but he resisted the sudden urge.

"YOU'D BETTER BUY ME A NEW BEER OR I'M GONNA WEAVE YOUR HEAD INTO THAT FUCKING WALL."

Stevie cringed again as he pressed the pause button. This guy was furious and intimidating to say the least, with his shaved head, black goatee beard, and a set of shoulders on him designed for power lifting. What concerned him even more was his usual reaction to people who spoke to him in this way.

"No worries big guy, I'll get you a new pint."

He was impressed by his calmness as he watched and even more impressed with the gorilla. He might've been getting a fresh beer, but it wasn't going to suddenly absorb the huge stain down the front of his shirt.

"A pint of Guinness and a pint of lager for this big guy here," said Stevie to the young female bartender, who had a frightened look on her face as a result of the tension in the air.

She delivered the lager first, waiting for the Guinness to settle. Stevie took the lager and began to hand it to the brut of a guy. No sooner had he put his shovel of a hand out to take the gift, Stevie watched with repulsion as he threw the full contents of the glass over the guy's face.

"DON'T EVER TALK TO ME LIKE THAT AGAIN YOU FUCKING ARSEHOLE," screamed Stevie, throwing a right hook which connected with what looked like extreme force to the jaw of the shaved-headed brute. The apparent strength transpired into that of a butterfly landing on an eggshell and only seemed to infuriate the guy even more. Just then, Stevie watched as his head jerked upwards and he was staring at the white popcorn-style ceiling, but could see an elbow around his neck; someone other than the recipient of his feeble punch had him in a headlock. His body was quickly turned around and he was now heading towards the exit door. The room may have been packed, but the young patrons parted like the Red Sea, clearing an almost perfect runway for his departure. Stevie watched in horror as he saw himself hurdle down the three steps and into the street, falling over, but quickly returning to his feet. He turned around to see the doorman, Ronnie, staring angrily at him.

"Now get the hell out of here before I call the police, and don't come back, you're barred," said Ronnie, before returning back into the building.

Stevie pressed the stop button on his computer and took several deep breaths. It certainly explained why his knuckles had been sore and also the graze on his right elbow. Ronnie was only doing his job, and it was just as well he did, otherwise Stevie would've likely spent the evening in the Emergency Room or even the morgue if the big bear of a guy had been able to get his hands on him.

Stevie lay on top of his quilt and reflected on the events he'd watched. His life was certainly spiraling out of control. If it hadn't been for Gordon's beer goggles he would've had no idea how bad things had become as well as how often, and he would've no doubt just continued on with his crazy ways. His drinking had to stop or at least be reduced to moderate consumption. His mother and father would be appalled by what he was doing to himself if they could see him now. He had to put aside any lingering mental trauma and find some stability in his life, and it had to happen sooner than later, or joining them in an early grave was more of a probability than a possibility.

Where Am I?

It didn't take long for Stevie's plan of cleaning up his act to hit the back burner. It was only two days since his big revelation, but he figured he'd have a final blowout as a result of a work's night out. What he should've done was come up with a valid excuse for why he couldn't attend and stay home for a sober evening, but it was the company's ten year anniversary party and the food and drink was free all night. Dangling a carrot of free beer in front of Stevie was like attaching a cube of diced steak on a hook, hanging it from a fishing line in the Amazon River and politely asking a piranha not to take a bite.

He wished the boys could've come along with him, partly because most of the work folks were as interesting as a politician delivering a speech on healthcare reform, but also for moral support and keeping an eye on his behavior, but it was restricted to employees only. As a result, he *really* didn't want to go, but free beer was free beer and completely negated the impact of the less than desirable company.

Due to his lack of interest, Stevie didn't exactly get dressed up for the occasion. He managed a shower, but passed on a shave and formal attire. He was sure many of the company brown-nosers would be decked out in their dressed trousers and pressed shirts, but he wasn't one of them. He hated the company men and women, those who put on the corporate façade during work events, attempting to create an impression of someone they actually weren't behind closed doors. He hated fake individuals with a passion. If people didn't like him for who he was they could go and fuck themselves. Needless to say he opted for blue jeans and a black Calvin Klein t-shirt.

The taxi ride over to the event involved the usual bullshit conversation; isn't the weather a bitch, how's your job going, and aren't house prices escalating out of control. Stevie couldn't hand over the cab fare quickly enough, as pointless, forced conversation in order to kill time and awkward silence bored the crap out of him any time they occurred.

The venue for the evening wasn't exactly the Ritz Carlton. The company may have been forking out for the food and drink, but they'd obviously opted to save a few pennies with regard to the location. The Coach House hotel in Blantyre had definitely seen better days, and the use of the word hotel was stretching it a little as it only had eight rooms to let. In its day it was known as an upscale, quaint setting, ideal for taking a loved one for a nice Sunday lunch; renowned around the area for their award-winning steak and ale pies. Those days were long gone as a result of a change in management who were obviously lacking any business savvy as well as the concept of customer satisfaction, and were reluctant to put any significant money into their operation. It was amazing they were still open for business.

Stevie eyed the Tudor-style building up and down before he entered, and shook his head in disgust. Previously the outside walls had been pristine white with glossy black wooden windowsills and frames, and immaculate symmetrical guttering lining the roof. Now though, the perfect white was more of a smoker's living room white, verging on a sick washed out yellow. The gutters were falling apart and there were several rust-like stains streaked down the side of the stone walls where the rain water had been leaking down over the years. The glossy black paint on the windowsills was chipping away and they were a haven for accumulating spider webs. It really was a tragedy.

The interior had so much potential but had faltered as much as the exterior. The small lobby area looked like it was stuck in a 70s time warp, and Stevie chuckled to himself as the floral carpeting wasn't unlike one his grandmother used to own. The place smelled old as well; an almost damp fustiness to it that attacked the back of his throat, causing him to feel a little squeamish. The young dark-haired girl behind the reception desk looked slightly alarmed as she witnessed Stevie struggling to keep down his lunch.

"Can I help you sir?"

"Nothing an air freshener and a clothes-peg for my nose wouldn't sort out," said Stevie, wandering over to her while holding his nose.

"I'm sorry sir. We had a problem with a burst pipe yesterday. Hopefully the damp smell will go away soon. I guess my senses have just acclimated to it."

"Anyway, I'm here for the party. Can you tell me where I need to go?"

"Certainly sir, go straight down the hallway and take the last set of double doors on your right. The party is in the large function room. It'll say Coach Suite on the door."

"Cheers sweetheart, take it easy."

Stevie made his way down the hallway, thankful the stale smell was deteriorating with every step away from the lobby. It was the same retro carpet throughout and the narrow walls of the passageway were clad with cheap-looking light wood paneling.

As he approached the function suite his heartbeat picked up in pace. He wasn't sure why, but he hated walking into busy rooms when he knew he didn't care much for the crowd, and detested the feeling of all the sets of eyes on him. No doubt there would be muttering about the casual way he was dressed, but he just hoped it wouldn't be a scenario similar to an old western film when the villain entered the swing doors of the saloon; instant silence including the piano player drawing to a halt.

He took a deep breath as he readied himself for entrance and opened the door and walked into the large rectangular-shaped room that was *way* too brightly lit in his opinion. Fortunately not much attention was given to his arrival which calmed down his initial anxiety. Funnily enough there *was* actually as piano player, but he showed less than zero attention to his presence. Stevie was a little perplexed as to why they had someone on a grand piano in the far corner of the room, and even less enamored with the cheesy, soothing, pre-dinner melodies that were being churned out. They only added an unnecessary formal layer to the proceedings, causing him to feel even more scruffily dressed than he had before.

It was clear he was one of the last people to show up, as available seats were few and far between. He caught Maggie's eye - the forty something office administrative assistant, more than endowed in the chest department – as he strutted towards the bar for a well-deserved free beer. There was an open chair to her left at one of the large circular tables seating around ten people. She smiled as he approached and patted the seat of the empty chair with her hand. He wanted a drink badly, but figured by-passing Maggie's invitation would've been extremely rude, and would've been something that would've pissed him off substantially had the shoe been on the other foot.

"Hi Maggie, how are you?"

"Doing well Stevie. I'm having a nice time so far, but the two margaritas might have something to do with that."

Stevie sat down, but was itching to get to the bar.

"Well you can't beat a couple of cocktails to get the night off to a fun start."

"I love your glasses by the way, very sophisticated looking. I've never seen you wearing those before, but they really suit you."

"Yeah, they're a new addition. I just got them a few days ago," lied Stevie.

"Well they look cute."

"Watch my seat for a minute Maggie; I'm going to grab myself a drink. Can I get you anything while I'm up there?"

"Another margarita would be nice," she replied, shaking her empty cocktail glass.

Stevie approached the bar, but for some reason glanced back at the table, only to notice Maggie staring back at him. She gave him a wink and he reacted with a friendly smile. Maggie wasn't looking too bad, and he felt a little guilty as he always referred to her face in his mind as being as rough as a raccoon's scrotum; tonight though her face seemed to be showing fewer lines than usual. Perhaps some additional make-up had been applied to fill in some of the minor crevasses, but she was looking decent in his opinion and that was even before he'd consumed any alcohol. Her body was killer as usual though, and as normal, she was decked out in clothes fit for any trashy young woman hanging out on a street corner. She was sitting there legs crossed in a mini-skirt, toned legs on display for all to see. Her tight long-sleeved black spandex top hugged every curve, and only enhanced her oversized fake breasts. She'd also straightened her usual dyed blonde wavy hair for the evening, and between that and her unusually smooth facial features, it took at least five years off her and she could've easily passed as forty for the night. One thing was for sure, he was going to be giving her a good stare up and down during the night, capturing all with his beer goggles and sharing the delights at some point in the future with the boys.

"A pint of Guinness and a margarita please chief; in fact, make that two margaritas," said Stevie to the male bartender.

"So no Guinness, just the two margaritas?"

"No, still give me the Guinness, and the two margaritas on top of that."

"No worries mate."

The bartender sat the settling pint of Guinness on the bar and went off to work on the cocktails. By the time he returned with the two light green drinks the Guinness was nothing more than a glass with remnants of some white foam in the bottom of it.

"I take it you were thirsty," said the young guy, looking genuinely surprised by how quickly Stevie had finished his pint.

"I always get thirsty when the company is paying for it," said Stevie, giving him a wink. "Better pour me another while I'm here."

"You got it mate."

It was common knowledge that Stevie was an alcohol glutton, but the word "free" combined with the prospect of fooling around with an older woman who was a little rough around the edges only magnified the need.

He made his way back towards Maggie, taking tiny steps like he was walking a tightrope, making sure not to spill any of the contents of the three glasses that were forming a triangular shape together between his two hands.

He had requested to Maggie to save his seat, but as he looked over at her on his way back, she was guarding it with the intensity of an alligator watching her newly hatched babies.

"Well hello stranger," said Maggie in a seductive tone.

"Well hello there sexy lady, can I interest you in a cocktail?"

"I'd love one," said Maggie, relieving him of one of the glasses.

Stevie questioned himself. What was he doing flirting already? He quickly surmised that it was no big deal. He *was* single after all and Maggie had initiated things, and she was looking fairly appealing, so what the hell, there didn't seem to be anything else of equal excitement taking place in the room.

There were eight others at the table. He knew two of them extremely well, both a couple of egotistical fannies who thought they were the dog's bollocks even though they were lower down the chain of command than he was, and that was saying something. Their names were Crawford and Roderick, but Stevie had them tagged as Big Gay and Little Gay. They were both straight, but he'd never seen one without the other and had often pictured them snuggled up like Bert and Ernie from Sesame Street under the comfort of a pink Barbie and Ken decorated bed quilt.

The others at the table were not really known to him. He'd seen most of them around the work cafeteria as they munched on their garden salads and fruit while he was getting stuck into some fried and greasy option. He was happy about it though as it was ample excuse not to interact too much other than the quick informal introduction he'd given. The majority of them were sipping on cokes and orange juice, but three of them were supping on *half pints* of beer. It was apparent that their healthy lunch options cascaded over to their entire social lives as well. Stevie could tell they weren't exactly itching to talk with him either. He'd seen the subtle change in their pupils as they sized up his attire and he'd almost heard a few disapproving sighs also as he put his Guinness *and* margarita down at his place setting on the table. The reaction delighted him as he knew it meant they'd be avoiding him like the plague and it was a free pass to focus his attention on Maggie.

The chit-chat between Maggie and him was increasing in intensity, and her naked left knee was now resting against his right, and occasionally moved discreetly in his direction, unseen by all, but he knew it was more than an accidental nudge.

Their flirting and occasional secret touch continued until the waiter arrived to take the dinner orders. The choice of starter was mushrooms sautéed in garlic butter or lentil soup. Both Maggie and Stevie opted for the soup, perhaps thinking ahead to the prospect of some deep French kissing, and deciding the garlic butter would skank up their breath too much. Of course, the lentil soup would only encourage severe flatulence, but it seemed the lesser of two evils.

The main course choice was not dissimilar to many an airline in-flight meal selection; chicken or beef. The beef was done with onion gravy, so they both elected to go for the chicken in white wine sauce.

Stevie wolfed his food down as though he'd been held in solitary confinement for the entire week prior to the party, and

Maggie picked at hers like a fussy child, citing she was watching her figure and wanted to leave room for a few more cocktails.

Stevie let out a huge involuntary burp after swallowing the last of his mashed potatoes that had been used to mop up the remainder of the white wine sauce.

"Excuse me," he said holding up his hand as an apologetic gesture to the table.

There was no reply other than a few expected disapproving head shakes. The only interruption to the awkward silence was the chuckling from a slightly drunk Maggie.

"It could've been worse, it could've come out the other end," said Maggie out of the blue to the entire table of prudes as she burst into laughter again, this time with Stevie joining in.

Maggie's comment was greeted with as much enthusiasm by the stuck-up folks as Stevie's belch, most of them appearing as though they didn't know where to look. A thin woman by the name of Molly who worked on the sales team even turned bright red and quickly excused herself to the bathroom. Even Stevie was beginning to feel uncomfortable, not with Maggie, but with the stuffy environment he was surrounded by.

"Anyway folks, I'd like to say it's been a blast, but I'd be lying. Enjoy the rest of your evening," said Stevie, picking up his glass of Guinness, taking Maggie by the hand as she looked puzzled by the goings on, and led her in the direction of the bar.

As they walked away Stevie could virtually hear the relief from the table as their muttering commenced.

"Sorry about that Maggie but those prissy arseholes were bugging the shit out of me. The guys really need to get out of work mode and relax a little and the women seem like they need a good hard shag to loosen them up. Sorry to be crude Maggie but I felt like a fucking leper sitting there."

"Don't worry about being crude in front of me, I actually like dirty talk. Anyway, I agree with you, they were no fun at all."

"Good, at least we're on the same page and you don't think I'm a complete dick."

"Well I didn't say I *didn't* think you were a complete dick," said Maggie, again laughing.

"You know something Maggie, you're actually quite a funny lady."

"I do know how to separate in work and out of work behavior."

"I like that. Let's sit at the bar and I'll buy you a free cocktail."

"I feel *so* honored."

"You should sweetheart," said Stevie, cheekily sticking out his tongue.

They sat at the bar shooting the shit. The tables full of empty glasses and dirty plates were cleaned up and the lights were dimmed as the DJ began the music.

"I hate my boss," said Stevie. "Look at him dancing. He really thinks he's the dog's bollocks. He's really just a smug prick."

Stevie was capturing all the dance moves with his glasses and was very eager to show this to the boys also. It was hysterical as his boss, Rob Andrews, attempted his 70s moves to the sound of the *Bee Gees* classic "You Should Be Dancing." He just looked like a dork. He was clad in a white shirt with a grey waistcoat barely clinging onto his puny shoulders. Stevie figured one slight jerk too many would have it at his ankles like a pervert's underpants. As usual Rob had his elevated shoes on, pushing him to the high heights of five feet eight inches. He was dancing with Deirdre from the accounts team, a monster of a woman with the appearance of Jabba the Hutt in a brown wig and a pink dress. It looked as though she thought Rob was the dog's bollocks also as she giggled every time he attempted to twirl her around. She was likely just happy someone had asked her to dance, so Rob could not be faulted on that front.

"What do you think about swinging?" said Maggie out of nowhere.

"Depends. You talking about couple swapping or like Tarzan making his way through the jungle?" replied Stevie with a smirk, fully aware which one she was referring to.

"Tarzan making his way through the jungle! Stevie, you are hilarious. Couple swapping, obviously."

"Can't say I've given it much thought, but I'm a great believer in however people want to live their private lives is their business and it should never be judged. As long as they are happy and having fun. Why do you ask?"

Stevie was really intrigued to find out where this was going.

Maggie's cheeks were a little more flushed than before and Stevie wasn't sure if it was embarrassment kicking in or the additional alcohol, or a combination of the two.

"When I was married my husband and I used to go to one of those clubs every week."

"Really?" said Stevie, almost choking on a mouthful of his beer.

"Yes. We didn't always do it though. We were married for just over ten years before anything like that ever happened. We were always best friends, but all the passion evaporated after about four or five years. We wanted to stay together because we got on so well but the sex was non-existent, and even during the times we did give it a go it was lifeless and we were just going through the motions. We talked about it and decided to try the swingers scene."

"Wow, wasn't expecting you to say that. How did that work out for you?"

"Best thing we ever did. As I said, we were literally *just* best friends and there was no jealously whatsoever. We'd go to a club in Glasgow called *Sway* on Friday and Saturday nights. We were nervous at first as we didn't have a clue what we were doing. That first night we sat in the *Liquor House* bar around the corner and drank it up for some Dutch courage. It was really pleasant though and much different from what we had expected. If anything, we felt a little bit low on the class level. Most of the folks there were lawyer and doctor types, very sophisticated and extremely laid back and friendly. I guess what I am trying to say is that it wasn't seedy like we were sort of expecting."

"This is fascinating stuff Maggie, please tell me more," said Stevie as he signaled for two more margaritas and a pint of Guinness.

He genuinely was fascinated and hadn't for the life of him thought he'd be spending the evening at the bar, with Maggie of all people, particularly talking about her previously open and adventurous sexual escapades.

"Well we timidly walked into the place at first and there was a foyer area not unlike a small hotel or dance club. A cute young blonde girl, no older than twenty two greeted us with a smile and a pleasant introduction, and asked us if we were members. We told her we were not and were almost ready to leave, but she told us we could pay twenty pounds per person for a first visit and if we discovered it was something we were interested in we could pay for a membership. Well, we looked at each other, shrugged our shoulders and paid the money. We figured we'd come this far so should at least check it out and then decide what we wanted to do going forward."

"Makes sense to me. I'm a great believer in trying something and then deciding whether it is for you or not, rather than not trying it at all and then wondering what it would've been like," replied Stevie, still listening intently.

"Yeah, that's what I believe in as well. Anyway, the young girl ink stamped the back of our hands and the doorman ushered us through a set of double doors and into a cozy lounge area just like a typical wine bar or something. Everything was a shade of blue though. The comfy sofas were blue, the low tables in front of them had tinted blue glass for their surface, the drinking glasses were tinted blue, the lighting was blue, and even the bar staff and waitresses were decked out in blue uniforms."

"And I'm sure the atmosphere was blue," said Stevie, wanting more of the juicy details rather than a room description.

"I was just about to get to that. As we were walking through the double doors past the bouncer I did see a sign saying 'clothing optional,' but I didn't give it much more thought beyond that. The place was packed and my jaw almost hit the floor as I would say that about seventy five percent of those there were either walking around naked, sitting at the bar naked or laying back comfortably on the sofas, again naked. We slowly approached the bar, my husband's face lit up like a Christmas tree. On display were big dicks, little dicks, funny-looking dicks, old dicks, young dicks, circumcised dicks, uncircumcised dicks. Think about a dick and it was there."

"I'd rather not if you don't mind Maggie," said Stevie laughing. "I'm strictly a vagina man myself."

"Well for every dick there was an exposed pussy. There was shaved pussy, landing strip pussy, hairy pussy, *too* hairy pussy, wrinkly pussy, small labia, large labia. You picture it and it was there."

"I am Maggie, but you messed up my excitement with the *too* hairy pussy."

"It was though. I was half expecting a flock of birds the fly out."

'I hope you don't model yourself on that now?"

"One word Stevie; Kojak."

"My favorite."

"We can get back to that later. Shut up and let me finish my story you crazy boy."

"Sorry honey, I'm all ears."

"Well, we sat at the bar and ordered two Jack and Cokes. Either side of us were a naked couple, both checking us out. Most of the folks seemed like regulars so they probably sniffed out the newbies like a hound on a fox. We knew why we were there though. Let's face it, we hadn't had sex in months and I have needs. Holy shit, the twenty pound entry fee was small in comparison to the amount I'd spent on Duracell batteries the month before. Anyway, the couple to our left wasn't exactly pulling for a slot in Vogue magazine. He wasn't too bad looking. He was in his early fifties with a shaved head and his body was in decent shape and he was hung like a Cheshire horse, but he smiled at me and his teeth weren't very nice, so any inclination I may have had jumped right out the window. She was rough though, about five years his senior, probably a looker in her day, but as my husband said, she needed a good iron to make her even moderately presentable. The couple to our right though was a different story altogether. My Greg certainly thought so. They were *so* different in appearance than us. We were both fair haired with pale skin; it was before I'd become obsessed with sun beds. They were more around our age, hair as dark as coal, hers long and straight and his short and cropped at the sides with a slight spike on top. They were really beautiful with a Mediterranean flavor to them, and obviously no strangers to a workout. The blue light only highlighted their blemish-free naked skin even more. Greg gave me a nudge before asking them if he could buy them a drink. I couldn't look at them at the time and rejection would've had me wanting to curl up in a ball, so I stared in the other direction and my eyes caught sight of the disappointment on the faces of the older wrinkly couple. My heartbeat started to race and my head became extremely light as the tanned beauties said they'd love a drink. I instantly felt turned on as the reality sank home that this hunk could be stuffing me like a turkey and ridding me of my bottled up frustration before the night was over."

"This is great stuff Maggie. Was the other chick digging your Greg?"

"She was over him like a rash. My main concern was that the bronzed Adonis wouldn't be into me after closer inspection, but as I later learned about the scene, there is rarely any extended flirtation if both members of the couple are not comfortable with the swap."

"Go on."

"Well we moved seats. Well, Greg switched places with Eduardo, so he was to my left, Greg was to my right, and Tatiana to his right. Within seconds it was as though Greg and Tatiana weren't there, or at least strangers absorbed in their own little world. Eduardo had me in a trance with his deep voice and penetrating eyes as he told me about the chain of estate agents he owned. I've never been a gold digger but his obvious success in life only added to his attractiveness as well as the tingling in my knickers."

"You've a wonderful way with words!" said Stevie, absorbing her crudeness; he himself discovering some activity in the underwear region as a result.

"It gets better Stevie. He asked me what I did for a living and I told him I was an account manager. I figured if I told him the truth and said administrative assistant he might've jumped ship. Greg and I had it figured out before we went. If the place was a bit scummy we would go with the truth. If it was high-end we would lie our arses off. Greg was a senior electrical engineer for a major corporation. It was close to the truth if being a house-call electrician for a small six man outfit for over ten years counted."

"One question Maggie, and sorry to interrupt again, but while this was going on, are you now naked like he is?"

"No, I still had all my clothes on."

"And that subject never came up?"

"Not at all. He just conversed with me like we were two people chatting in a coffee shop on a Saturday afternoon."

"This might be one of the most interesting stories I've ever heard," said Stevie, delighted his glasses were capturing all the details as he had his doubts the boys would ever totally believe him if it just came from his spoken word.

"Anyway, the conversation kept flowing as we sipped on our drinks, then out of nowhere he asked me if I liked oral sex. I was a little taken aback but the amount of alcohol in me had my defenses down, much like our conversation now," said Maggie with a smile as she rested her hand on Stevie's knee. "I said I loved oral sex and he said giving or receiving and I said both, and often at the same time. He seemed cool and collected as he took a large swig of his Jack and Coke, but his free hand shot down and he placed it over his penis. I could tell my response was beginning to get him slightly aroused."

"Oh my God, that's one problem about sitting around naked talking dirty. Shit, I think I'd die if I suddenly got an involuntary boner in a situation like that."

"Well he started to become a little uneasy but he was very open about it. He looked at me and then down at his penis and asked me if I wanted to continue our conversation in one of the back rooms of the club. I hesitantly said sure, and turned to give Greg a look, but he and Tatiana were in a world of their own, oblivious to all around them. Eduardo stood up, and thankfully he'd managed to get himself under control. He interrupted Greg and Tatiana, seemingly taking them by surprise and snapping them out of whatever subject they were engrossed in. Greg was up out of his seat like an audience member of *The Price Is Right* whose name had just been called. I was half expecting him to run through the blue curtains like he was charging down the studio stairs, throwing his arms in the air and shouting the word championship. Tatiana was up quickly also. I later discovered they'd already been discussing that option and had been thinking about approaching the subject with me and Eduardo."

"Sounds like we're getting to the really juicy stuff now."

"Well I'm not sure I'm going to tell you all of that."

Come on Maggie, I was hoping to at least find out some of your likes and dislikes."

"Oh you were were you," she replied, now seeming really intrigued by what was on his mind.

"My aim is always to please," said Stevie, deciding to make his intentions fairly clear since he now knew she was definitely on the freaky side.

"If you put it that way then you have a deal," said Maggie, extending her open hand for a shake which was promptly grasped. "OK, well we swigged down the leftovers in our glasses and made our way towards these thick blue velvet curtains. Eduardo and Tatiana took the lead as they were veterans at the club and it seemed like it wasn't the first time they'd gone through this drill. Greg and I were like a couple of school kids ; me directly behind Eduardo and him right up Tatiana's arse, both of us glued to their firm buttocks. Eduardo held open one of the curtains and ushered us all through. It was as though we'd entered a different world. For one, everything was now red. They told me it was the color of love, but it was lust and certainly not love that was going on in their minds and the same could be said for everyone else in there. Stevie, it was like nothing I'd ever witnessed before other than some of the cheap porn that Greg used to keep in the corner of his drawer that used to store his socks and pants. The painted walls were red, the carpet was red, the sofas set against the walls of the room were red velvet, and the mattresses on the floor in the middle of the room were red."

"Mattresses?"

"Yes, mattresses. There were naked people in full view messing around on them. There were guys rubbing their wives backs while sipping on a beer while some other guy was doing her doggy style. One guy even handed his wife a glass so she could take a quick slurp of his drink between thrusts. I was appalled in a way yet incredibly aroused at the same time. I just wasn't expecting it to be so in my face."

"Holy shit Maggie this *is* like something out of a porn film."

"I know, but it was like Eduardo and Tatiana didn't even see the proceedings. They just calmly asked us if we wanted to have more drinks in the open area or whether we wanted to go back to some of the private rooms. I was quick on the draw for that one, saying it was our first time and I wanted to try the private rooms first. Poor Greg had a look of relief on his face. I think he caught sight of a big black guy receiving a blow job from a older fat lady. His dick was as big as a baby's arm clutching an apple and I don't think Greg was quite ready to display his little thing in the shop window for all to see. We headed up a thin red corridor to the left that had a bunch of doors on each side. I think there were ten on each side, but counting them accurately was the last thing on my mind. The whole club was huge, and much bigger than it appeared from the small discreet entrance door on the outside."

"So all of you ended up in the same private room?"

"No, but that was an option. Tatiana asked if we all wanted to be together or have two separate rooms. Again I was quick on the draw, saying that I'd prefer separate rooms and maybe if there was a next time we could all go in together. I didn't feel too comfortable with all four of us being together and I wasn't sure how that was expected to go anyway. I didn't know if it meant we were *all* expected to do things to each other and I could tell Greg was in agreement. He doesn't believe in more than one sausage at a time being involved in proceedings and I'd never done anything to a woman before so just incase that was the expected entrée we opted for the separate thing."

"I have to say I agree with Greg, although I have heard that there are a lot of guys who are straight that do like to just watch some other dude pork their wife. It's not my cup of tea, but as I said, each to their own as long as they're having fun and nobody is getting hurt."

"Anyway, there were two available rooms towards the end of the corridor, opposite each other. Eduardo suggested we meet back in the red lounge where all the shagging was going on in about an hour. Well, he just said red lounge, I added the other part," laughed Maggie. "The corridor was like rows of individual bathroom stalls. If a room was taken the door was locked and a red circle appeared below the silver handle. If it was vacant the door was either open or there was a green circle on display if it was closed."

"So you went in one with Eduardo and Greg into the other with Tatiana?"

"Yes, and off we went with a quick wave and a see you later. The interior of the room was *way* beyond any expectation I may have had. It was top of the line stuff. The entire room was about fifteen feet wide and about twenty feet deep. The walls and carpet were all white and everything else was black."

Maggie waved her glass at the bartender for a refill and continued.

"In the far left corner there was bed without a quilt and only a top sheet on it. Beside it was a black cabinet that Eduardo told me was filled with extra white top sheets that could be used to change out the current one. However, he did say it was club policy that after you are finished with a room you are required to take off the dirty or used sheet, put it in the black clothes basket at the end of the bed and put on a new fresh one from the cabinet." She smiled broadly. "That part I thought was a great idea."

"Anyway," she continued. "In the right hand corner beside the entrance wall was a Jacuzzi. A Jacuzzi. I could hardly believe it. It too was black on the outside, black wood panels to be precise, and the inside was like a shiny white bathtub; the warmth from the water was heating the entire room and you could see a hint of steam rising from the surface. Beside it was a large black fridge."

She stretched her arms expansively. "Eduardo pointed out to me that this was just like a larger version of a hotel mini-bar but more technically advanced. He said they used to have a waitress service that went door to door, but the members complained about the interruptions it caused while they were *doing it*. So, each membership card was swiped on a panel on the front of the fridge which unlocked it. When the door opened it was like a big vending machine; enter the code of the item you wanted and it spat it out at the bottom flap for you. Then the item is electronically charged to your account and you are billed monthly."

The bartender came over with drinks for both of them, but Maggie continued with her story as if they were the only ones in the room.

"It really was smart. Anyway, Eduardo asked me if I fancied some champagne, which I immediately agreed to, and then he asked me if I wanted to join him in the tub." She made a wry smile. "Well, you know what us women are like when it comes to hygiene, and I had been sweating a bit due to all the nerves, so I said I thought it was a great idea. Eduardo grabbed the chilled bottle of Moet et Chandon from the fridge, took two champagne flutes from one of the black shelves beside it and climbed into the tub and pushed on the button for the water jets as I tentatively started to undress."

"Don't know why you were tentative Maggie, you've got a killer body."

"Compliments will get you everywhere young man, but he was a relative stranger to me. Before I got into the swing scene I'd never really been one for one night stands or anything."

"But you are now?"

"Depends on my mood."

"What sort of mood are you in tonight?"

"Wouldn't you like to know?"

"Actually I would."

"Well maybe if you let me finish this story you'll find out."

"OK I'll shut up for now."

"Well I was finally standing there in nothing more than red nail varnish and a smile. Eduardo was laying back in the hot tub with both arms outstretched around the edges and two glasses of bubbly sat on the side. You look good enough to eat he said, blowing me a kiss with his soft lips. Well after that I virtually jumped in beside him as my juices were beginning to flow like

Niagara Falls. I clumsily splashed around a little before grabbing one of the glasses of Moet and gulped it down in one and then I lifted the other and threw that one back as well. I could see Eduardo was taken aback, but it really did the job of removing any final nerves. He was about to say something when I tossed my arms around him and planted my lips on his and fired my tongue straight into his mouth. He quickly got into it and the passion was electric. We kissed and fondled and were only in the water for a few minutes. I didn't want it going too far in there because there was no way I was screwing him bareback and I didn't trust rolling a condom on him and then being underwater, so we got out, dried off half-arsed with a couple of the towels and jumped onto the bed. We were straight into a sixty-nine position. We had been kissing very briefly but he whisked me around like a rag doll and before I knew it he was in my mouth and his tongue was giving my clit more attention than I had ever given it myself with my vibrator."

Stevie could hardly believe how open she was being, as well as graphic. He'd asked her for *all* the details but in his mind he hadn't actually believed she would've adhered to the request. Even the young bartender seemed to be cleaning glasses a little closer to them than he had previously, one ear to other patrons and one on Maggie's words. Stevie was going to tell him to mind his own business but decided against it, figuring he would've done exactly the same in his position and he *was* pouring him free drinks.

"It was wonderful and he had a good inch and a half on Greg in terms of length and it was as thick as a can of Red Bull. Fortunately he wanted to move onto the real deal after five minutes or so as I was starting to get the initial symptoms of lockjaw. He got off the bed for a second and opened a drawer at the top of the black cabinet with the clean sheets in it and pulled out a few Trojans. He asked me if I liked regular, ribbed, or flavored. I said just pull one on and get on top of me."

The young bartender almost dropped the glass he was drying with his towel, only clarifying Stevie's earlier prognosis.

"You can spare me any further detail. That's as much as I need to know," said Stevie.

The bartender developed a frown and moved off to serve someone.

"Did Eduardo live up to expectation?"

"It was incredible."

"Did you hook up with him again?"

"Every Friday night for about a year then they moved to England. It was the last we saw or heard of them. We still went every Saturday after that though. We got together with a lot of nice people, some of the guys were great lovers, but others were mediocre to say the least, but overall it was fantastic and a real thrill."

"You really do miss it don't you?"

"That's an understatement, and my current boyfriend is a real drag."

"You've got a boyfriend?"

"Yeah, his name is Robert. We've only been seeing each other for about six months but he is *so* conservative. All I get from him as foreplay is enough licks down there to wet the back of a stamp and then it's nothing but two minutes of missionary before he rolls over and starts snoring. I wouldn't even think of telling him some of the stuff I've just told you never mind suggest to him we give it a try."

"He sounds a real barrel of fun."

"Yeah, I'm not sure we'll make it to seven months."

"What happened with Greg anyway?"

"He ran off with one of the women he met at the club. Unfortunately for me her husband was one of the guys I'd been with who wasn't exactly a magician with his wand, so I couldn't even keep anything going with him. After that was when I stopped going back to club *Sway*."

"Do you fancy getting out of this place for a while? Maybe go for a walk or something. This party is doing nothing for me."

"Let's have one more cocktail first then we can go grab some fresh air."

The party was now in full swing and it seemed everyone other than Stevie and Maggie were enjoying the atmosphere. The dance floor was becoming busy as the DJ spoke into his microphone, gathering some recruits and coordinating the traffic.

"You must be kidding me," said Stevie, giving Maggie an elbow and pointing over to the floor.

The cheesy-sounding DJ was having everyone form into lines; about eight in each and four feet between them. There were forty people in total and a real mixed bag of ages, weights, and heights, and as it turned out, natural rhythm and knowledge of the song.

"OK people, let's get ready to do THE LOCOMOTION," hollered DJ Boy, a little too excited by it in Stevie's opinion.

"*Everybody's doing the brand new dance now, come on baby, do the locomotion…*" were the blaring lyrics from the sound system.

It may have been a brand new dance when it first appeared on the scene in the early sixties, but it was anything but now. For some though – the late eighties generation – it felt as though it was brand new as many of the youngsters had never heard of it before and those who actually had probably thought the late eighties Kylie Minogue cover version had been the original.

There was a dance that had become attached to the song, with pre-set moves, and was the reason the DJ had everyone set like they were line dancing at a Country and Western bar. It kicked off and it was very evident this was one scenario where the elderly didn't look like the fools. Two of the women from human resources that were pushing retirement age if they weren't already there were in their element, swinging their hips, stepping forward, backwards, to the side, clapping their hands in front and to the back of them and turning ninety degrees at the appropriate time and beginning the moves all over again.

"Look at my donkey of a boss," whispered Stevie to Maggie.

Little Rob Andrews was back on the floor again and was directly behind old Betty and Morag – the two experts from the HR department – attempting to duplicate their every movement, but was at least a second behind them as he mimicked. By the time they were already changing direction he was still clapping and at one point almost fell face first into Betty's arse as he attempted to catch up. It was plain for all to see that he *wasn't* one of the many orange juice drinkers in the room.

"You've gotta swing your hips now, come on baby, jump up, jump back..."

Stevie and Maggie made their way out of the function suite before the end of The Locomotion; strategically planned as all eyes were on all the Muppets flailing around on the floor and would help divert any unwanted attention and the resulting office gossip.

They stepped out of the hotel into the crisp Scottish night, Maggie staggering slightly as she took the last of the entrance steps, but fortunately Stevie was there to prevent any unwanted fall.

"My hero," she said, eyes now looking extremely glassy.

Maggie was plastered and Stevie wasn't far behind. The fresh air had instantly become a drunkenness acceleration factor and he could feel his head beginning to spin. It was hardly a surprise. He'd already put away six or more Guinness and about the same again in tequila cocktails.

They headed down the street, passing the graffiti-ridden steel shutters covering the windows of the unisex hairdresser's and butcher's shops.

"Where are we going?" asked Maggie, fighting through her double vision.

"I have no idea sweetheart, but let's keep walking and get a bit further from the party."

Blantyre wasn't the nicest of places. It had its good and bad areas like any other town around the county, but this specific location wasn't the former. The graffiti was the first indicator and the occasional broken bottle of Buckfast on the pavement was another, but Stevie and Maggie were beyond the point of drunkenness that they gave a shit.

The street darkened as they passed a couple of street lamps where the bulbs were out; Maggie almost falling over a dog as it urinated against one of them. The quality of a neighborhood could often be measured by the number of apparent stray dogs roaming around. The one in question had a collar and was obviously owned by someone, but it was common in lower-class areas for people to treat dogs much like cats. If they actually had a job or were just heading out to the pub to blow off financial worries they'd often send the dog out the door to fend for itself. Most of the dogs were some form of mutt, usually a mix between a black Labrador and some form of sheepdog. It wasn't any surprise the dogs were all mixed breeds. There was probably a time when pure breeds had walked around the streets by themselves, but most of the folks in the area barely had enough money to fuel their drink habits never mind have any spare coin to shell out on having their pets fixed so it was just a matter of time before little mixed pups appeared on the scene to further dilute the original species.

"I can't believe people just let their dogs roam around," said Maggie as Stevie saved her yet again from a fall.

"I know, but I think it's just the done thing around here. They're probably all too drunk or too broke to give a shit about them."

"It's still terrible. If I owned one it wouldn't be out anywhere without me being attached to it at the end of a leash."

"I hear you sweetheart, but not everyone is as responsible as you and me."

His statement was tinted with irony. Responsible was a word people rarely used in the same sentence as the word Stevie, and the fact they were both staggering around a dodgy street mentally undressing each other was hardly a dictionary definition.

There was a light ahead on the left hand side that shone bright in the darkened surroundings. As they approached, Stevie focused his weary eyes, discovering – to his delight – it was a late night corner shop. It was fully equipped with bars on the windows that only reiterated the area wasn't exactly fit for the Royal Family.

'Let's grab a bottle of wine and find somewhere to drink it," said Stevie as they reached the entrance.

"I probably don't need any more drink but I am in the mood," replied Maggie, glancing up and down at him.

They pulled open the door and a bell chimed to announce their entrance. It was a typical convenience shop, Pakistani owned, full of bread, canned soups, frozen meals for one, cigarettes, and more importantly, alcohol. Hygiene was obviously low on their priority list; Stevie could've written his name on the dust and dirt covered floor with his index finger and it would've had similar clarity to scribbling on a fogged up window.

The shop owner eyed them up carefully as they made their way to the counter; the middle-aged guy wearing a turban seemingly more focused on Maggie than Stevie.

"Bottle of Thunderbird chief."

"Red or blue?" replied the guy, one eye on Stevie and the other on Maggie's cleavage.

"Red please mate."

The color referred to the color of the label which Maggie was oblivious to. Red was the stronger of the two and the question was like asking Stevie if he'd prefer to be given a free gold watch or one made of stainless steel.

The guy turned to grab the bottle and Stevie gave Maggie a head nod towards the owner. She shrugged her shoulders, unclear of what his body language was saying.

They made their way out of the grubby shop; Stevie turning to look at the shopkeeper one more time, whose eyes were glued to the wiggle of Maggie's perky behind.

They continued walking down the street in the same direction, Stevie holding the bottle of super-strength wine in his hand, encased in a brown paper bag.

"You know Maggie; I respect people's religious beliefs, but come on. After the eleventh of September and all the other shit since then, you'd think folks like that guy would take the fucking bath towel off his head, trim that fox's tail of a beard, and scratch off the old red dot on the forehead. I'm not trying to be racist or anything and *I* certainly don't care about his appearance, but I'm sure some of the deadbeats that live around here automatically associate him with terrorism."

"It doesn't really bother me one way or the other Stevie."

"Me neither, but look at his shop. I'm pretty sure he wouldn't need to have bars on the windows if he at least *tried* to embrace our culture a little."

"Yeah you're probably right."

"I mean, if a bunch of redneck Americans in cowboy hats and boots crashed a plane into the center of Islamabad and I lived there, it's highly unlikely I'm going to go riding a horse down the center of town the next day wearing a Stetson and swinging a lasso. It would be more likely I'd be wearing one of those towel things on a daily basis and rapidly growing some facial hair."

"You really crack me up Stevie," said Maggie with a drunken giggle.

"It's true though."

"I'm not disagreeing with you; I'm just saying you're funny."

'Want to go in here and find somewhere to drink this wine?"

Shortly after the shop was the beginning of a wrought iron metal railing fence that stretched for a hundred yards or so and was lined with thick oak trees on the inside of it.

"Sure, what is it anyway?"

"Looks like the local park."

"It's closed though."

There was an entrance gate with a sign on it stating the park open hours, which had expired hours earlier. A thick, rusty-looking chain was wrapped around the end of the gate and the nearest metal rail of the fence it was attached to, fastened tightly with a padlock about half the size of a brick.

"I think we can manage to squeeze through there," said Stevie, pointing to a section of the fence about twenty feet down from the entrance gate.

Someone or some *thing* had bent open two adjacent iron railings, just enough for a person to squeeze through. It looked as though The Incredible Hulk had broken out of a jail cell.

"I didn't even see that. In fact I'm not seeing anything too well right now," said Maggie.

"I figured there would be a break in the fence somewhere, especially around here. I'm pretty sure it's a popular spot for drinkers and those seeking a sneaky late night roll in the grass."

"And which one of those are we here for?"

"The drink obviously," replied Stevie, holding up the bottle. "But if you're a good girl maybe we can dabble in both of them," he said, giving her a wink.

"I think you mean if *you're* a good boy."

"I'm always good sweetheart. I'm just a little disappointed there's a break in this fence. I was hoping to lift you over it and get a little glimpse of your panties under that mini-skirt."

"Well you would've been disappointed then as I don't believe in wearing underwear."

"You really are something Maggie," said Stevie, gesturing for her to lead the way through the fence.

Maggie slipped through with the ease of a skilled limbo dancer working her way under a horizontal pole, but Stevie had to work hard, sucking in his stomach, but still greasing the side of each pole so much that they left a nasty brown rust stain on the front and back of his t-shirt. He was feeling wasted though and virtually forgot about it as quickly as it occurred.

They made their way tentatively along the tree line. There was a small building over in the center of the park, but they could see it was more or less surrounded by a group of teenagers drinking their cheap alcohol and shouting drunken obscenities to each other.

"Let's go over here and keep out of the kids' way," said Stevie, signaling over to a clump of hedges.

The drunken teenagers were so pre-occupied with their shenanigans they had no idea Stevie and Maggie were even there. They quietly made their way in the opposite direction of the young imbeciles and pitched a spot on the grass behind the seclusion of the bushes. They swigged merrily from the bottle, passing it between them and it wasn't long before half of it was gone; Stevie consuming the lion's share.

"You do get used to the taste," said Maggie, now swallowing it down without the facial spasms of her first few hits.

"It's cheap and nasty but I like it," replied Stevie before guzzling down some more.

"I figured you'd like anything cheap and nasty."

"I like you and I don't consider you cheap and nasty," lied Stevie through his faltering eyeballs.

"I can be sometimes," said Maggie, moving in close to him from their seated position on the grass.

She removed the bottle from his hand, screwed on the metal cap, and sat it on the ground next to them before pouncing on him, pushing him onto his back and landing clumsily on top; her open mouth latching onto his like a plunger in a toilet bowl. Their tongues jostled, Maggie forcing hers deep inside him as she slipped her hand down onto the crotch of his jeans, cupping him tightly before pulling her head away from him.

"Wow, you're pretty much ready to go right now aren't you you young horn-dog," she said as she slowly slid her way down his body, her head now level with his protruding manhood.

Stevie relaxed, putting his hands behind his head as he looked up at the clear night sky and half moon as Maggie's saliva-filled mouth worked on him. The stars were out in all their glory as his drunken eyes searched for the Big Dipper. As he attempted to focus, his head started to spin, white stars appearing more and more, hundreds of them, and they were not the ones located in the sky. He fought hard to maintain consciousness but it was a battle he was destined to lose.

The wet tongue slurped on his cheeks, nose, and mouth, and the foul stench meandering up his nostrils was enough to snap him out of his drunken blackout. What the hell was Maggie doing?

"JESUS CHRIST," screamed Stevie as his eyes opened and focused on what was *actually* happening to him.

The sun was now up and a fine layer of dew covered the grass. The dog they'd witnessed peeing on the street light pole the night before had been feasting on the stale booze-ridden saliva drooling from the corner of his open mouth and down onto his left cheek.

"GET THE FUCK OUTTA HERE," he shouted to the shaggy grey mutt as he flapped his hands around in front of him before wiping his face.

The dog was initially startled, but quickly and calmly made its way off in the direction of the public bathrooms where the underage drinkers had been previously loitering.

Stevie got to his feet, head pounding, but he paid little attention to the headache as the surprise of the entire situation had his brain focused elsewhere. There was no sign of Maggie. There was no sign of anything other than the dog. He glanced at his watch; it was 6:56 am. He was completely disorientated and racked his library of a mind for any reference material on the events that had taken place, but no information was to be found. A cold shiver attacked his body. The sun was out, but as usual the cold Scottish wind was there in all its glory. He was only clad in jeans and a t-shirt and the chilling draft seemed to be more concentrated on his penis than anything else. Looking down he realized that his little man was dangling for all to see and the waist of his jeans were hanging tentatively up by the edges of his hips. He frantically flipped his shrunken dick back into the comfort of his boxers and fastened his trousers. What had happened? Where was Maggie? Why had she left him there? Had he had sex with her? He grabbed his black leather wallet from his back pocket – much relieved it was still there – and opened the small flap at the front. He hoped and prayed they hadn't had sex as the two condoms he had placed in there earlier were still in view. He scratched his head as he made his way out of the park via the gap in the fence and back to the main road.

Stevie made his way back in the direction of the hotel, keeping his eyes peeled for any signs of a taxi. The morning surprise had his mind confused and his mouth was as dry as a nomad's sandal and his tongue felt as though it needed a shave. He worked to create some saliva in his mouth to neutralize the desert conditions, but the taste of the stale wine almost caused him to gag. A cold sweat covered him as he walked and his body ached all over. Suddenly his previously retarded mind had a moment of inspiration, but only made him feel like a dummy as it hadn't immediately occurred to him. His glasses were still perched firmly on his face. Like usual they would be able to fill in the blanks for him when he eventually made it back home.

The warmth of his flat felt similar to that of returning home after a walk on a winter's day. It had taken about twenty minutes for a cab to appear and his bones felt as though he'd spent the night trapped in a meat freezer. A piping hot bath was the order of the morning but his traumatized head had him snatching for his laptop as the number one priority. He switched on the kettle for a warm mug of coffee as the computer booted-up and he grabbed a dirty blue sweatshirt from the pile on top of the laundry basket to at least provide some interim insulation. He heaped in two spoons of Nescafe and the same again with sugar into his favorite mug and added the boiling water. The fridge door creaked as it opened and he removed the carton of milk and sniffed the top; not causing him to gag so figured it was safe to add a splash. A quick stir of the contents was made, his bloodshot eyes briefly following the swirl of the brown liquid before throwing the spoon into the sink on top of the already accumulating dirty pile of dishes.

Stevie sat the coffee on the arm of his chair and connected the chip from his glasses to the computer and began the download process. He cringed as he pressed play. His main concern was the time since the blackout, so resisted the urge to glare at Maggie's tits and arse again during the work's bash as well as listening to her story about the swingers club, and went straight to the moment when she was down on him as he stared up at the stars.

The footage on screen wasn't triggering anything for him. All he could see was the clear sky and hear the eager slurps from Maggie. This continued on for two minutes or so before he heard her voice.

"Stevie, are you *asleep*? Stevie, STEVIE."

The sight of Maggie's face came into view as she'd obviously worked her way up his limp body. She slapped him on the face three times – the last with much greater force than the first two – but his glasses moved very little other than the vibration generated from the smacks. He was dead to the world. Maggie stood up over him, her fake breasts and annoyed-looking face still in the shot.

"Goddammit Stevie; I really needed some sex tonight. I guess I'll need to head back to the party and see what I can find."

She turned and moved out of sight and Stevie was left looking at a picture of the peaceful sky. He figured if she'd had any idea she was under surveillance she would've refrained from making such a comment, but it did confirm her earlier statement that she could be cheap and nasty.

Stevie fast forwarded the action in the hope that she returned to make another attempt at waking him, but the only change as the film sped on was the ever so gradual lighting of the surroundings as the sun began to rise. Suddenly, and taking him by surprise, was the face of the shaggy grey dog. He was happy he was alone as the disappointment on his face was impossible to hide.

Message for Maggie

Stevie spent most of the day on the couch dozing in and out of consciousness, not unlike a regular Saturday. He was still a little appalled that he had awoken in the park earlier in the morning and it was really bothering him that his drinking was leading to such events. He could've been robbed, been victim of homosexual rape, or even murdered, and he would've been none the wiser at the time.

His mood was dull, but the saving grace on the horizon was he was heading off to Ibiza with the boys the following morning for one week. He was looking forward to escaping from daily life and the generally bleak Scottish weather. A warm and relaxed change of pace was just what he required to get his mind back on track.

Maggie was completely unaware he was going to be out of the office the following week; the subject had never arisen during any of their conversations. He'd decided to call work and leave a message on her extension that he was safe and well. He had no idea of her home or cell number so it would be Monday before she'd likely pick-up the voicemail. Stevie was tempted not to bother notifying her, picturing her alarm at the beginning of the week as she saw nothing at his desk other than an empty chair, but figured he wouldn't go down that juvenile path.

Being the procrastinator that he was, he decided to leave the call until later. The boys and him were not only catching an early flight in the morning, but were also popping to the bar that evening for a few pre-holiday beverages. It would've been far more sensible to have a quiet night at home in order to be fresh for the airport, but they had all agreed it would be better to go for at least a couple; sitting at home all excited with their holiday moods would've driven them up the wall.

Instead of the call to Maggie, Stevie worked on washing some clothes so he actually had something clean to throw into his suitcase *and* wear to the airport. At this moment in time the only wearable clean items around the flat was a string vest, a red tennis headband, and a pair of oven gloves hanging over the handle of the cooker. The current situation was *that* bad.

One load turned into two. The first was just shorts and casual t-shirts for during the day. Those were the essentials so he prioritized first incase any power cut hit his street. No outages occurred and he fired the second load of wet clothes into the dryer after removing the first batch. These were the evening attire; blue and black jeans, a few short-sleeved collared shirts, and four designer t-shirts. He folded the first load of freshly dried items right there and then to avoid the need for ironing – an activity he enjoyed about as much as the discovery of a hemorrhoid – and put each directly into his tatty old black suitcase that still had the baggage tags on it from his holiday the year before.

A quick shower, shit, and shave and he was all set, so grabbed his phone to finally make the courtesy call to the office and leave Maggie the news.

The office was closed on weekends but they were up to date with technology and had the robotic-like automated voice system with speech recognition.

"I am sorry, but the office is currently closed. Our hours of operation are Monday to Friday from 8:00 am until 6:00 pm. If you know your party's extension and wish to leave a voicemail, please enter their extension now. If you wish to leave a message and do not know your party's extension, press one now."

Stevie pressed one.

"If you know the name of the person you wish to leave a message for, press one now."

Stevie pressed one again.

"Please state the name of the person you wish to reach."

Stevie had a temporary brain fart, briefly forgetting her surname, but quickly recovered.

"Maggie Bond," he said, slowly and politely into the receiver.

"If you said Maggie Bond, please say yes, otherwise say no."

"Yes."

He'd remembered it was Bond due to his enjoyment of Sean Connery and 007. She had no doubt been smoking hot in her prime and very Bond-girl-like back in the day. Now she was more like a 1980 version of Honor Blackman rather than the Pussy Galore image from the film Goldfinger back in the sixties.

"Hi there, you're through to Maggie Bond. Unfortunately I'm not available to take your call at this time. Please leave me a detailed message after the tone and I'll get back to you as soon as I can."

The beep sounded and Stevie went into his rant.

"Hi Maggie; it's Stevie. It's about seven o'clock or so on Saturday night. Yes I did manage to drag my drunken arse out of the park, although it was only about twelve hours ago since that happened. I just wanted you to know that I am fine and eventually got home. Hopefully you'll forgive me for passing out on you. For what it's worth, your mouth skills are fabulous. Maybe you'll give me a chance to redeem myself one of these days. Anyway, take it easy and apologies again. By the way, when you got back to the hotel after you left me in the park, did you manage to find anyone to take care of your needs?"

He left it at that and ended the call. He was beginning to love certain things that his glasses uncovered at times and knew his final comment would have her confused for most of the week.

Mental Evaluation

There were several theories behind Stevie's current lifestyle and general behavior, mainly between his friends, but also from rumors and speculation amongst work colleagues who didn't *really* know him. He'd always enjoyed a drink, it was part and parcel of Scottish pub culture, but he hadn't always indulged to the degree he did now. His father's death had undoubtedly triggered his slide down the slippery slope, but it was more than that now, it had become an addiction just like tobacco for some, heroin for others, and habitual masturbation and porn surfing for many sex addicts.

Alcohol for many was an escape route during times of stress. It was viewed as a way to calm the nerves, let the hair down, and put any worries temporarily on the back-burner. Stevie had found this to be a successful outlet. It may have been a momentary escape, but it was an escape nevertheless, and certainly beat the continual mental torture he'd endured prior to using it as a channel.

Part of him wanted to curtail the habit but he was still plagued by the horrifying dreams, the frightening visuals of his father hanging by the neck, so he struggled to restrict the urge. Before he knew it he was hooked, craving the cold bitter taste of Guinness and the face-pulling shots of pure alcohol.

What he needed was some stability in his life. A good woman could no doubt put him in his place and get him back on track, but cheap and meaningless sex was as much a part of his lonely existence as his cigarette and beer consumption. He did enjoy companionship, brief as it currently was, but he battled against loving and depending on anyone. He'd loved his parents deeply and unconditionally, sharing many an evening with them, sharing his fears and troubles, being there when they needed him and they were always there when he needed them. That closeness had been harshly torn from him, ripping out his heart, leaving a wound that was struggling to heal. The pain was still evident and he couldn't bring himself to form another new bond of such strength. The mere idea of having to potentially go through another tear-filled and painful loss repelled any inclination he may have had. It was sad but true, and was going to take someone *extremely* special to break him from his current ways.

Off To Sunny Sunny Spain

The time for the boys' annual vacation had finally arrived. It had been around two months since the pre-holiday talk had commenced, and their excitement had been gradually building ever since. Those sixty days had appeared to crawl by, but like an active volcano of glee, the eruption of joy had finally exploded into the atmosphere.

"The airport bar had better be open. You can't beat a few cold beers to settle the nerves before take-off," said Stevie, as the taxi made its way towards Glasgow airport.

"Stevie, it's just after six o'clock in the fucking morning! As long as there's somewhere to get a coffee and a bacon roll I'll be as happy as a pig in shit," stated Gordon from the front passenger seat as he raised his disapproving eyebrows in the direction of the driver.

Colin and Sean were coma-like, propped against the back left and right interior doors respectively like a couple of overused mannequins. Colin had originally agreed to drive them all there and leave his car in the long-stay car park for the week long trip, but the couple of beers the previous night had – funnily enough – multiplied by five and none of them had been fit to put a key in the ignition. They could've chanced it, but Stevie Wonder would've probably been a more roadworthy navigator as things currently stood.

"Well, you can have your coffee and I'll have my beer. Everyone has their own hangover cure that works for them."

"How you can even mention the word beer right now is beyond me. I'm almost going to puke just thinking about it."

The little fat cab driver threw a look of alarm towards Gordon while simultaneously flicking down the passenger seat electric window.

"Don't worry chief; I'm not going to actually be sick. I was just trying to show my alcoholic friend here how much beer doesn't appeal to me right now."

"Thank fuck for that," said the driver, with a hint of relief very evident in his tone. "I only came on at ten o'clock last night, and some drunken slag puked all over the backseat right behind me. It took me about twenty minutes to clean, as well as a full can of air freshener and driving around aimlessly with the windows down for half an hour to get rid of the smell. God only knows how much money the bitch cost me. She was really messed up on the drink. Of course, the guy's cock she was sucking on at the time didn't exactly help her gag reflex I suppose. I should always follow my instincts. I knew she was a prime candidate to lose her dinner, even before she got in, but I gave her the benefit of the doubt. The blow job shenanigans were great though. It was making my night at the time as well. Why they thought I didn't notice what was going on is beyond me."

"Well, you don't have to worry about me sucking any cock mate," replied Stevie, leaning forward from his middle position and resting an elbow beside each of the front seat headrests. "Although the state these two Muppets are in right now I could probably blow them both while tickling their balls and they'd be none the wiser."

Gordon and the driver erupted with laughter and Stevie followed suit. It was like the infectious type that happens in a group of stoners after the delivery of even the most mediocre of punch lines.

The hilarity caused Colin to peel open his crusty eyelids, but Sean remained like a stone sculpture.

"Laughing at my expense I suppose," mumbled Colin through an emphatic yawn.

"For once we weren't," said Gordon, catching Colin's eye from his view in the rear-view mirror.

"We weren't, but you might want to check the arse of those beige trousers you're wearing after we get out of the taxi. There might be some squashed-up carrots tattooed on them now. Some drunken slapper last night barfed all over where you're sitting."

"For fuck sake," said Colin, quickly jumping back to the land of the living, lifting his buttocks off the seat and rubbing them with his right hand.

"They're just messing with you man. I gave it a good clean last night. Just be thankful it's leather seats I have in here," replied the driver with a wry smile.

At that point, Stevie delicately unzipped the fly of Sean's jeans and held his index finger vertically to his lips. The boys successfully fought their laughter into submission as Stevie delivered a slap to the side of Sean's cheek.

"What the fuck?" roared Sean, flapping both hands around in the air like he'd just walked into a swarm of bees.

"We're nearly at the airport, asshole," said Stevie; the word asshole being more of a term of endearment than an insult.

"Shit, I was just having the weirdest of dreams there."

"Someone wasn't trying to blow you, were they?" said Stevie, looking at him quizzically.

"Are you psychic or something," said Sean, genuinely freaked out with the reply.

Right at that moment Sean glanced down at his groin and virtually had an epileptic fit, resembling more of a man locked in a closet with a rattle snake than a sleepy guy in the back of a taxi.

"Easy Tiger, I was just messing with you. Some chick was gobbling a guy back here last night though. You probably subconsciously heard us talking about it," said Stevie.

Again the laughter flowed. The mood was good, but Sean looked perplexed.

They were only ten minutes from Glasgow airport and a silence fell upon the car as they crossed the Kingston Bridge. The city had seen much transformation over the years. The days when the River Clyde was one of the World's pre-eminent shipbuilding centers were long gone, now replaced by rows of waterfront yuppie apartment buildings and structures such as the Clyde Auditorium, better known as "The Armadillo;" due to its similarity in shape to the animal with the same name. It was a wonderful city, modern yet strangely old fashioned. Entwined within many of the contemporary structures were a multitude of magnificently preserved Victorian buildings lining the elegant streets. On a fine sunny day there weren't many places that could make you as proud to be from Scotland.

"Right boys, that'll be twenty-two pounds even," said the driver as he pulled up to the terminal building and stopped his meter. "Enjoy your holiday."

"I've got this lads," said Stevie. "Each of you can just buy me a pint at the bar."

"That might not be a good deal for us considering airport prices," said Sean, only half joking.

The line for the check-in desk was relatively quiet. The boys had arrived over two hours in advance of their departure time, beating most of the other holiday-makers joining them on the Ibiza flight.

They checked in without any issues and proceeded through the security checkpoint. For once Stevie managed to pass through the metal detector without alarm bells ringing or being pulled aside for a "random" bag check.

They put their shoes back on and proceeded to the bar closest to their departure gate, Stevie pleasantly surprised to find that beer was on the menu even at this early hour and began a steady consumption until their flight was eventually called.

They all had a little holiday alcohol buzz going as they took their seats, which resulted in an extremely short three hour flight as they all slept most of the way, particularly Sean, who quickly dozed off just as in the taxi, and was asleep even before the wheels of the plane had left the tarmac.

The plane hit the Ibiza runway with an almighty thud. It was as though the senior pilot had handed the reins to his trainee, and although successful, a B- was sketched onto the report card.

Like typical eager Scots, less than a handful of people waited for the beep of the seatbelt sign before leaving their seats and opening the overhead compartments. Apparently for them the moment the airplane came to a halt at the gate was their formal approval.

The boys were actually part of the handful that'd waited in their chairs. The hustle and bustle of those rummaging for their carry-on bags above them was similar to that of a bedside alarm clock on a Monday morning.

"We're here boys, wakey wakey. Grab your shit and let's go," said Sean, turning from coma to excited lottery winner within the blink of an eye.

The other three followed suit, with Gordon pushing his way into the masses in the main aisle and stretching back a row to pull out Colin and Sean's bags as they were unable to leave their seats due to the excited and impatient crowd packing the aisle.

It wasn't long before they were saying goodbye to the flight attendants and heading towards baggage claim, but they were in no hurry; they were just happy to be away from the real world as they knew it, even if it was for only a week.

They followed the procession of people in the direction of the bag carousel. It wasn't too difficult to identify that the flight was from Glasgow as the boys scanned those around them. There were the usual folks who'd decided traveling in Rangers and Celtic shirts with shell suit bottoms was a great idea, while many others had decided to dress for Spain even before they'd boarded the plane, wearing an array of brightly colored shorts and cut-off vest tops, putting their milk-bottle skin color on display for all to see, hoping to travel back like bronze figurines, when really the best they could ever hope for was a blazing red with minimal skin peeling.

"I'll bet you ten quid my suitcase is one of the last ones off," said Colin as they stood around the conveyor belt with a couple of the complimentary trolleys.

"Well I'm not taking that bet," replied Stevie as he pointed at a black case making its way towards them wrapped with three strands of bright orange tape.

"Stevie, why the hell do you do that with the orange shit? You've got a tag on the handle with your name on it," said Gordon.

"Dude, how many people have black cases?"

"Can I assume that's a rhetorical question?"

"Of course, but you know what I mean. Half the people on the plane have black cases by the looks of it," he said as they looked at all the bags revolving around the track. "Who knows how many Spanish dudes who shouldn't even be in here are sniffing around looking to snag something. Do you really think they are even giving consideration to the one with the luminous orange tape on it? It's unique and just gives some added security."

Gordon shrugged his shoulders.

"Exactly, you've just proved my point chief. How many Spanish dudes do you think are sniffing around a security polluted airport looking for a score?" replied Gordon.

"Can I assume that's a rhetorical question?"

"Fuck you Stevie, you paranoid prick."

"Did I get my bag without any problems?" said Stevie, lifting it from the moving rail.

"Do you see anyone in here running around screaming, claiming someone must've skipped off with their shit?"

"No, but you can never be too safe," he replied, and Gordon just shook his head.

Gordon and Sean's bags followed suit and the place began to clear out.

"I told you," said Colin, scratching his head and pacing up and down impatiently.

"Colin, I'm sure it'll be out in a minute. I hardly think the Glasgow and Ibiza baggage handlers collaborated in a conspiracy against you," said Gordon.

Sure enough, Colin's blue case finally pushed open the rubber flaps and made its entrance onto the carousel like a lone entertainer gracing the stage. They loaded it onto one of the trolleys and headed outside to find the coach transporting them to their resort.

Outside the breeze was warm and a pleasant change from the chill of the typical Scottish wind.

"This is the life," said Stevie. "I tell you, I could get used to this."

"You're not kidding chief, beats our shitty weather any day of the week," replied Sean, looking up with a smile at the early afternoon sun.

There were four coaches lined up outside.

"This must be ours," said Gordon, as they drew level with the one marked "Sunshine Tours" in large red writing against its white exterior.

Beside the open door at the front was a young blonde girl wearing red shorts and a white t-shirt – matching the coach company colors – with the name "Mandy" tagged next to her right breast. She was holding a clipboard and ticking off names as she let people filter aboard.

"Ello boys, welcome to Ibeefa," she said, over enthusiastically in her Cockney twang. "Ah'm Mandy, and you boys are?"

"Party of four from Scotland. I'm Gordon and these fine fellows are Stevie, Colin, and Sean."

Mandy scanned down her list and marked their names with her yellow highlighter.

"Ah faught that was your naymes," she replied. "You're the last ones on me list."

"Yeah, I'm not surprised," said Colin. "My case took forever to come out as usual."

"At least it came out, ay. Anyway, this is Carlos our driver," she said, as a middle-aged, short, Spanish gentleman with a moustache that could've doubled as a hairy caterpillar, climbed down the stairs and joined them. "Ee'll get your cases packed away and we can get this party started."

Carlos threw the bags into the large compartment in the side of the bus and the lads boarded, grabbing seats near the middle, and the bus headed on its way. Mandy stood at the front facing the excited holiday-makers, with a microphone in hand.

"If you're 'appy to be on 'oliday let me 'ere ya," she said in her rough London brogue as she pointed the mic towards the back of the bus.

A few people gave a half-hearted "YAY."

"Ah, cam on, I can't 'ere ya," was her answer, again pointing the mic back at them.

"YAAAAAY," they all shouted simultaneously.

"That's betta."

Her jovial antics continued relentlessly for the entire forty minute journey, pointing out landmarks and giving them a rundown of the bars and clubs that were essential visits during their time on the island. She was cute, and the accent was sexy for a short while, but after about ten minutes or so, became more annoying than anything else.

"I bet she's been banged more times than a barn door on a windy day," said Stevie to Gordon beside him.

His words must've came out a little louder than planned, as Colin and Sean in front of them chuckled and the sound of laughter also rang from behind them as well as from several rows on the other side of the main aisle.

"Sounds loyk we're 'aving fun back there. That's wot I like to 'ere," said Mandy into her microphone, completely unaware she was the centerpiece of their festivities.

Eventually they reached their destination in the town of Sant Antoni de Portmany, everyone glad their ears would finally be receiving a reprieve from Mandy's constant bickering. The boys gave one another a strange look as Carlos pulled into a small square-shaped car park at the side of a peach-colored building.

"Well I'm sure the interior is better looking than the outside," said Gordon, hoping his optimism would rub-off on them all.

"Maybe this isn't our place. Maybe they're just dropping a few unlucky folks off and ours is further up the road," stated Sean, taking optimism to an entirely new level.

"Yeah that's it dickhead," replied Colin. "Look what it says, 'Beach Water Luxurious Apartments.' That's the name of our place."

"Well it's about time they updated their sign and replaced the word luxurious with cockroach infested. I couldn't give a shite though. Look, we'll be out most days at the beach or by the pool, or out on the beer. We'll be out every night as well so we're only going to be using it for the shower or a few hours kip, and hopefully to gag a few chicks, so it's not worth getting your panties in a wee bit of a fankle."

"OK everyone listen up," hollered Mandy. "Make your way out, collect your bags from Carlos, and they'll take care of ya at reception. Fanks for choosing Sunshine Tours and 'ave a lovely 'oliday."

Check-in went smoothly and they headed outside to a courtyard area that housed a kidney-bean-shaped swimming pool and had a littering of tall palm trees throughout. Looking onto the pool were the back windows of each row of apartments; ground floor and a second floor, with the upper level having balconies. The boys were on the second floor, Gordon and Stevie in one room and Colin and Sean next door.

The interior of the rooms, as expected, were anything but glamorous. They were minimalistic to say the least, with barely more than the two single beds and a set of drawers beside each. Upon initial inspection though they were relatively clean and would serve their purpose for the week.

A couple of days progressed as planned; sunning themselves by day and drinking heavily and picking up women by night.

Ibiza never halted and the sun would be beginning to rise when they finally left the clubs, more or less drinking themselves sober and stumbling back to the apartments for a spot of breakfast to recharge the batteries before the cycle continued all over again.

Time ticked by faster than they wanted though, and the realization that a return to work and their regular lives was starting to hit home.

Stevie walked bleary-eyed down the stone stairs of the apartment building, almost falling flat on his face and dropping the multi-colored beach towel that was thrown over his shoulder as he caught the sole of his brown sandal on the uneven final step.

Applause reigned from the outdoor breakfast area in the courtyard from the other three lads who were feeling a lot fresher than their toasted counterpart.

"It's alive!" jibed Sean, in a deep tone reminiscent of the Frankenstein horror movie.

"Only just," replied Stevie, wearily wiping away the morning crust from his eyes. "She might've had a squint rivaling Sammy Davis Jr. and a face that would've struggled to tempt the Elephant Man from a burning house, but she was *without doubt* the best ride I've had in a long time; up for anything. I was going down on her and even got away with the old Shocker move."

"Shocker, what the hell is that?" asked Gordon, looking extremely puzzled.

"Is it not what Sean Connery calls football when he's in America," chuckled Colin.

"Yesh, very good my shtupid young friend," replied Stevie in his best Sean accent.

"Well, can you tell us already? The excitement is killing me!" said Sean sarcastically.

"You know, the old two in the pink and one in the stink."

They all laughed emphatically.

"Ah, the old trusty two in the humper and one in the dumper," piped in Gordon.

"Two in the poon and one in the moon," said Colin.

The intensity of the laughter increased and the other diners in the breakfast area were staring, wondering what all the hilarity was about. The boys looked at Sean.

"What? You want me to come up with one."

"Well we all did, wanker," replied Gordon.

"I don't know. Two in the slit and one in the shit," was Sean's response.

Tears rolled down their faces, so much so that Gordon knocked a sausage off his plate as he doubled over, but quickly applied the three second rule.

"Sean, you've taken that too far," said Stevie, trying to maintain a straight face. "That's not the visual I want to have the next time I try that maneuver."

"What, you're going to do that Neanderthal again?" said Gordon.

"I meant in general, but never say never. I put in a fine performance on her if I do say so myself. One of those nights when you're as drunk as a skunk but can still get a stiffy like an iron rod. I lasted for ages. Gave her a right good pile driving as well. If you see her this morning she'll probably be wheeling herself around.

The mood was good as they munched through their fried breakfasts. It was nice to relax and take time away from the stresses of home.

The next few days followed a similar pattern: breakfast, beer, and babes.

Ibiza was a crazy place that never stopped to catch a breath. Ironically the quietest time of the day in the sun-filled resort was from morning until mid-afternoon. It was warm and breezy, with gorgeous white sandy beaches, but the majority of the visitors weren't there to work on their tans. Most of them were there for the nightlife. The place was renowned around the globe for its nightclub scene, attracting world famous DJ's who charged an arm and a leg to mix, spin, and scratch their vinyl record collections for a two hour evening set. These guys and gals were viewed as Gods on the little Spanish island.

The majority of club-goers would dance the night away until six in the morning, hyped-up on Speed, Ecstasy, or whatever drug-fuelled concoction they could get their hands on. Sleeping hours for the masses usually commenced around seven or eight in the morning until they surfaced their buzzing heads mid-to-late afternoon.

The four boys though were not part of this regular crew. None of them had much coordination or interest for dancing, and even less when it came to drugs. Their usual method of operation was to consume a few beers and work on hooking up with some promiscuous young ladies, with the aim of being back in bed – preferably not alone – before 6:00 am, then back up for the hangover cure breakfast around nine or ten, before heading back to bed for another couple of hours kip.

The week was nearing its climax, and the prospect of a return to work and normal day to day life was getting them down.

"Well boys, it's our last night tonight. What do you fancy doing?" said Gordon, genuinely searching for ideas.

"That chick I was trying to fire into last night said there was some huge outdoor rave going on tonight. It's not really my thing but it might be worth a look."

"I'm in," said Colin.

"I'm up for it as well. We've done pretty much the same thing every night so far, so a little change of scenery sounds good to me," said Sean.

"OK, the rave it is then," said Gordon, nodding his head in agreement with Sean.

They all lay poolside, towels spread out across the white plastic sun-beds like thin sheets on top of a mattress. They were all tired. It had been a hectic week, putting their bodies and liver through an intense workout, so some downtime before the evening proceedings was all they were up for.

The pool area by the apartment complex was essentially occupied with the 18-35 crowd, but there were a couple of families intermingled in between, likely a result of a dirt cheap holiday deal where you find out your living accommodation upon arrival. There was no doubt they were disappointed with the outcome, but that was the gamble, although they were attempting to make the most of things.

Two brothers around ten and twelve years old were floating around on a couple of inflatable beds, giggling and splashing each other like the kids they were. They were *way* happier looking than their parents, who continually drew them disappointing looks every time they saw them glaring at some of the female topless bathers.

Stevie and Colin were like larger versions of the two kids, propped up on their loungers, dark sunglasses firmly attached; appearing to be reading magazines, but their vision was locked in like a laser-sight on a bank robber as the cute blonde with her DD's on display applied sun cream to her freckly red-headed friend.

"Right guys, let's get a pose together for a quick photograph," said Colin, pulling the digital camera out from under the shade of the molded plastic bed.

They reluctantly obliged and took stance at the edge of the pool, Gordon the six feet five inch monster in the middle with arms wrapped around the shoulders of Stevie and Sean. Colin flipped the camera setting to record and appeared to be pointing it in the direction of his smiling buddies. He wasn't, instead zoomed in on the early twenty year olds applying the lotion. It wasn't apparent to the three lads, but seemingly obvious to the girls, as the blonde whispered in the ear of the redhead and then began rubbing the white liquid across her already erect nipples. Colin knew they were onto him but continued on unfazed. He knew that altering the camera now would've been an admission of guilt. Anyway, if he continued on like nothing was untoward, the girls could never be 100 percent as to what was actually materializing, so he remained as cool as a cucumber, knowing he had a secret stash for the spank bank after the vacation was over.

The girls *were 100 percent* onto the antics though, but they were glory seekers, posers, and seemingly lapping up the attention. Blondie planted a kiss on Red's neck as the lotion application continued, and one of the young boys – eyes popping out his head – lost balance on his inflatable raft and fell face first into the water.

"Could you hurry the fuck up," complained Gordon. "I'm standing here like a right fag with my arm around two dudes."

"Keep your Speedos on; I've nearly got the shot. OK, I'm done now!"

"Well give me a look then," replied Gordon impatiently.

"You should all take a look at this one; it's a work of art."

"Are you turning into a complete pussy or what? Three virtually naked guys is a work of art to you!" exclaimed Stevie.

"Take a look before you start thinking I've become a sausage lover."

The three of them crowded around the camera screen; Colin holding his left hand over the top of it in order to block out the glare from the sun.

"Holy shit!" was all Sean could say, and Gordon and Stevie looked at each other, mouths open, before glancing over at the two sexy girls, who sportingly waved.

"WAS I THAT OBVIOUS?" shouted Colin to the girls.

"WE MIGHT LOOK LIKE A COUPLE OF BIMBOS, BUT WE'RE ACTUALLY QUITE SMART," said Blondie.

"WELL, THANK YOU FOR PLAYING ALONG."

The girls returned to their horizontal positions on their sun loungers and continued on with the tanning. The boys were still in awe.

"For fuck sake; put that thing away," said Gordon to Stevie, almost in shock as he looked around incase any of the other folks at the pool area had noticed, but fortunately they were still in a state of disbelief from the breasts and lotion combo.

Stevie's erection was pitching a tent in his light blue swim-shorts, attempting to poke its head through like a baby python entering the world for the very first time.

"How was I supposed to stop that? Sounds to me like you're all partial to the occasional slice of cock if that didn't cause a *little* bit of movement from your tiny peckers."

"It's called self-control, hard-on boy. It just means we don't usually fire off a warning shot as soon as we see a piece of arse," replied Sean.

"Screw you guys, it's perfectly normal. Anyway, I think I'll leave you guys to it down here. I'm gonna go take a lie down before we get ready to go out tonight, so I'll talk to you all in a little bit."

"You should've brought your beer goggles with you mate and you could've captured all that without any of them noticing," said Colin.

"Yeah, I thought about bringing them, but knowing me I would've left them here or something. Anyway, I'm on holiday, so I decided to give myself a free pass from scrutinizing my life."

Stevie lifted his towel and sun lotion and began to walk away. He turned back after a few steps.

"Hey Colin, any chance I can take your camera with me?"

Stevie stood in the shower, eagerly anticipating the evening events. He flicked away a cockroach with his left big toe as he applied some Head and Shoulders to his greasy scalp. The apartment was fairly clean, but the bugs had become a problem shortly after their arrival. He dried himself off and slipped into the same pair of jeans from the previous night. He'd packed efficiently, having one remaining clean t-shirt which was more luck than by design. A quick application of hair gel, a brush of his teeth, and a few slaps of aftershave to his cheeks and he was ready for the final night blowout.

They funneled onto the coach with another forty or so of the apartment residents and made their way on the short ride to what seemed like the middle of nowhere. The roads were winding and the sun was dropping, and wasn't long before the night was pitch black other than the headlights of the coach hitting the road in front of them.

"I hope this rave doesn't turn out to be a pile of pish. It's not like we can just decide to walk back to town if it is," said Stevie.

"I think it'll be fine," replied Sean. "Have you seen some of the talent on the bus? Those chicks from the pool earlier are here as well and I'm sure it's only going to get even better when we get there."

He wasn't wrong either. The bus was stacked with its share of hot available ladies, most of them decked out in their most revealing of attire; cleavage and tanned legs on view for every male to drool over.

The trip was a noisy affair, with most of the passengers obviously having had more than a couple of beverages before boarding, and a chant of "if you're happy in Ibiza clap your hands," was being belted out by most of the English folks, clapping their hands together in a timely rhythm.

The topless girls from the pool were sitting on the back row with two of their friends, giggling and yelling - and occasionally joining in with the clapping – as they sipped on an assortment of Bacardi Breezers they'd brought with them, and had the guys on both sides of the second back row hanging over the headrests, vying for their attention.

Stevie had noticed all the girls alright, especially those from earlier, but was a little pissed off with their own location near the front of the bus.

"I hear you Sean, but I had my sights set on that blonde with the big tits from the pool this afternoon. Half the guys up the back there are giving it big licks with her and her friends. Basically she can choose whoever she wants tonight, so by not being up there right now and turning on the charm I'm already a bit snookered."

"Get a grip Stevie. You'll be all over her like a rash as soon as she gets off the bus, so I'm sure you'll be back in the running," said Gordon, becoming a little irritated with his juvenile antics.

In the distance they could see a lit up area that appeared no larger than a football pitch stuck out in the middle of a desert. As the coach pulled up there were six fifty-foot floodlights surrounding the place and the heavy beats from the DJ booth could be felt vibrating throughout the bus, only riling everyone up even further.

"I think that's our cue to get this party started," said Colin, pulling a few unimpressive techno dance hand moves as he kneeled on his seat.

Surprisingly the disembarking process was fairly well organized; front row first then progressively to the back. Stevie sparked up a Marlboro Light and Colin followed suit. Everyone else was filtering into the venue but Stevie and the lads held off for the ladies from the back row.

"How you doing girls?" said Stevie, directing his question at the attractive blonde.

"Oh hiya," she replied. "Girls, these are the guys from the pool I was telling you about earlier."

The two they hadn't met already just giggled nervously, obviously aware of the breast ogling situation from the afternoon.

"I'm Stevie by the way and this is Colin, Gordon, and Sean."

"Glad you could make it out tonight. I'm Tara, and this is Audrey," she said, pointing to the freckly redhead from before. "And this is Stacy and Ruth."

. They certainly were an attractive bunch. Tara had a crimped look to her long flowing blonde locks and was clothed in nothing more than a red bikini top and a dark blue mini-skirt. Audrey was similarly dressed but Tara's red and dark blue colors were substituted with yellow and green that only emphasized her fiery hair. She had a generous application of make-up to her face that covered most of her freckles, but the ones on her arms and shoulders we still very evident. The other two, Stacy and Ruth, seemed a little more reserved, which was probably the reason they hadn't been flaunting their breasts by the pool. It wasn't that they didn't have the bodies for it though. Ruth was a tall brunette with small but perky boobs and Stacy was naturally dark skinned, almost like she was the product of a mixed race marriage, and had a Jennifer Lopez shape to her arse that made the black Lycra trousers she was sporting appear to be applied with a lick of paint.

"Well it's nice to meet you all," replied Stevie. "Come on and I'll buy you all a cocktail."

Tara gave all her buddies a glance and they responded with a shrug of their shoulders.

"OK then, if you're buying let's go."

They followed the crowd up a long winding pathway that split the palm trees on either side. Lining the trail intermittently was tall wicker lantern poles with flames burning bright on top. At the end of the path the area opened out into a huge oval-shaped arena, literally stacked with masses of people bouncing around, blowing whistles to the beats and waving around luminous glowsticks as though they were conducting the DJ's along as they mixed their records.

The DJ area was on the far side and was an elevated stage with two sets of decks on board with a blue vinyl tent-like covering overhead. The main dance area was directly in front, and behind it facing the booth was another large elevated stage full of people also dancing the night away. This area appeared to be full of folks who really knew how to move, putting their skills on display, and Stevie quickly identified this was one place he wouldn't be gracing with his presence.

"Looks like the bar area is over there," said Gordon, towering above most of the heads and signaling towards a large marquis to the right.

"Lead the way Big Man," replied Stevie, ushering Tara along with a gentle arm around her shoulder.

Stevie's hand slipped from Tara's shoulder as they made their way through the crowd towards the drinks tent, but as it hit his right side she grasped hold of it and gave him a warm look as she did so. There were a lot of people around as they jostled their way – led by Gordon – through the crowd and he wasn't sure if the hand holding was a result of her instant fondness for him or just the added security he provided.

As Stevie looked around he was more than a little surprised by the mix of people. Initially he'd been expecting the mass of individuals to be solely British holiday-makers, but upon closer inspection the ratio of Spanish to people from back home was closer to two to one respectively. He was a bit uncomfortable himself as groups of locals eyed up Tara and the girls on the way past, uttering comments in their native language that he had no comprehension of. The only one appearing in a comfort zone was Gordon, spearheading the way forth as people in front watched him pushing towards them and parting immediately as he got within range.

They entered the drinks tent that wasn't as busy as the venue suggested, and easily slid to the front of the manufactured bar.

"Pretty quiet here considering the crowd," said Sean.

"I'm sure most people are downing more drugs than they are drinks," replied Gordon, flashing his hand in the air for a bartender.

"Works for me," said Colin. "I'm sure we'll manage to drink enough to make up for all the dope heads."

"Well I know I will," replied Stevie.

"Right, what you all having?" asked Gordon as one of the male bar staff approached.

"Whatever beer they have," said Colin, as Stevie and Sean gave a nod of confirmation.

"What about you girls," said Gordon, directing his question at Tara.

"Just some kind of cocktail for all of us, like a Cosmo or something."

"Four beer and four Cosmopolitans," said Gordon deliberately to the dark haired guy, holding up four fingers.

"No worries mate," replied the guy as they all looked rather surprised at each other.

"I'm English mate," said the bartender. "They call me Rodney," he said, holding out his hand towards Gordon.

"Sorry chief, I just assumed you were Spanish," replied Gordon, feeling a bit of a fool.

"Not a problem mate, I get it all the time."

"What brings you here?" asked Gordon.

"Just came on holiday one year and never went home."

"Well there are worse places you could be spending your time."

"Yeah, the ladies are spectacular, but it doesn't look like I need to tell you lads that. Nice to meet you anyway, you're drinks will be up in a sec."

And off Rodney went, grabbing four bottles of San Miguel from the fridge and began shaking up the ladies mix.

"There you go mate, that'll be five thousand six hundred Pesetas."

Gordon paid and left a sizeable gratuity which obviously pleased Rodney.

"Listen Big Man, even if there's a queue the next time you get here, just give me a shout and I'll sort you out."

"You're a good man Rodney, cheers," said Gordon, giving him a salute with his bottle.

"You up for a dance?" said Tara to Stevie as she gulped down her red-colored drink.

Beer Goggles

"Maybe in a little bit sweetheart. I think me and the boys here are just going to work on a couple of beers first. I'll probably come over and watch a few of your moves just to see what I need to contend with when I decide the moment is right."

"You don't have much competition believe me. I just think I'm a good dancer when I've got a bit of a buzz going."

"And you have one going now?"

"We had one going before we got off the bus."

"So is that why you're hanging around me now?"

"Don't you think it might be because I think you're cute?"

"Do you always answer a question with another question?"

"Do you?" she replied with a laugh and a cheesy grin.

"I can see you're going to be trouble."

"I was about to say the same about you."

"I love a smart arse. Alright, we'll follow you over there. I'll be waiting around, just come back and see me when you're ready for a refill."

"You can bet on it," she replied, squeezing his hand before they made their way back in the direction of the DJ stage.

The boys made their way lazily behind them, Gordon again taking the lead.

"Looks like you might be in there already," said Sean to Stevie.

"Well I'm not one for counting chickens before they've hatched but I'd say it's looking more than a little promising."

"True, but it's looking pretty sweet from where I was standing."

"What about you?"

"Who knows," replied Sean. "That black-looking chick Stacy has an arse to die for though. Shit, you could break walnuts off the thing. Maybe if you get in there with the friend we'll all stand a better chance?"

"I hope you're right mate."

They stood around the dance floor with several other male onlookers as Tara and friends shook their stuff in time to *Utah Saints*. The mixing from the DJ's was simply seamless and even had Stevie shaking an involuntary leg.

"Got your eye on any of them Big Man?" asked Stevie, as Gordon surveyed the floor more like a bouncer than a mere bystander.

"Not really, but as you know I've got a bit of a soft spot for redheads."

"Mate, you'll be in there like a dog eating beetroot if you want. I could already see that Audrey one giving you the stare. I'm pretty sure she's into the big dominating type. Think the way you weaved your way through that crowd earlier had her creaming in her pants."

"You really have a way with words don't you?"

"Not really Big Chap, I just call it the way I see it. There's no need to be modest all the time you know."

"Fair enough, but I'll agree with you after it happens, OK?"

"Sounds good to me mate, but if I was a betting man I wouldn't want to put on any money against it if I were you."

The girls danced their tails off as the tunes changed to the early nineties anthem "Don't You Want Me," by *Felix*. Tara and Audrey were really getting into it and causing quite a stir as each of them took turns squatting and kissing each others belly buttons. Sean could hardly control himself as he nudged Colin beside him.

"I'm not fucking blind you know," replied Colin, swigging on his beer until it was dry.

Stacy flashed Sean a smile.

"Right boys, you ready for another beer?" asked Sean, appearing to become more than a little hot under the collar.

"Thought you'd never ask," replied Stevie above the heavy beats.

"Tell me you saw that?" was Sean's response.

"Of course I did," said Stevie. "As I was telling the Big Man here, we're all in there. Looks like the Tara lass is digging me, the redhead is after the Big Fella, and by the looks of it the black chick wants a piece of you Sean-lad, so as long as Colin is content with Ruth we're golden."

"Too right I am," said Colin. "She was the one I had my eye on anyway."

It may have been true or just a function of not wanting to appear to be settling for the dregs, but either way Stevie was thinking like Hannibal Smith: "I love it when a plan comes together."

"Anyway, I'm going for the drinks. With an arse like she has I need a few more beers or I'm likely to blow a load before I've even pulled it out my shorts," said Sean.

"I'll come with you," replied Colin.

Stevie and Gordon remained behind watching the girl's seductive moves and growing more eager by the second to have them in their arms.

The mixing continued, switching to the old school classic "Hardcore Uproar." As the piano marathon kicked in the lighting switched to an ultraviolet color and the whistles and glow sticks kicked into overdrive.

Even the Spaniards were rocking to the tune, shaking their heads like they were at an Iron Maiden concert rather than a rave.

The hair on Stevie's arms began to rise as he watched a group of five or so Spanish-looking lads mix in amongst Tara and the girls. He glanced briefly at Gordon who appeared enamored with the mixing and scratching from the DJ booth. Before he could give him a nudge he looked back to the floor only to see one of the Spanish lads groping at Tara's arse and squeezing on one of her breasts. It was as though another life form took over his body as he bolted in her direction and wrenched the molesting hands from her and punched him directly in the face, dropping the culprit to the floor like a sack of potatoes. He grasped his hands around her, shielding her from them but was instantaneously smacked on the back of the head forcing him to turn around to defend himself. As he pulled his arm back to deliver another punch he felt a blow land in his stomach, causing him to double over and hit the floor and the blood immediately started to flow from him.

Stevie was more or less dead to the world but he could hear the screams and felt the trampling feet around him, bruising him further as panic set in amongst those on the floor. The final thing he remembered was the cries of Gordon shouting "COME HERE YOU MOTHER FUCKERS."

Police Suck, Doctors Rock

Stevie's eyes opened in slow motion, his eyelashes battling to break free from the crust that had built up. He was warm and snug under the blankets and felt safe, smiling as his vision focused in on the boys looking down at him with their worried faces. Surprisingly, Stevie was fully aware where he was and the reason why. He could still picture the scene of the fuzzy-looking ceiling of the ambulance even though it had been through blurred vision, in shock and virtually unable to talk, but he remembered Gordon sitting by his side as he lay on the stretcher, gripping his hand tightly and mouthing the words "stay with me mate" every other minute as two male paramedics attended to him, yapping away in Spanish.

"Morning boys," said Stevie in a sluggish tone. "I take it I made it then?"

Gordon bent down and hugged him tightly and Stevie let out a huge painful groan.

"Sorry mate, sorry," said Gordon, realizing he'd just leaned against the freshly stitched wound. "You just had me so worried last night man. I wasn't sure for a while if we'd ever get to talk again."

Gordon's eyes quickly filled with tears as he pictured how things could've possibly played out.

"You can't keep a good man down lads," said Stevie with a laugh that quickly turned to an excruciating grimace.

"How are you feeling chief?" asked Colin, his eyes glassy also.

"A little bit sore mate but not too bad."

"Well you're gonna be a lot worse when the drugs wear off," said Sean, doing his best to keep his emotions in check.

"What happened with those guys who jumped me?"

"Not sure man. I smacked one of them but as soon as I did two of the others flashed a blade at me before helping the prick up off the floor. I was gonna take the knife off the Spanish fucks and beat the living shit outta them, but I glanced over to you on the ground and saw the ever growing pool of blood around you and decided to let them go. It all happened so fast. At the time I didn't even know they'd plunged you. As soon as I did though I wanted to kill every one of the tossers, but they were off like greyhounds after a rabbit."

"That's alright mate. I really don't give a shit whether they catch them or not. I'm just happy I'm here to ask the question."

Sean and Colin simultaneously bowed their heads and their cheeks began to turn red.

"What the fuck's going on with you two?" asked Stevie; his brow becoming a little furrowed.

"They feel bad," piped up Gordon. "They were at the bar grabbing us all some beers and missed the whole incident. They feel guilty they weren't there to lend a hand."

"Right, enough of that shite. We're all here aren't we? No excuses and no blame. Let's just get our shit together and get out of here as soon as we can. I love every one of you with every ounce of strength I have, although that might not be saying a hell of a lot at this very moment in time, but we'll be back in The Crown before we know it, laughing about the entire thing. Tell you what though, it makes for a super story."

Just then, two official-looking gentlemen in dark suits entered the hospital room, one pleasant-looking young guy and one pushing retirement age with a face on him that looked all business.

They walked towards the left side of the bed, staring at Stevie. The boys were on the other side and just looked at each other.

"Can we help you?" said Gordon, drawing daggers at them both.

The younger guy turned towards Gordon, but the older one appeared oblivious to the question.

"I detective Gonzalez and this detective Mendes," replied the young cop, briefly flashing his badge. "We need ask some question about attack."

His English would've had the Queen shaking her head in disgust, but they were from a foreign country and it was significantly better than any of the boys Spanish. They knew un, dos, tres or cuatro, followed by cerveza, but that was about it, so they had no cause for complaint.

"Well can you make it quick? My friend here has had quite a traumatic experience and is a little tired," said Gordon sternly.

The older of the policemen turned his head slowly towards Gordon.

"We take as long as we need," he said abruptly before returning his attention to Stevie.

Stevie could virtually see the vein on the side of Gordon's temple expanding and beginning to pulsate.

"It's OK Big Man, take it easy. Let the guys ask whatever they want," replied Stevie, attempting to neutralize the atmosphere.

Without as much as a formal hello to Stevie, detective Mendes the little Spanish Hitler began.

"So why these guys attack you?"

Stevie explained the scenario with the girl and how they were being forceful with her and that he was intervening on the situation to ensure her safety.

"And you do nothing to provoke such attack?"

Gordon's vein was now verging on bursting.

"You trying to say it was his fucking fault!" he said, as Colin and Sean each grabbed one of Gordon's shoulders.

Detective Mendes remained unfazed, not even looking at Gordon.

"Big Man, let me handle this. Look detective, I was just protecting the girl. I'd never even seen those guys before they stabbed me last night."

"This girl you mention, what she do to these people?"

"Nothing. She was dancing with her friends minding her own business and they came up to her and started laying their hands on her."

"What she wearing?"

"She was wearing a bikini top and a short skirt, but what the hell does that have to do with anything?"

Stevie was beginning to understand Gordon's previous frustration with this guy.

"I just try to gather all facts."

"Well it sounds to me like you're trying to find an excuse for some arsehole sticking a knife in me," replied Stevie, the sound of extreme agitation very evident.

"What going on in here?" said a voice in an irate manner from the entrance of the room.

Dr. Javier Lopez was an intimidating man; a very nice man, but had an aura about him so large that you could virtually smell the importance and respect he commanded.

Both detectives and the boys turned to him and almost stood to attention.

"Detectives, I understand you doing your job, but this man need rest. He suffer much trauma and not need any more stress right now."

"Thanks Doctor, but I've got one question for them," said Stevie.

Dr. Javier Lopez gave him a confirmatory nod.

"Are we all free to leave the country whenever we want, or in my case when the good Doctor here gives me his clearance?"

"Well, do you want press charges if we find these men?" replied Mendes in his broken English.

"No, I just want to get the hell out of here and back to Scotland as quickly as possible and forget this shit ever happened."

"In that case you free to go when you want."

"Thanks, that's what I want."

"Fair enough sir," said Gonzalez. "That make less work for us."

"Good to know you are both so motivated!"

And with that the detectives turned and left.

"So Doctor, how long do I have to stay in here?"

"Maybe two or three days."

"So there's no way I can make my flight back home tonight?"

"Absolutely no way. You need rest and some healing. You lucky. There was no real damage to internal organs. If there had, your stay would be longer."

"OK Doc, you know best. Thanks for helping me."

"Just doing my job. I check on you later. I need go and look at another patient."

"Well thanks again anyway."

Doctor Javier Lopez said a pleasant goodbye to the boys and continued on with his rounds.

"Right, you boys better get on your way and get packed. I don't want you guys to miss the plane just because I have to."

"Don't talk so much shite," said Sean. "We're going to stay here with you until they're ready to release you."

"No chance lads. You heard the Doctor, no internal damage so I'll be grand here myself. Anyway, you'll lose the flight and we'll all have to buy new return tickets. They're not transferable."

"Listen, all of you," said Gordon in a stern tone. "This is what is going to happen. You two catch the flight as planned and I'll wait with Stevie. He's right that there's no point in all of us having to splash out on return tickets. And Stevie, I don't want to hear any of your pish. I'm staying with you and that'll be the end of it. Even when they give you the OK to leave it's not like you're suddenly going jump out of that bed like a fucking athlete. You're going to be sore for a bit and will definitely need some help with luggage, going up and down stairs, and other shit like that, so cut the tough talk and accept it."

"Fair enough," replied Stevie, as Colin and Sean remained silent.

They all just stared at the Big Man as he delivered a scowl. He was like a disciplinarian of a headmaster addressing three playground trouble-makers.

"OK, that's settled then," said Gordon, and they all nodded in agreement.

The Stark Realization

He felt the blade slowly penetrate his stomach, making a popping sound like a grape had just been crushed. Next he felt the serrated steel as it tore its way through his abdominal muscles, ripping and snagging on every layer of flesh, but it continued on its journey undeterred by any obstacle. Finally he felt the thick hilt stop suddenly against his skin and a rumbling and bubbling noise built up before exploding as an upward fountain of red, squirting out and splattering everything within a ten foot radius.

He lay there on his back becoming weaker and weaker, his head becoming lighter and lighter as the blood eruption continued as strong as ever. His white shirt was now a soaked maroon version; the only piece of it remaining unchanged was the bright green crocodile Lacoste emblem by his left nipple that had an expression on its jaws that gave the impression it was cackling at his distress.

His vision was deteriorating, fading into a blur more and more as each pint of warm iron-filled red liquid drained from within him. He could make out a dark outline of a figure standing tall above him, very, very tall. He traced the silhouette from the head down to the shoulders, two arms, two legs, then four more legs. Two legs then four legs; what the fuck? He squinted hard, trying to ignore the continual geyser from his stomach, his eyes slanted like a Chinese man, determined to figure out the deformed beast standing before him.

The two legs were definitely human, a pair of black dressed shorts stopping just above the kneecaps and hair on the lower halves not unlike his own. The four legs below the feet were like thin sticks by comparison, thin wooden sticks. It was a chair. His slits for eyes jolted upwards towards the head. It was his father with a rope around his neck.

"This is the best way it could end for you Stevie. It will save you the years of pain, suffering, and illness that is ahead of you. Don't fight it now, let all the blood go. Come join your mother and soon to be me. Save yourself the journey you are destined to take. Avoid the drunken depression, the heartache of nobody wanting to deal with your antics, the liver cirrhosis, the night sweats, the weight loss, the anxiety of whether you'll get the liver transplant you're going to require, and if you do, wondering if your body will accept or reject it, wondering if you'll be able to treat the new organ like it needs to be or whether you'll view it as a fresh start to begin your ghastly ways all over again. Of course you would. Nobody will be there to support and love you. No decent loving woman wants a long-term life with a drunken loose cannon. Sort yourself out or let the blood continue to flow and just die. See you in heaven, unless you are banished to hell."

He stepped from the chair and fell, stopping suddenly as the snap from his neck echoed in the air.

Stevie's eyes opened wide and his hands grasped at the wound, trying to push down with his palm and stop the flow. He looked down. There was no flow. His shirt was still white. There was no sign of his father. There *was* a chair in the corner, but it was his armchair and not a four-legged wooden variety. He lay on his sofa, heart beating so hard he could almost hear it as clearly as a doctor with a stethoscope. The wound was real, but it was the recently stitched one and there was no blood to speak of.

Stevie was scared and felt an eerie chill running through him, every hair on his body tingling and standing on end. Suddenly he wanted to speak with Gordon more than he ever had.

Nurse Becky

It had been almost a week since Stevie's eventual return from Ibiza; a holiday that started so well but finished so horrendously. Either way it would never be forgotten for a plethora of reasons.

The week had been a long and boring one, basically spent in the solitude of his flat drinking himself senseless, occasionally intermingled with a few visits from the boys bringing over Chinese take-away and cans of cheap lager.

The one positive from it all was a three or four week reprieve from the office. The doctor had said three or four weeks off depending on how he was feeling, which Stevie immediately calculated out as going to take all four of them. He hated most of his colleagues, but had been pleasantly surprised by the numerous get well cards he'd received in the mail from them. The two bunches of flowers though had confused the hell out of him, as he'd always considered those to be the gift for a female at such a time of illness and recovery, and thought that if they'd wanted to send presents, a half bottle of vodka or Jack Daniels would've been significantly more appropriate as well as less expensive.

Stevie slipped on his last clean white t-shirt and a pair of dark blue jeans, and sat down on his armchair with his socks and shoes in his hands. The pain from his stomach wound was excruciating as he bent over and pulled the socks on. The tying of the shoelaces was equally as delightful. He let out a huge groan as he got to his feet, before throwing on his trusty black leather jacket and headed out the front door.

It was times like these he wished he were a bungalow owner, as he still had to negotiate the two flights of the building's stairs before making it out into the open air.

The grunts and groans continued as he progressed slowly down each step, pain bolting like short, sharp shocks in his abdomen with every movement. Fortunately the doctor's office was only a few minutes walk away. He'd contemplated taking the car, but the prospect of climbing in and out of the front seat and potentially twisting his abdominal muscles sent alarm bells ringing in his head, so he decided the short walk was the way to go. It was finally the day to have his stitches removed and that was at least one thing keeping him happy.

It was a fresh, yet warmer than usual day in Uddingston, and the sun was even attempting to peek its head out from behind a thick dark cloud. His progress was slow but steady, walking almost from the knees down in order to prevent as much upper body movement as possible.

He made the mistake of inhaling deeply as he passed the Tunnock's biscuit factory, which resulted in more pain, but he could hardly be faulted. The smell of caramel and melting chocolate escaping through the factory vents was always a talking point in the village and something that had to be enjoyed.

The doctor's office was a cold and grey colored place that fitted in nicely with all the miserable-looking people sitting in the waiting room. The only form of enthusiasm was coming from two young kids in the corner playing with the toys as their young mother looked on, appearing glad of some reprieve from their energy.

No sooner had Stevie sat down and began flicking through a tatty-looking copy of Golf Monthly, his name was called.

"Stevie McDonald," shouted the crabby old receptionist; obviously who loved her job and the constant bickering from patients complaining to her about wait times.

Stevie made his way to the desk, conscious of all the eyes on him, wondering how he was being seen before them.

"That was quick," he said with a smile.

"Well, you don't need to see the doctor. The nurse will be taking care of you today. Room number three, through the door and take your first left," said the grumpy, expressionless old lady.

Stevie hobbled his way through to room three and gave a gentle knock on the door.

"Come in," said the perky female voice.

Stevie stepped inside and struggled to keep the look of glee from his face, but could almost feel his eyes attempting to pop out of their sockets as he ogled at the young nurse sitting behind the brown wooden desk.

"Take a seat and I'll be with you in a minute," she said sweetly, turning her attention back to her paperwork.

Stevie was speechless.

The young nurse was in her late twenties and had long blonde hair pulled back in a ponytail. She was dressed in a set of light blue scrubs and was wearing a pair of black rimmed designer glasses.

Stevie watched her intently as she finished up her note taking. He was surprised and delighted to see she wasn't wearing an engagement or wedding ring. Her skin appeared to be flawless. She was make-up free as well, so her beauty was all natural. Stevie could only imagine how stunning she would be when dressed up for a night on the town, with her face done up and her long blonde hair flowing onto her shoulders.

"Sorry about that Mr. McDonald, but I just had to finish up a few details from the last patient," she said, giving him a smile that exposed her perfect white teeth, before closing the file she'd been working on.

"Call me Stevie," he replied, trying to remain cool.

"Hi Stevie, I'm Becky," she said, standing up from her chair and extending her hand for the customary shake.

"Nice to meet you Becky."

Her hand was a dainty one that felt so delicate in Stevie's shovel of a palm, but it was in line with her entire body. She stood around five feet three with what appeared to be a slim yet toned physique, but it was a little tricky to tell with the scrubs on.

"So you're here to have some stitches removed. Where did you cut yourself?"

"On my stomach."

"OK, well pop over to the bed over there and let's take a look."

Again Stevie let out a groan as he got to his feet and hobbled over to the padded table in the corner of the small office.

"You really are in pain," said Becky, giving him a sympathetic look.

"I'll be grand in a couple of weeks."

Stevie winced as he took off his leather jacket and sat upright on the padded table.

"OK, pull up your t-shirt and give us a look."

Stevie lifted the shirt and held it just below his pectoral muscles.

"Wow, that's quite a wound you've got there. What happened?"

"Well it's a bit of a long story, but I was in Ibiza on holiday and some Spanish guy stuck a knife in me."

"Holy shit Stevie. Pardon my language, but I don't get too many stab victims coming to see me."

He couldn't tell if her comment was a disapproving one or not, but he *really* had the hots for this girl and didn't want her thinking he was just some thug, so decided he had to elaborate.

"Yeah, it's an incident I wish I could forget. We were at a rave and there was a bunch of Spanish guys harassing a young English girl. I decided to step in to her defense and they didn't take too kindly to the intervention. They began throwing punches at me and the next thing I felt was the blade in my stomach. I don't remember much after that other than lying in the ambulance and then waking up in the hospital."

"You poor thing. That was a very brave thing you did and you should be commended for it."

He was back on track with Becky and she now had a motherly look to her that suggested she almost wanted to give him a hug.

"Well sometimes you gotta do what you gotta do."

"Be careful next time, but hopefully there won't be one. OK, let's get these stitches out for you."

She placed her left hand on the right side of Stevie's stomach around the wound, and with the small clippers in her other hand, began cutting the stitches.

It was a simple process and part of Stevie wished there had been hundreds of stitches rather than eight, in order to extend the time Becky was next to him. She smelled unbelievable. Her perfume had a fresh, fruity aroma that even kicked the arse off the caramel and melting chocolate coming from Tunnock's factory vents. Her head was level with his chest as she clipped away, and Stevie breathed in deeply to inhale as much of her as he could, ignoring the pain it was causing him. Even her hair had a flowery scent to it and was evidence of her morning journey to the shower. He faded away briefly to his little dream world, fantasizing about a shower for two, rubbing sweet shampoo into Becky's long locks as the warm water flowed over their heads. He was just about to move onto soaping up her body when he was snapped back to reality.

"OK Stevie, you're all set."

It was just as well there were no more stitches to be removed, as he was already beginning to feel a little movement in the groin of his jeans and didn't feel that sticking her in the chest with an erection was the most impressive way to go, even if he was prepared with a line regarding the irony of her tending to his stab wound as he stabbed her in return with his hard-on.

"That's me done?"

"That's you done Stevie."

"So do you live around here Becky?" said Stevie, determined to continue their interaction for at least another couple of minutes.

"Not too far. I've got a little one bedroom flat over in Hamilton. What about you?"

"I've got a one bedroom place as well that's about walking distance from here. It's a decent place and the folks in the same building are pretty decent. Plus it's handy if I want to walk over to The Crown bar for a pint. Do you know that place?"

"I'm not too familiar with the bars in Uddingston."

"Well, it's right at the cross beside the solicitor's office. I'll be there on Saturday night if you fancy popping over here for a drink."

"Well, I'm not too sure my boyfriend would appreciate that, but he and I aren't exactly seeing eye to eye at the moment, so I'll think about it. I could always bring a couple of friends with me I suppose, but I can't promise anything."

"That's good enough for me Becky. Alright sweetheart thanks again, and I really hope you can drop in for a glass of wine or something on Saturday. I'm paying of course."

And with that Stevie went on his merry way, turning back for a final glance of Becky as he left the room. She smiled and seemed genuinely flattered by the invitation, and her body language as she played with her hair and said a final goodbye indicated she was definitely attracted to Stevie.

He was on cloud nine as he made the short walk back to his flat, so much so that he barely noticed the pain. If only he'd been wearing his beer goggles, that was his only regret, but those were usually reserved for nights out on the drink incase he blacked out. He would've loved to have replayed the appointment with Becky in the comfort of his own home on the big TV screen, but one thing was for sure, he'd be at The Crown this Saturday night on the off chance she showed up.

Saturday Night at The Crown

It was finally Saturday night and Becky was all Stevie had been thinking about since they'd met. He'd returned many times to his daydream of them in the shower together, taking it further than before. The vision of them washing and fondling each other seemed so right and so lifelike. He imagined carrying her dripping wet body out of the shower and into the bedroom, throwing her down on the mattress and exploring every inch of her. He hoped and prayed he would see her tonight, if only so he could ease up on the wrist workouts and huge quantities of tissues he was ploughing his way through.

Stevie entered the bar and was delighted to see the boys were already there and had snagged the seats in the immediate corner by the jukebox. That way he could have an ideal vantage point of the entrance door and quickly spot Becky and friend if they decided to show up.

The place was packed and a little rowdier than usual; the majority of the patrons already tanked up on beer and spirits and had likely been there all day watching the afternoon football games.

Sandra was behind the bar as usual and had seen Stevie arrive. She already had a pint of Guinness flowing into a cold glass for him. He greeted her with a wink and a hello before thanking her for the beer and headed over to his buddies. Sandra's eyes followed his arse like it was a hypnotist's finger as he made his way towards the table; an action the boys didn't fail to notice.

"I think Sandra the MILF wants another piece of you mate," said Colin.

"She's only human lads."

"Yeah yeah stud boy, what woman wouldn't want to get you in the sack," said Gordon sarcastically.

"Was she any good by the way?" said Colin, digging for details.

"Not bad at all. She's got an arse and a set of hips designed for doggie-style. Anyway, most of these older chicks are pretty horny."

"You gonna venture back again?" said Sean, looking more than a little intrigued.

"I might do. It's always nice to have something to fall back on. It might be tonight if this chick Becky doesn't appear."

"So, fill us in on that one," said Gordon.

"Guys, she is su-fucking-perb. Fantastic looking, great little body, excellent personality, and she smells like a fucking fruit salad. One major problem though, she's got a boyfriend. She told me they weren't seeing eye to eye right now, so hopefully she's just been looking for something better to come along to give her an excuse to send him packing."

"And by something better you mean *you*?" said Colin bursting into laugher closely followed by Gordon and Sean.

"Kiss my arse Colin. Anyway, enough of your pish, just get up to the bar and get a round in," said Stevie, adjusting the beer goggles on the bridge of his nose.

"Do me a favour Stevie, can you go and get this one in and order me a bottle of Rolling Rock."

"Right ya numpty, when did your last servant die? Anyway, what's with the Rolling Rock shite? Turning gay on us?"

"Yeah, that's it dickhead. No, that Sandra chick is wearing a really short skirt tonight and I'm convinced she's not wearing any undies. I was up at the bar before you came in and I was almost sure I got a wee swatch of her arse crack when she bent over to get a bottle of beer from the top shelf of the fridge. Now, in the same fridge, the Rolling Rock is on the *bottom* shelf, so I figured if she has to bend over *even further* we'll be able to see for sure and you'll capture all the action with the old beer goggles."

"Aye alright then, but you had me at arse crack," chuckled Stevie, turning and making his way gingerly to the bar.

"Another Guinness Stevie?" said Sandra as Stevie squeezed in between a couple of young guys.

"Make that two Guinness sweetheart, one Belhaven Best, and a bottle of Rolling Rock."

Sandra scuttled off and poured the Belhaven and the first of the Guinness and brought them back over just as Colin appeared by Stevie's side.

"The other two will be with you in a second Stevie," said Sandra.

"Cheers sweetheart."

"Thought I'd come over and help you carry the drinks," said Colin, grinning from ear to ear.

"Yeah, I'm sure that's your motive ya dirty bastard."

Sandra started the second Guinness pouring and made her way towards the fridge. Stevie and Colin gave each other a quick look before returning their attention back to the action. You could've cut their anticipation in two with a blunt knife.

The fridge in question was directly facing them, so if anything was going on under the denim mini-skirt they had the best view in the house.

Sandra opened the fridge door in what seemed like slow motion, before bending at the hips and pulling a bottle from the bottom shelf. Stevie wanted to turn immediately to Colin, but maintained his stare on Sandra, uttering the words "fuck me."

Not only had Colin been correct about seeing her arse crack, but her labia were on display like a couple of medium rare beef curtains.

"Will that be all for you Stevie," asked Sandra putting the other Guinness and the now infamous bottle of Rolling Rock on the bar.

"That's all for now darling, but I'm sure I'll be back for the same round very shortly," replied Stevie, struggling to keep his laughter in check.

"Outstanding," said Colin as they rejoined Gordon and Sean at the table.

"So her arse crack *was* on display then," said Sean.

"Arse crack! Shit, the whole downstairs area was on display for all to see. Some size of flaps on her as well. You could've tied a fucking reef knot with them," replied Colin in his excited tone.

"Well at least tell us you captured all of it. I wouldn't mind getting a wee look at it after we're done here tonight," said Gordon.

"Oh I got it alright. We can play it back on my TV later if you'd like."

"You can definitely count me in for that," said Sean, looking like the moment for viewing couldn't come soon enough.

Stevie's mind went back to thoughts of Becky. He stared at the door, perking up in his seat every time it opened, but each time led to more disappointment.

The hours passed by and still no Becky, and closing time was fast approaching.

"Tell you what Stevie, you've been a right bundle of laughs tonight!" said Gordon.

"I know guys; I was just really hoping she would've showed up. Maybe I'm an idiot, but I really thought she would."

"Some you win and some you lose mate," piped up Sean.

Sandra rang the bell and shouted last orders.

"Will I get us one for the road," said Colin.

"I'm good chief. Think I'll just head back home," said Stevie in a depressed sounding tone.

"Holy shit man, you really are disappointed," said Colin, giving Gordon and Sean a puzzled look.

Stevie turning down a drink was as likely as the Queen pausing to break wind during her annual address to the nation, so it was no surprise the lads were taken aback.

"Let's just go back to your place for a nightcap then and we can get a wee gander at your recording of Sandra's arse and snatch," said Sean eagerly.

"I'm up for that," replied Colin.

"Me too," said Gordon.

"No worries. Let's go then," said Stevie, still sounding a little down.

They swigged down their last mouthfuls of beer and headed for the door.

"Have a good one Sandra," said Stevie.

The place was more or less empty now other than one or two of the alcoholic regulars who weren't completely sure if they were there or not, and Sandra looked bored, leaning on her side of the bar with her elbows, palms holding up her chin.

"What are you up to now? Going out clubbing or something?" replied Sandra curiously.

"Nah, just heading home for a quiet one," said Stevie.

"Well, I'll be getting out of here soon if you'd like to *do* something," she said, raising her eyebrows and a slight smirk crept onto her face.

Stevie's eyes lit up, instantly snapping him out of his negativity. He turned and whispered to the boys.

"We can watch that footage another night. Think I'll try and find out if a reef knot is actually possible."

A Chat With Dad

"*Stevie, I am so sorry. I was a coward and didn't realize what my death would do to you. I wasn't thinking clearly, and my inner pain was too much for me to cope with. I just didn't want to go on without your mother. She was my life. We are now together again though and we are both worried about you. Your drinking habits are spiraling out of control and you are heading for an early grave. You need to find yourself a good woman and pack in all the one night stands. You need to experience the kind of love your mother and I have together. Son, it's magical, and I am finally happy again. I love you Stevie. We both love you my boy, but hate seeing you destroy yourself. You have so much to offer a girl, so much to offer the world. Stay strong son. Find love, enjoy life in moderation, and we will be a family again one day.*"

"What the fuck!" said Stevie, suddenly awakening, covered in cold sweat as usual.

One thing was different though. His heart wasn't racing at warp speed like it usually did when his father entered his dreams.

Funnily enough it had felt almost therapeutic, and a severe contrast from the usual graphic nightmares. It seemed so real and made sense to him. Maybe it had been real. Maybe there *was* a place after life on Earth. Maybe they *would* be a family again. Real or not, the advice was sound. He did have to turn his life around and he knew it. He'd known it for some time, but it was like an addiction. He had to stop though, and that time was now.

"Good morning."

The words startled Stevie. He'd been so caught up in his thoughts he'd forgotten that Sandra had spent the night.

"Hey, good morning," replied Stevie calmly, hiding his surprise like an Oscar winning actor.

"You were a bit restless last night. You were tossing and turning all over the place. At one point I thought I was going to have to go and sleep on your couch, especially after you accidentally cracked me on the side of the head, but you calmed down after I punched you in the ribs."

"Really? I'm sorry, I was dreaming about my dad," said Stevie pressing the right side of his ribcage. He was painful and tender, so he knew Sandra hadn't been tormenting him about his antics.

"That's OK Stevie. I understand things are still tough for you," replied Sandra, drawing him a concerned and sympathetic look and began stroking his upper arm.

Daylight streamed horizontally through the blinds and lit up Sandra's face. She really was a genuine and caring lady who'd had her fair share of tough times. She was pushing forty and the morning light was displaying the fine wrinkles around her eyes and her long red hair mixed with the yellow rays of sun gave off a beautiful tangerine glow.

Stevie stared back into her eyes. He knew her life had been mixed with ups and downs and it was beginning to show on her features. He almost felt sorry for her like she did for him. He leaned in to give her a soft kiss but she turned her cheek away.

"Where's the cat?" she said.

"What cat?" asked Stevie, completely baffled.

"The one that took the shit in your mouth. Go brush your teeth Stevie, you reek of stale booze. Then I'll kiss you."

"You might want to do the same yourself."

They both laughed.

Stevie put toothpaste on his blue brush and took it into the shower with him as Sandra entered the bathroom.

"Can I borrow your brush when you're done," said Sandra. "I hadn't exactly planned to spend the night here."

Stevie removed the brush from his mouth and spat a huge white gob of paste and saliva into the shower grate and opened the Perspex screen door.

"There's one right there you can use," replied Stevie, pointing to the floor beside the toilet seat.

"The fucking toilet brush! Is that your idea of getting me back for the cat joke? Anyway, *you* could've used the toilet brush this morning and it would've *actually* freshened you up considerably."

"Fuck you dick breath," said Stevie, laughing his arse off.

"Great put down Stevie considering it was your dick that was in there. You might want to think things through before you come back with any more *fantastic* lines."

"Here, take the damn brush," said Stevie, quickly rinsing it in the warm spray and handing it to her. "Now hurry up and brush them and get in here for round two."

The Golden Pole

Stevie's wounds had fully healed, but his alcoholism had not been deterred. He had taken some time away from it the previous day, but not through design. It was more the result of spending the afternoon and evening in bed from of a massive hangover. By the time he had surfaced from his virtual coma, it was around last orders at the local bar, so he'd decided to just return to bed.

It was Colin's birthday tonight and the plan was for the four of them to take their celebrations to *The Golden Pole* strip club for the evening. Colin had demanded that his friends not buy him any gifts, but instead "sponsor" his first lap-dance at the club. They all had quickly agreed, as a trip to the shops was the last activity they'd wanted to endure.

Stevie was literally foaming at the mouth as he made his way into the shower. He needed a beer and a shot of whiskey. That combined with his appetite for scantily clad women had his juices flowing. He scrubbed his arms and legs furiously with the worn out yellow sponge caked in shower gel, before moving onto his crucial one, two, three, application: penis, balls, arsehole. That was the usual order. Sometimes he mixed it up by interchanging steps one and two, but three was always last. He was on a mission this evening and was fully planning on not being alone at the end of the night, so genital hygiene was of primary importance.

The Golden Pole was a dark and dingy-looking place; the only element of light being the stage area where the naked girls paraded around and performed twirling moves up and down the twenty foot, sturdy looking poles. Most of the girls were born to put on a show, fixing their seductive stares on groups of testosterone-fuelled men, or older lonely-looking single gentlemen, occasionally licking their lips to entice them further. It was like these "dancers" had special powers, reeling these pathetic guys to the edge of the stage with an imaginary fishing rod, and taking a few notes from their eager stack of cash.

Men were such wankers. Many of them *actually* believed these girls were digging them, and would spend a fortune on visits to the stage to get some verbal interaction, or indeed back behind the curtain covered booths where they might manage a quick squeeze of their tits – if the price was right. Some of the skankier ones could even agree to you slipping them a couple of fingers if their mood was right.

The boys were a little boisterous as they entered the club, gaining an unappreciative stare from the gorilla-like doorman. He eyeballed them all closely and their jubilation quickly turned to silence.

"I.D please," he said sternly to Sean, who had been last to enter.

Sean, although in his later twenties, had a face as smooth as a baby's bottom, and had about as much chance of growing a beard as he had of convincing an American vegetarian that haggis was a tasty and suitable meat substitute.

"Mate, ah'm twenty eight," replied Sean, staring into the eyes of the neckless guy, as the other lads looked on, dying to laugh at their buddy's distress.

"I.D please," the bouncer repeated, cool as a cucumber, and not even flinching from his original expression.

Sean dug deep into his back pocket and pulled out his brown leather wallet, reaching in and handed him his license.

"Chief, he just made that on the computer earlier and laminated it before we left the house. It's probably still warm," said Colin, surprisingly maintaining a straight face.

"Screw you Colin, I'm three months your senior you prick."

"Your friend does have a point though, it is still warm," replied the bouncer.

"Come on man, it's been in my back pocket. We were sitting in a roasting hot taxi for about twenty minutes on the way here. The dick of a driver had the heating cranked up to full capacity. Christ, the beads of sweat are still running down my arse crack."

"I'm just playing with you, have a nice night guys," said the doorman, glancing at the other boys and flashing them a wink; a slight smirk appearing on his previously expressionless features.

The boys made their way past the buffet of hot food; an addition at most strip clubs designed to soak up some of the alcohol in order to promote more drinking and in turn more lap dances. They passed the main bar and the girl parading on top of it, letting each patron sitting there slip a dollar in her thigh-high garter belt.

They surveyed the scene of the open plan main room before taking a seat at one of the small circular-top wooden tables covered with a black cloth that draped to the floor. The four surrounding seats were comfortable; red suede material, with a sunken look to them as the back and side armrests were high in comparison to the seating position, but they were designed to make it comfy for any of the girls should they decide to keep you company and sit on your lap.

Stevie gazed attentively at the stage. The lights briefly dimmed before a spotlight appeared against the back curtain. Like a vision from every man's dream world, a tall, naked, Latin woman with silky smooth skin and flowing long black hair emerged. The spotlight illuminated her pearly white teeth as she flashed a smile at the excited masses.

As the stage light returned, she tentatively made her way on her six inch transparent platform heels to the center of the stage. The clear soles on the slutty shoes were enormous, and the type you'd half expect to see a goldfish swimming around in.

The boys all briefly glanced at each other without saying anything, other than Colin lip-synching the word "wow." It was a more than adequate description as she ran her perfectly manicured right index finger down her thin sliver of dark pubic hair, all the way to the prize on every guy's mind. Suddenly the sound of Britney Spears "Hit Me Baby One More Time" flowed from the sound system and her vigorous dancing routine kicked into full flow.

The lads were situated one table row back from stage-side, and giggled like a bunch of school kids seeing a pair of breasts for the very first time as the South American goddess pranced around for a few seconds before scaling the golden pole nearest the boys. She reached the top with the ease of a trained marine before flipping upside down and descending at a rapid rate of knots. A gasp, not dissimilar to a crowd watching a tightrope walker suddenly lose their balance, flooded the room. Crashing her head into the wooden stage seemed inevitable, but she adjusted her grip just in time and screeched to a halt no more than six inches from the floor.

It was obviously a maneuver that had gone through many a sore skull as well as a lot of practice, but the excitement level it created probably outweighed that of most Scottish division one football matches.

Stevie was like a kid in a candy shop. His beer goggles were capturing everything, and he was already looking forward to replaying again at home.

My loneliness is killing me, and I, I must confess…

The sweet tone of Britney's voice continued on as the Latin girl flicked her long, dark, locks of hair around like a fan at a heavy metal concert, while running her hands up her inner thighs. The place was in a frenzy and three people had already made their way stage-side, holding outstretched paper bills out to gain the stripper's attention. Not to be outdone, Stevie made his way over and dangled a five in his hand. The others were holding ones.

There were now four of them waiting eagerly, ogling her closely and absorbing every move of her seductiveness. She certainly was a cool customer, continuing on with her dance moves and teasing them all into surrender.

When I'm not with you I lose my mind, give me a siiiiiiiiiign, hit me baby one more time.

The four of them at the stage were a real mixed bunch. To the left hand side was an elderly gentleman, probably in his late sixties and obviously short-sighted. His brown rimmed glasses were perched on the end of his nose as he gazed over the top of them, watching the girl's every movement with a creepy look of desire invading his face.

At the opposite side of the stage was a little fat balding gentleman who'd obviously consumed a few too many beverages. He was attempting to focus on the Latin princess's moves, but was definitely fighting the blurred vision as his eyes continued to squint. Each time the bronzed beauty moved from side to side, he would do the same, often having to grab the edge of the stage to prevent from falling over. As a result of his over exuberance, the few grey strands of hair he had "discreetly" situated in a comb-over across the top of his fat white cue-ball were now hanging down like a side ponytail; a look that all strippers found particularly appealing.

To Stevie's right was a girl replicating the dancer's moves, and was being cheered on by her friends at the table directly behind her. They were obviously on a work night out and had actually come out straight from there. It didn't take Sherlock Holmes to work it out, and the fact they applied their trade at one of the local hospitals or medical centers was a given as well, as they were all sporting matching light blue scrubs outfits.

Stevie checked out the young lady mimicking the stripper's moves, before returning his attention to the naked female body. His head jolted quickly back to the nurse, so much so that his beer spectacles were nearly thrown from his face.

"Holy shit, what the hell are you doing here?"

It was Nurse Becky, the little doll who'd removed his stitches.

"Stevie, how are you?" she exclaimed, just as surprised to see him as he was her.

The gorgeous stripper made her way towards the five pound note that Stevie was still holding out in his hand, but just as she arrived, he made his way over to Becky, oblivious to the Latin girl's advance.

Becky threw her arms around Stevie and gave him a huge hug. A few of the patrons averted their attention from the naked dancer and over to the interaction taking place between them.

Becky didn't appear too far behind the fat balding guy with the side ponytail with her alcohol count. Her words were slightly slurred and any inhibition had been thrown away like shit off a shovel.

"Been here a while I take it," said Stevie, picking up on her slur and bloodshot blue eyes.

"Not really, I'm just a bit of a lightweight when it comes to drinking. I've only had four bottles of Budweiser, but I'm feeling a bit of a buzz."

"Well it's good to see you Becky. You are looking great."

He wasn't kidding either. Not many women could look sexy in a set of scrubs, but she was doing a fine job. She'd obviously applied a little make-up and brushed her long blonde hair, but to look this good in a work outfit was impressive, and Stevie could only imagine the improvement had she *really* made an effort.

"You're looking really good yourself."

"Well, I'm sure most of the guys in here are looking well considering you've probably been examining crusty old geriatrics with erectile dysfunction problems all day."

"Stevie, you really are disgusting. Charming in a strange way, but you are still disgusting," she said with a smirk and a slight hint of blush formed on her cheeks.

It may have been the alcohol, but Stevie had seen this type of reaction before when talking to women, and previous experience told him that she did like him. His excitement bubbled inside like a mud pool and he fought back a grin, although the potential indicator provided him with extreme joy. He *really* had it bad for her.

"So is this all your work buddies?" said Stevie, trying to alter the conversation flow and gather his thoughts.

"We used to work together in the Hamilton medical center before I moved over to the Uddingston surgery. Come over and meet them," replied Becky with drunken enthusiasm.

"Sounds good," said Stevie, following her lead, before looking over at the boys and giving a shrug of his shoulders.

"Everybody, this is Stevie. Stevie, this is Monica, Anabel, Sarah, Brian, and Matt," said Becky, working her way clockwise around the table.

Stevie made a brief mental note of the names, but knew they would all likely be quickly forgotten, perhaps with the exception of Sarah, who was on par with Becky in the looks department.

"Nice to meet you guys. Your friend here is a dab hand at removing stitches."

"Oh, you're the Stevie with the stab wound," said Sarah.

Stevie was a little taken aback with the comment, and wasn't quite sure whether it was a frown upon him being involved in such an incident or evidence that Becky had been talking to her about their brief meeting in a positive light. The fact she was smiling was indication of the latter though.

"Yes, I'm the very one. Tell you what though, it'll be the last time I jump to anyone's defense," replied Stevie, immediately attempting to put out the flames should his former assumption of Sarah's comment be the case.

"Yeah, she said you were a nice guy," said Sarah, flashing a wink at Becky.

"Shut up Sarah, you'll be giving him a bigger head than he already has."

Becky was becoming redder by the second, and Stevie was getting slightly uncomfortable. It wasn't the female attention that bothered him, but more the fact that Brian and Matt – who had said nothing more than a quick hello – were giving him a funny look. Was one of them involved with Becky? He couldn't be sure, so told them all it was nice to meet them and he would catch-up with them again later, before returning to the boys at their table.

"Who the hell was that?" inquired Gordon. "She was a bit of alright, and her friends were a bit tasty as well."

"That was the nurse I talked about, the one who took out my stitches. She is an absolute sweetheart. As for the tasty friends you're probably referring to, that was Brian and Matt."

Colin and Sean erupted into laughter, and even Gordon got a kick out of the remark.

"You really are a prick Stevie. A lovable prick, but a prick all the same," said Gordon.

"By the way Stevie, do you know that stripper who was just on stage had come over to get your money right as you went over to that Becky chick?" said Sean.

"Who cares? I'm sure she does just fine in the money department. Anyway, I'd take Becky over her any day."

"*Seriously*. You'd rather bone that nurse than the naked sensation that was just up there? I mean, don't get me wrong, Becky is a very attractive chick, but that stripper was a once in a lifetime type of girl. Shit, her farts probably smell like roses!" exclaimed Colin, genuinely surprised by Stevie's statement.

"Colin, there's just something about her. I really think she is the type of girl I could really settle down with."

"Oh my God, I *never* thought I'd hear those words coming from you of all people," replied Gordon, even more surprised than Colin had been with Stevie's first comment.

"Sounds like somebody might be falling in love," said Sean with a teasing tone in his voice.

"I think you might be right," replied Stevie, giving yet another glance in the direction of Becky.

The night was going well and the boys were having a whale of a time. The beers were flowing and various dancers graced the stage. The beer goggles were capturing a multitude of girls, but Becky was being filmed every bit as much as the strippers. Stevie had even made Sean switch chairs with him as his original seating position had him facing away from Becky and company.

Stevie was happy to see that Becky had slowed down on the booze and was now sipping a large glass of iced water through a straw. If only he'd shown the same self control when it came to alcohol consumption.

He'd been following her antics closely ever since they'd spoke, and as the evening wore on, he became convinced that Brian and Matt were just friends of hers.

"Fuck me, I need to piss again," said Colin, which was no real surprise considering he'd been throwing back the beers as though prohibition was being reintroduced the following morning.

"Well go and take one then," said Gordon.

"I know, but it's just bullshit. By the time the night is over I'm gonna have given the bathroom attendant more money than I've given any of the dancers. That wanker expects a pound every time he hands you a cloth to dry your hands. Maybe I should make him give me a lap dance. Christ I could've got myself one with as much as I've sprung on him already."

"Just take a piss and walk straight back out again. That's what I do," replied Gordon.

"And not wash my hands. You really are a dirty bastard."

"Hey, my dick is probably cleaner than those taps you're touching in there, and the rate you're going I'd probably be about fifteen pounds better off by the end of the night."

"Yeah, but the guy is expecting it now and I kinda feel bad for him. I mean, he's working in a toilet, so I'm pretty sure he isn't exactly rolling in cash. At least I smell and taste good I suppose. I make sure I get my moneys worth. I grab a handful of those mints and make sure I take a spray of the aftershave every time."

"Is that what that fucking smell is," said Sean. "I thought someone had pissed themselves. If it's aftershave I can only assume he isn't exactly carrying top of the line stuff back there. It reminds me of my grandfather. It must be Brut or Old Spice. You'd be better with some Eau de toilette, and I mean proper toilet water. Just take a handful from the first urinal and splash that on your chops and you'll probably smell the same."

"Anyway lads," said Stevie. "I'll leave you all to your bickering. I'm off for a piss myself."

Stevie made his way past the circular-shaped bar with the blonde naked stripper parading around on top of it, virtually demanding money from each patron sitting there sipping on their drink of choice. Behind the bar on the back wall was a line of little booths where the lap dances took place. Only a couple of them were vacant; the others had their blue glittery curtain drawn, and Stevie was convinced there was more than dancing occurring in a few of them.

As he approached the door in the far corner labeled with the little man and woman stick figures on it, he glanced back towards Becky's table and caught her eye. She'd obviously been following his movements and he flashed her a quick smile which she reciprocated before he disappeared through the door.

The door led into a darkened corridor. The ladies room was the first door on the right and the gents was second. He closed his eyes as he entered the bathroom then opened them slowly, trying to regain focus. The restroom was extremely bright and a major contrast to the dimly lit interior of the club.

Like Colin had stated, the bathroom attendant was obviously hustling for tips. Upon Stevie's arrival his eyes lit up and he immediately reached for one of his dry white hand cloths that were piled high beside his array of mint sweets and after shave bottles. There was almost a sad, yet hopeful look from the guy. He wasn't young by any stretch of the imagination, probably in his mid-to-late fifties, dyed black, untidy hair and had a few burst blood vessels on each cheek that likely indicated a fondness for alcohol not unlike Stevie. Perhaps the loneliness and sadness in his eyes was all part of the act of squeezing a few extra pounds from his customers. Maybe he was a retired salesman or something, used to putting on a show and was currently living off a healthy pension with no debt and used this gig as an excuse to get out of the house and see some tits and arse (or more likely cock from where he spent most of the evening). Regardless, his persona had already sapped in Stevie and he removed two pound notes from his back pocket with his free hand as he stood in front of the white porcelain urinal, chasing around an old cigarette butt with his fast-flowing stream.

"How's business?" said Stevie to the attendant as he zipped up his fly.

"A little slow tonight," he replied in a fairly downbeat tone while presenting a forced smile.

If the guy was putting on an act he was definitely a contender for an academy award.

He turned on the hot water tap for Stevie and held out his bottle of green liquid soap, squirting a large dollop into Stevie's open palms and handed him one of the white drying cloths when he was done.

"Here you go chief," said Stevie, throwing two pound notes into the tiny wicker basket he had sitting beside the sink.

One thing Stevie did know about bathroom attendants was that they always frequently emptied whatever they used as a money container. Even if they were raking it in they always attempted to create the perception that times were tough. Having just a couple of notes on display was far likelier to be rewarded. Generosity was probably not on the cards if a huge bundle was there for all to see. Whatever the real situation was, Stevie figured he was still doing better than this guy so was happy to part with his money.

"Thanks boss," replied the attendant, this time flashing a genuine smile.

"No worries mate. Can I grab one of your mints?"

"Take a couple."

And with that Stevie unwrapped and popped a mint into his mouth and made his way back to join the festivities.

As he turned back into the dark corridor he let out a shriek. "AAARGH."

There was someone waiting directly outside the door and he was extremely embarrassed by his outburst as the person spoke to him.

"Did I scare you?"

"Yes you did," he said, suddenly realizing the familiarity of the voice.

It was Becky.

"Holy shit Becky, what are you doing hanging about here?"

"Waiting for you."

"Why are you waiting for me?"

"Because of this."

She threw her arms around his neck and lunged towards him, planting her lips on him. He was taken completely by surprise but instinct took over and he used his tongue to flick the red and white striped mint from the roof of his mouth to the side of his cheek, figuring a game of pass the sweet wasn't the best idea for a first kiss. It might have made for a great story but would've only killed the sudden spontaneity.

He turned her body slightly and pushed her against the wall. There was nothing slow and soft about their embrace. They were virtually mauling each other, like a man and woman who'd known each other for a long time, finally succumbing to the obvious connection and sexual chemistry they'd had since they'd been friends.

Their tongues clashed like a couple of swords, saliva almost dribbling onto the floor, but they were enjoying every second. They sensed someone passing them and the gents' door opened and the bright light from the bathroom briefly lit up their embrace. They pulled back for some well deserved air.

"Well that was unexpected," said Stevie, looking into her beautiful blue eyes.

"It might've been for you but I knew exactly what I was doing."

"You *certainly* know what you are doing."

"I'm glad you liked it."

"Liked it! I loved it."

"We should probably get back. They think I was just going to the bathroom. You go out first and I'll follow you out in a minute or so."

"OK, I guess I'll see you around."

"I hope so. Here, take this," said Becky, pushing a folded piece of paper into his hand. "Call me tomorrow."

Stevie returned to the table, receiving a prolonged look from each of the boys.

"Either you were taking a shit or you *really* ended up getting that guy in there to give you a lap dance," said Sean.

"Well it wasn't the latter."

"Seriously chief, we thought you'd fallen down the pan," laughed Colin.

"Hey Stevie, you'll never guess what this prick did," said Gordon looking at Colin and shaking his head. "He was so adamant that he wasn't going to pay for another piss that he went to the doorman and told him he needed to step outside to make an important phone call. Did he bollocks. He went around the back of the building and pissed up against the wall."

"Colin you are an absolute tinker and a tight arse. You couldn't even give the poor guy in there one pound. Shit, throw him fifty pence or something. I'm sure you can afford that and he would be happy with at least getting some money. It's people like you who give us Scots the reputation of being miserable when it comes to cash. You're one of those guys that Billy Connolly was referring to when he talked about some Scotsman who accidentally dropped a ten pence coin from his pocket, bent down to pick it up and it hit him on the back of the head."

All of them burst into laughter, including Colin.

Over the next couple of hours the beers continued to flow, the dancers continued to dance, and Colin continued to pop out to make important "phone calls." Many a seductive glance was shared between Stevie and Becky, but on each of his subsequent visits to the bathroom he'd been disappointed that he hadn't found her outside again waiting for him. He figured she had perhaps sobered up a little and didn't want to risk being found out by any of her friends. It was unclear to him how close any of them were with her current boyfriend, if at all. She'd obviously got away with it the first time so probably didn't want to mess with success.

It was pushing towards the closing time of 2:00 am and Colin ordered a round of drinks for the road from the mobile waitress. The waitresses were all smoking hot and dressed in a standard uniform that would've been at home on any dominatrix: black leather mini-skirt and knee length boots, fishnet tights, and a red vinyl-looking corset on top.

Many of the current dancers had started off waiting tables in the club. The waitresses definitely made good money on tips, especially if they were extremely flirtatious with the already frisky male clientele, but it wasn't a patch on the dough that the strippers pulled in. Most of them likely had no initial inclination they would migrate over to removing their clothes, but when they discovered the earning potential and got used to being around the environment, it became a natural progression.

The boys agreed that pretty much all dancers fell into three categories: those who needed the attention because daddy was never around growing up, those who were single mothers going through college and looking to have enough money to immediately wipe out any student loans after graduation, and those who just craved dicks and balls. It was a game the boys played every time one of the dancers graced the stage, classifying them as an *Attention Seeker*, *Money Grabber*, or *Slag*.

The *Slags* were easy to make a quick call on. They were typically not the trimmest of the bunch or facially gifted, but were without doubt the most fun behind the seclusion of a curtained booth.

Differentiating the *Attention Seekers* from the *Money Grabbers* wasn't quite as easy to determine. Usually it took a few minutes of watching them prance around in order to make a reasonable judgment. Generally they looked the same in terms of their model-like qualities, but the *Money Grabbers* put very little into their routines, deciding instead to parade around doing the occasional vertical leg kick but barely breaking a sweat, and relying on their looks and seductive glances to entice guys to part with their money.

The *Attention Seekers* were the ones many guys were there to see, excluding of course those with the primary objective of receiving a cheap hand job from one of the *Slags* before the evening was over. Not only were they beautiful and had bodies you could've cracked walnuts on, but it was as though they had Duracell batteries lodged in every orifice such was their energy and intensity. It usually turned into more of a circus act than a stage dance as they charged around like a female version of Kevin Bacon in Footloose, flicking their long hair around and darting up and down both sets of golden poles not unlike an army cadet at training camp, as well as rubbing their exposed crotch at every spare opportunity. *Attention Seekers* they may have been, but they earned their money well and created a buzz in the place that kept all the regular punters returning for more.

Colin was chatting to one of the waitresses and Sean and Gordon were fixated on one of the remaining dances while sipping on their drinks. Stevie however, had one eye on the stage and the other on Becky's table, particularly now that it looked as though they were calling it a night. Their sexy waitress was in progress of clearing all the empty bottles from their table and Becky and friends were on their feet, exchanging money, obviously ensuring they each had their portion of the evening bill covered.

Stevie wanted her *so* bad. He was confused though as he'd never experienced heart palpitations like this before while staring at a woman. He knew it must be love at first sight and prayed it wasn't a one way street.

The group of them was now making their way towards the exit, but thankfully in Stevie's mind they had to walk past his table in order to do so. Brian and Matt were at the front and passed by without an acknowledgement. Sarah, Anabel, and Monica batted their eyelids and said nice to meet you, which certainly gained all the boys attention. Becky was last in the line and said "hope to see you soon Stevie," as she passed, turning around afterwards and looking at him while holding her thumb and pinky finger to her ear.

"Could you *be* any more in there," said Sean, sounding uncannily like Chandler Bing. "I assume from what she just did that you got her number."

Stevie rolled onto his left arse cheek like he was breaking wind and reached into his back pocket, pulling out the folded up piece of white paper and opened it up to expose the number, making sure the beer goggles clearly captured every digit on the page. He may have been slightly intoxicated but was sensible enough to make sure that even if he lost the paper he had a back-up plan that would enable him to make the call. He wanted her badly and was already visualizing dialing her the following day.

The one drink for the road turned into one more, which was hardly a surprise. The only surprise was that it was Sean's idea and not Stevie's. Sean had become a little drawn to one of the *Slag's* by the name of Sunshine; obviously her stage name and no resemblance to her birth certificate. He'd slipped her a few pounds already when she'd been clumsily dancing around one of the poles. Her face was pretty to a degree, but her cheeks had a slight pouch to them, almost like a cute little hamster that had them loaded with peanuts. She was still a sweet looking girl though, but strip club was the last place of employment you would've guessed had you seen her in a bikini at the beach or swimming pool. Her thighs were built for construction work and had a texture to them not unlike a layer of cottage cheese on a slice of toast. Sean though was one of the guys looking for a cheap blow or hand job. It wasn't that he didn't land himself a *fairly* regular hook-up, but the entire seedy setting and cheapness of it all added a layer of dirt to the situation that he found an extreme turn-on.

The song with the lyrics "I Like Big Butts and I Cannot Lie" finished up and Sunshine took herself and her big butt down the stairs at the left hand side of the stage. The boys could virtually feel the ground vibrate as her foot hit each step, but Sean had a glint in his eye and was as keen as ever.

As Sunshine thumped past the boys table, Sean called out to her.

"You got time for a lap dance sweetheart?"

Sunshine turned around slowly, *attempting* to be seductive.

"You keep calling me sweetheart and you've got a big chance of more than just a lap dance," she replied.

Her response only cemented the *Slag* categorization, and Sean got up from his chair, beer in hand, and Sunshine led him towards the seclusion of one of the curtained booths.

The boys chatted amongst themselves as a new song from the DJ kicked in. Lap dances were based on songs, each dance or song as it was cost fifteen pounds. It was a weird method but not one anyone every *really* questioned. Stevie had made the point before that you could get really screwed if some two minute instrumental dance number came on and you just happened to be unlucky enough to land it. Colin had laughed, saying that with Stevie's extraordinary good luck with women he'd likely ask a stripper for a dance just before the DJ threw on the live version of Led Zeppelin's Stairway to Heaven.

Another song started and there was no sign of Sean returning, so they ordered another beverage; their last, as they were told by the waitress they were getting ready to close the bar register.

A third song began and still no sign of Sean.

"There's no way he's staying in there this long just so she can dance around or grind up and down his leg," said Colin with a sound of disappointment to him that signaled he'd wished he'd grabbed one of the *Slags* for a final send-off.

"Well let's just hope he's at least getting some head for the price he's obviously paying," said Gordon, and they all laughed before taking another gulp of their already half-empty beers.

A fourth song ended and Sean reappeared from the depths of the curtained abyss, smiling from ear to ear as he counted out a bunch of notes and placed them in the eager hands of Sunshine. Had there been a smiling contest, Sunshine would've easily taken the prize. He gave her a kiss on the cheek and made his way back to the table.

The boys burst into a fit of the giggles as Sean arrived table-side.

"Oh my God; nice night to wear beige trousers," said Colin, pointing at Sean's crotch.

There was a visible damp patch - not dissimilar in shape to a geographical map of India – on display for all to see. Sean quickly covered it up with his left hand and immediately sat back down in his chair.

"Did somebody get a little overexcited back there?" said Stevie, doubling over in the process.

"Shut the fuck up and stop bringing as much attention to the table," Sean complained.

There wasn't much attention to bring though, as there was only a light scattering of people remaining, and most were too drunk to care. Even the wait staff was oblivious; too eager on getting things tidied up so they could be done with their shift.

"So semen stains, give us the details then," said Gordon.

Sean pulled his chair nearer to the table and leaned in closer to them and gave a whispered account.

"Well, she started grinding on me in rhythm to the music and I was already pitching a tent by that point. I had to adjust myself as she really started picking up the pace on me and I thought for a minute she was going to break my dick. Her pussy was right on me and as I adjusted myself into a more favorable position, I accidentally rubbed the back of my knuckles on her lips. She let out a slight groan and I apologized, but she told me she liked it. Before I knew it I had two fingers inside her and she started to unbuckle my belt. She reached her hand inside, grabbed hold of me, and began tossing me off. So we were just frantically playing with each other. I was trying to shoot a load as quickly as possible so I could save a few quid, but you know what it's like when you've had a bunch of beers, it can take ages. The first song was over and she asked if I wanted to keep going for another song or not. There was no way I could stop there. So four songs in total and sixty pounds later, here I am with the evidence on my trousers."

It was a top class report and the boys got a real kick out of it. Stevie was even becoming slightly aroused by it as he'd visualized Becky doing the same to him behind one of the curtains. That would have to wait, but he was delighted his goggles had captured Sean's embarrassing moment should they want to replay it during a future ball-busting poker night or something.

"So she really let you finger her then?" asked Colin, again looking like he'd really missed out on something.

"You think I just made it up?"

"Maybe you did."

Sean quickly reached out and put his middle and index fingers under Colin's nostrils. Colin acted disgusted and waved his hand in front of his face, but he'd paused just long enough before doing so in order to have a little sniff. His appalled expression quickly faded.

"Actually that was really nice," he said surprised. "I was expecting something more like tuna, but that is pretty sweet."

"Don't tell him that," said Gordon. "He'll never wash that hand again."

Stevie just sat there and captured all proceedings with his glasses.

They bullshitted for a few minutes as they finished off the remainder of their drinks. Between the finger smelling and the crude insults, it replicated the juvenile antics from years before in the school playground.

"Right, are we ready for the off?" asked Stevie.

"Yeah, let's call it a night," said Colin.

They made their way to the exit, stopping at the front desk so the girl could call them a taxi. They thanked the gorilla-like doorman and headed out into the cold of the club car park.

The night was cold, but it was beautiful all the same. There wasn't a cloud in the sky, the moon was there in all its glory, and the stars littered the pitch black background.

"I hope this taxi shows up soon, I'm freezing my balls off," said Stevie, fiercely rubbing his hands together.

"You're not kidding chief," replied Gordon.

"Shouldn't be too long this time of the morning," said Colin.

Sean stood silent with his fingers under his nose.

The quiet and crispness of the night was suddenly interrupted and briefly startled them all. It was just the door of the club opening and the bathroom attendant appeared with his remaining mints in their plastic container under his left arm, and was carrying a small black sports bag over his right shoulder; the various aftershave bottles from its interior clinking together with each step he made.

"Have a good one gentlemen," he said to them, digging a set of car keys from his pocket as he walked.

"Take it easy," they all said, with the exception of Colin.

They watched his every move as he made his way to the far side of the lot where three cars remained. They looked at each other and then back at the attendant but said nothing; for now. He unlocked the door of a brand new white Jaguar, started it up, flicked on the headlights and drove off into the night.

"I fucking knew it!" exclaimed Colin. "And you were giving me a hard time for being tight and not giving the *poor guy* my money, and how it was ridiculous coming outside and pissing on the back wall instead."

The others remained open-mouthed and speechless.

The First Date

S tevie awoke with a smile on his face that would've been at home on any toothpaste advertisement. He knew his rendezvous at *The Golden Pole* with Becky hadn't been a figment of his imagination, but he jumped out of bed like he was late for work, grabbed his glasses from the bedside table and went through to the comfort of his armchair to replay the evening on his laptop.

He watched the exotic, naked Latin dancer maneuver her way up and down the pole and prance around the stage. She was nothing less than magnificent, but his mind was wandering to thoughts of Becky, so decided to fast forward to the moment he saw her. As soon as the initial sight of her flashed on the screen he pressed play. When her eyes met with his he frantically pressed pause. Hundreds of goose bumps appeared on his arms and every last hair stood at attention. He hadn't originally noticed, but she seemed *extremely* happy the moment she set eyes on him. Maybe she had been a little inebriated and generally in a good mood at the time, but her face seemed to light up as though she'd been thinking good things about him since his visit to the doctor's surgery. It was a huge, pleasant, yet unexpected surprise.

He paused the film again during their initial embrace. Although all he could see on screen was the back of her scrubs as they hugged, he could almost still feel her tight grip around him.

The tape continued and was extremely revealing. The beer goggles captured everything clearly; where he was directly looking *as well* as his peripheral vision. The interaction with Becky's friends told him everything he hadn't seen. Her male buddies were looking at him disapprovingly, and her girlfriends looked intrigued. It was clear Becky was digging him. The girlfriends were likely enamored by what Becky had told them and the guys no doubt had a thing for her and were pissed off they'd bumped into him, ruining any possible chance they had with her.

The tape continued, and again he had to pause. He was looking at the right hand side of the stage, but the glasses also captured Becky's table. She was staring lustfully at him, but during the night out he'd been oblivious to the fact.

Enough was enough, he had to call her. It was still early, around 10:30 am, but she was all he could think about. He debated for a few minutes about possibly waiting until the afternoon, but their kiss was at the forefront of his mind. He could still taste her sweet lips and tongue, and knew if he didn't dial her now the hour and a half until afternoon would feel like an eternity, so he picked up the phone.

"Hello," said the husky female voice, obviously awakened by the ring of the phone.

"Is that you Becky?" replied Stevie.

Her voice was so gruff he wasn't sure if it was her or whether she'd given him a bogus number.

"Yes it is. Who's this?" she said, sounding a little more than out of it.

"Great, I'm that forgettable. It's Stevie you drunken tart," he said, deliberately laughing out loud to ensure she was aware he was joking around and didn't take offence to his jibe.

"Hi Stevie," said Becky, her tone picking up several notches. "Sorry, I was still half asleep. I was hoping you'd call, I just didn't think it would be until later. I figured you'd be having a long-lie today."

"Usually I would, but I've been thinking about you a lot and woke up early."

"Really?"

"Yeah, really. I hate sounding like a complete dick but I'm *really* attracted to you Becky."

Stevie could feel the embarrassment working its way onto his cheeks, and his heart pounded as Becky paused considerably before responding.

"I feel the same way Stevie."

The red remained on Stevie's face, but it was no longer that of embarrassment. It was now a warm glow of sheer jubilation. This was a new experience for him, new feelings, but he liked it.

"Well I'm glad to hear that. I was a little bit worried about putting myself out there and being shot down like a guy in front of a firing squad."

Becky giggled. He even loved the sound of her laughter.

"I might have been a little drunk last night Stevie, but I would've thought the way I was kissing you would've been a bit of a give away that the feeling is mutual."

"I suppose, but it's always good to hear it directly from the horse's mouth. Not that I'm saying you resemble a horse in any way."

"I figured that out," she said with her cute little giggle.

"So can I see you tonight?" asked Stevie, crossing his fingers.

"I'd like that."

"Sweet. Maybe we can go out for some dinner. There's a nice little Italian place over here in Uddingston if that sounds alright."

"Sounds yummy. Give me your number and I'll call you later this afternoon. I have a few things to take care of first; I need to break-up with Larry. I should've done it long before now, but I guess I've just been stuck in a rut and I'm the biggest procrastinator at the best of times, but this gives me the kick up the arse I should've had a while back. The spark has been gone for a long time and he just doesn't treat me the way I deserve. It's time for me to get on and enjoy my life."

Stevie gave her his number. He could hardly wait to talk to her again later.

He was *so* upbeat when he came off the phone, but it suddenly turned to worry. What if the call with her boyfriend Larry didn't go as planned? What if he expressed his undying love for her and told her all the things she'd been longing to hear? Would she forgive him and call back with an apology for leading him on, but she was going to give it another go with this fool? Stevie wasn't sure he could handle that scenario. It was making him sick to the stomach at the thought. He really believed Becky was the real deal, and a woman who could set him straight and rid him from his current errant ways. Rejection though could potentially push him *even further* down the present slippery slope.

He calmed himself down. He was getting way ahead of himself. He needed to distract himself until she called, which could be anywhere from one to four hours. He contemplated The Crown for a couple of pints, but knew a couple wasn't even in his vocabulary, so decided to go back to bed and sleep, that way he could remain sober and be prepared for their first date should it occur, and it would alleviate the numerous negative thoughts running through his hyperactive mind.

The phone rang and Stevie bolted upright on his mattress. He had been in a deep sleep but the ringer had a similar impact on him as the bang from a gunshot. His heartbeat raced as he tentatively picked up the bedside telephone receiver.

"Hello."

"Hi Stevie, its Becky," she said, sounding very chirpy.

Stevie prayed her buoyant tone was a good sign.

"Hey Becky; good to hear from you. Well, are we on for dinner tonight?"

He could almost hear his heart beating now.

"Yes we are. I'm now officially single again."

Stevie wanted to scream out loud with excitement, but made do with a silent fist pump in order to give the impression he was maintaining his cool.

"Fantastic. How did Larry take the news?"

"Very badly."

"Did he beg you for forgiveness and tell you how much he loved you?"

"Yes, but I was expecting it. We've been on and off for a while now and it's the same story he gives every time. He promises to change but never does and I'm tired of it. He was actually pathetic; crying like a kid losing a puppy. He prides himself on being a tough guy, but if you ask me they were likely crocodile tears. I wish him the best with his future, but it's time for me to move on. Anyway, enough of that, time to change the subject as you don't need to hear all this bullshit. I can come over to your place and pick you up. Would around seven o'clock work for you?"

"Works for me; I'm really looking forward to seeing you."

"I can't wait to see you too Stevie."

Stevie finished the call by giving her his address then lay back in bed. He was smiling from ear to ear and no matter how hard he tried, he couldn't get the grin off his face; it was like it was permanently painted on.

He still had around three hours until her scheduled arrival, but figured he should start getting prepared. First port of call was the underwear drawer which as it turned out, only contained two clean pairs of boxers. One was a pale blue pair that had originally been dark blue. They'd been through the washer as often as a restaurant table cloth and were about as old as the hills, so to describe them as hideous would've been verging on complimentary. The other was a white pair of Calvin Klein's with a few moth-eaten holes on the backside. Enough said.

He did have respectably clean black socks without holes or fading color as well as a smart pair of never worn black jeans. The shirt situation was even more pitiful than the boxer shorts though; in fact it was non-existent. All he had hanging in the wardrobe were the empty hangers where the shirts should've been. He glanced over to the brown wicker washing basket in the corner beside the window. It was overflowing with clothes; the lid balancing tentatively about eight inches above the rim and a shirt sleeve hanging over the edge like one of his lifeless arms dangling out the side of his bed after a crazy night on the beer. It was time to do some washing.

Normally he hated doing washing; he hated any form of housework, but under the current circumstances it was a nice distraction that would eat into the time until Becky's arrival.

He sat down and watched a couple of episodes of *Family Guy* before putting on the washing machine in order to use up a little more time. He was craving a beer, and had the time if he wanted, but was craving Becky even more; that's how bad he had it for her.

He emptied the washer and transferred the wet clothes over to the dryer, making sure he emptied the lint tray prior to starting it up. A previous fire scare had trained him that that *had* to be the procedure. Stevie decided that a nice hot bath was in order. The dryer was set for an hour, so a shower wasn't going to cut it. He needed to get clean and relax for a while at the same time.

The white tub had a layer of grime on it like a fine chocolate frosting on top of a sponge cake, so he decided to give it a scrub down prior to running the water. He really was a slob, but was beginning to believe that having Becky in his life could turn everything around. Right now he wanted to be particular; he wanted things to be pristine for her. He couldn't believe the transformation that was occurring *already*.

He could virtually see his face on the inside of the porcelain tub when he was done. The dirt had really been on there and the elbow grease required to remove it had the sweat running down his face. It tasted salty and he felt extremely grubby, but instead of jumping into the tub he decided to wash the pile of dishes clogging up the sink and vacuum the carpet, just on the off chance that Becky came back to his flat after dinner.

It was six o'clock, and he was finally lying back in the warm water of the tub. He was seriously considering masturbating in order to empty the chamber and prevent any unwanted premature gunfire should he and Becky end up in his bed, but he refrained for two reasons. Firstly, for once in his life he didn't want to have sex with her tonight. His life so far had been nothing but one night stands and meaningless casual encounters. Becky did not fall into either of these categories. This would be a new start with new priorities. Secondly, he hadn't contemplated the state of his bed sheets when doing the earlier washing and they were currently about as hygienic as the bathtub had been prior to its annual cleaning, and knowing his luck, Becky would be armed with a miniature ultraviolet light in her purse that she'd use to inspect the bed covers if he popped to the bathroom before any hanky-panky. He could virtually see the look of disgust on her face.

He washed himself meticulously, leaving no nook or cranny unexplored. It was 6:20 pm and his pre-date nerves were beginning to kick into overdrive. He took a few deep breaths before fully submerging himself in the water and flushing any shampoo remains from his hair, and then pulled the plug on the chain using his right foot. He started to daydream as he listened to the water slurp its way down the plughole, wondering what Becky would look like tonight. He'd only ever seen her wearing her work attire and the faintest powdering of make-up.

The last of the water disappeared and snapped him out of his trance. He climbed out of the tub, dried himself, and headed for the clothes dryer.

He opted for the smart but casual look; the pair of unworn black jeans and a white long-sleeved shirt with fashionable-looking silver buttons. Some gel to slightly spike up the front of his short brown hair was applied before brushing his teeth then gargling quickly with some Listerine. He looked at himself in the mirror above the bathroom sink. He thought he was looking pretty good as he slipped on the beer goggles. He paused, contemplating slightly, before removing the glasses. He didn't need them tonight. This wasn't going to be a drunken rowdy affair. This was going to be a civil occasion with some nice food and perhaps two or three drinks, but nothing that was going to lead to a blackout and no recollection of the evening events. Maybe if all went well with Becky he would never need the beer goggles again. Only time would tell, but it wasn't like he'd put the startling findings from them into any positive action plan anyway.

There was a sudden buzzing noise. She was here. Stevie quickly left his position at the bathroom mirror and answered the intercom.

"Hello," said Stevie, talking into the box on the wall.

"Hi, it's Becky."

"Hi Becky."

"Sorry I'm a little early."

"No problem, I'm ready. I'll be right down."

He'd considered inviting her up, but figured there wasn't much point in having her parade up two flights of stairs only to turn around and head back down.

Stevie quickly made his way down the stairs, heart pumping, eager to see her in the flesh. He opened the main front door of the building and there she was.

"Wow," he said.

It was more of an involuntary outburst than a planned opening line.

"Well thank you," she said, smiling and looking affectionately at him.

She was everything he'd hoped for and more. She had also opted for the smart but casual look, standing there in a pair of figure-hugging blue jeans and a long-sleeved shoulder-less red top that displayed her beautifully smooth skin. Her blonde hair was a little shorter than before, stopping just short of her shoulders with a newly cut, layered look to it. More make-up was evident compared to their previous meetings, but not as much as many women who lathered it on so much that it increased the entire size of their heads. Her lips looked divine; a bright red gloss on them that blended in immaculately with her shoulder-less top. The gold pendant around her neck was a classy finishing touch that just added value to the quality of the entire package.

"Becky, you look absolutely stunning. If it didn't look like you'd put as much time into putting on that lipstick I would kiss the face off you."

She laughed again, probably at his graceful way with words, and exposed her perfectly aligned set of white teeth.

"I'll take that as a compliment."

They hugged and Stevie planted a soft kiss on her cheek. She again smelled radiant; the same scent as the previous evening and it took him back to thoughts of their first kiss.

"Well, let's get this show on the road," said Stevie. "Will we take your car or mine?"

"We can take my car," said Becky, gently taking hold of Stevie's hand as they made their way around the corner of the building to the car parking area.

Stevie was happy she'd suggested her vehicle as he pictured the interior of his piece of shit car. He really was a slob. Like his bed sheets, he hadn't given much thought to the fact he could've been the one driving. His passenger seat was covered with magazines and unpaid bills, and the floor was littered with empty soft drink cans, chocolate bar wrappers, and cigarette packs. It probably smelled like a mixture of crap and marijuana as well, so avoiding any embarrassment was a serious bonus.

"Well well well, maybe I should consider a career in nursing. They must be paying you guys big bucks these days," said Stevie, more than surprised as she pressed the unlock button on her key chain remote for a black BMW 328i.

It was a fairly new car as well, paintwork shining like his rejuvenated bathtub.

"No, they still pay like shite. My grandfather passed away about six months ago and left me some money, so I decided to treat myself. He used to be a doctor in his day so he had plenty of cash. He was really the driving force for me getting into the medical field."

"Well I'm sorry to hear about his passing; sounds as though he really loved you though."

"Yes it was a shame. He was eighty-one though and had a good life. He'd been fighting cancer for a while."

They climbed into the pristine car; the interior as untainted as the exterior. The beige leather bucket-style seats hugged the body delightfully and the floors had been recently cleaned; faint stripes where the vacuum cleaner head had been were still visible as he looked down at his feet. There was also a smell of melon air freshener intertwined with the scent of her perfume.

The contrast between their cars was vast, and at completely opposite ends of the spectrum, but he figured Becky deserved it as it matched her overall appearance extremely well.

Stevie navigated for Becky, giving her the directions for the short three minute drive to Roscioli's, the best Italian restaurant in the village, albeit the only one.

They entered Roscioli's and were happily greeted by a chubby middle-aged Italian-looking gentleman – no stranger to a double helping of pasta and meat sauce – who quickly escorted them to a nice table for two in the far corner not far from the door leading to the kitchen and the marvelous smells of the fine cuisine.

The place was relatively busy, with only a couple of open tables. It was a small and intimate setting though and part of the reason Stevie had suggested it. He had never been before but Sean had recommended it as a winner for any first date. Stevie wanted the romantic ambience, the succulent food, and the flowing wine as well as conversation. If the setting was comfortable and enjoyable, he hoped Becky would feel secure with him and be eager to see him again.

Stevie flicked deliberately through the wine list, attempting to create the perception he knew what he was looking at, but would've been as successful with a selection had he closed his eyes and randomly stuck a needle into the page.

"Do you like red or white?" he asked.

"Red would be my preference."

"Nice choice, I'm a red guy myself," lied Stevie convincingly.

He hadn't actually had a glass of wine in some time. Truth be told, he didn't care that much for it. He enjoyed the flavor, but on the occasions he did participate, they often resulted in waking up during the middle of the night with chronic heartburn.

"A nice Merlot sounds good," said Becky, obviously a lot more knowledgeable on the subject matter than Stevie would ever be.

Stevie caught the waiter's eye and he was instantly table side. Stevie pointed to a bottle of red on the list.

"Excellent choice sir; the Roberto Voerzio is one of our best Merlots," said the waiter, taking the wine list from him and heading towards the bar.

Behind the bar were three large wooden wine racks side by side, stacked with a selection of bottles from all over the globe. Stevie had heard of two of them before – actual brand names, not just 'red' and 'white' – as he'd read the menu, and even then, they had been on the cheaper side of the scale, so highly inappropriate for first date impression purposes.

The waiter swiftly returned with the bottle of Roberto Voerzio, deliberately holding the label towards Stevie as confirmation of what was ordered, before uncorking it and pouring about two mouthfuls worth into Stevie's glass. Stevie had seen the likes on TV before and knew this was his cue to have a quick sip and give the waiter the thumbs up or down. He took a quick sniff before tasting and sloshing it around his mouth a couple of times before swallowing.

"Very nice, thank you," said Stevie, giving the waiter a nod to fill up both their glasses.

He felt a bit of a dick going through the whole wine tasting connoisseur routine, but figured it was a lot classier and politically correct than telling the waiter to just fill the glass up right away as he would've struggled to tell the difference between a Merlot and a double shot of pig's blood.

"Are you ready to order sir?"

"I think so," said Stevie, glancing at Becky.

"Yes, I'm ready."

Stevie went for the lasagne al forno and Becky opted for the spaghetti carbonara.

"This is really nice," said Becky with a lingering look.

"Here's to a lovely evening," replied Stevie, raising his glass and they chimed them together.

Sean's advice on the restaurant was superb. The setting for a first date *was* perfect, and everything a woman would've looked for. The lights were dimmed, the candle flickered in the middle of the table, and the soft instrumental string quartet music soothed in the background; only promoting a loving vibe.

They chatted freely and sipped on their wine as they waited for the food to arrive. It was *so* relaxed and was as though they'd known each other for years. It *was* only their first date, but Stevie knew he was falling in love already. Everything about her was adorable, and not just her looks and personality. He thought it was so cute the way she swept her hair behind her left ear and blushed when he made sarcastic or fun jibes at her, but she gave as good as she got which he also found wonderful. The one hope in his mind was that the same types of things were running through her head with regard to him.

"Thanks again Stevie, that was fabulous," said Becky, wiping up the final remains of carbonara sauce with a piece of garlic bread.

"Thanks honey, I enjoyed it also, but the number of kisses I was planning on giving you are dropping with every piece of garlic bread you're throwing back."

She swept her hair behind her ear before replying.

"The number I was planning on giving you evaporated completely when you were about halfway through that garlic filled lasagna."

He smiled inside and out; she really was a match for anything he threw at her.

"OK fair point. Why don't we call it even on the garlic? You've had some, I've had some, I've got some gum, so let's have some fun."

"Have you used that line before or are you just a bit of a poet? I agree though, let's call it even. I don't think I *couldn't* kiss you tonight even if I didn't want to."

He certainly hadn't meant such a cheesy line, and certainly hadn't used it before, but made a mental note never to use it *ever* again.

"I know what you mean Becky. It's all I've been thinking about since we got here. I'd even thought about dragging you through to the bathroom for a quick smooch before the food arrived."

Stevie signaled for the waiter who quickly hustled over to the table.

"I'll take the bill please," said Stevie.

"No problem sir; how was your meal?"

"It was great thank you."

"Yes it was delicious," said Becky.

Stevie settled up the bill, leaving a healthy tip for the attentive waiter, as much to show Becky he was a generous soul as it was a reward for the first class service.

They climbed back into Becky's pristine BMW and she started up the engine.

"Gum?" said Stevie, holding out a stick of spearmint Wrigley's.

"Does this mean you want to kiss me?"

"Yes it does."

"In that case I'd love a piece."

Stevie handed her a stick and frantically devoured a piece of his own. He gave it a few seconds for her to absorb some of the flavor then leaned over and locked lips. It started off as a few soft pecks before escalating into a frenzied animal passion. Their lips were a perfect fit together, synching up like a shiny Yale key in a pristine lock. She felt tiny in his strong arms as he pulled her close. It was a comfort he had never felt before. Other than the gearstick lodged in his abdomen, it was a soothing feeling never before encountered and a small price to pay for such an exquisite moment. There was no doubt Becky was having similar thoughts. Her grunts and groans as he worked his magic couldn't have possibly been fake, and the intensity of her soft tongue in his mouth wasn't something that occurred with someone not having the time of their life.

Their lips parted, but their noses remained close, positioned like a couple of Eskimo nose-rubbers. They stared deep into each other's eyes. It didn't take a genius to realize that Cupid had delivered an arrow to each of their hearts.

"Tell me this isn't a dream?" said Stevie, his stare not leaving her pupils and there wasn't a blink to be found.

"I hope it's not a dream. If it is I don't want to ever wake-up," she replied, planting the softest of kisses on his still moist lips.

Her words almost put Stevie into cardiac arrest. Was this the real deal? Was this the feeling he'd heard about all these years that had never crossed his path? If it wasn't, he doubted he would ever feel it.

"I think it's real sweetheart."

"I think you might be right."

There was a slight awkward silence as they both digested the moment.

"OK, let's get you home," said Becky, fighting to remain cool and keep the smile off her face.

It wasn't long before they arrived back in the car park of Stevie's building and Becky pulled into an open space. Again there was silence. It was apparent they were both contemplating the next move. Should they call it a night? Should they throw caution to the wind and follow the instincts and wishes of their respective groins? Stevie was first to speak.

"Well Becky, I'd invite you up for a cup of coffee or something but I think my mind would be on the something more than the coffee, so we should probably leave it for another day.

"That works for me Stevie. Call me tomorrow or I'll call you, whatever happens first."

"Take it easy honey and I'll talk to you soon. I had a lovely night by the way."

"Me too Stevie."

He pecked her on the lips and made his way to the front door of the building, turning to wave as she beeped her horn and drove off. He virtually floated up the stairs, wishing that time travel to the following morning was humanly possible.

Jealous Ex

Larry called in sick to work, even though he hadn't missed a shift in almost a year. He didn't usually drink, but he'd spent the previous evening at home drowning his sorrows. Surely Becky was just trying to teach him a lesson and they would be back together in a few days. Where the hell had she been last night anyway? He'd called her and left about half a dozen voicemail messages, the later ones not so nice in nature, mainly due to his drunkenness and loss of inhibition. Was she just ignoring the calls as she knew it was him? Had she went out for the night with her girlfriends? Surely she hadn't been out with another guy, but maybe that was part of the reason for breaking up with him.

Larry's anger and jealousy was building up more and more. The idea of her with someone else was making his blood boil and he began grinding his teeth together. He was feeling sick to his stomach and knew he had to talk to her and find out what she'd been up to.

Larry sat in his darkened living room, TV off, and the only form of noise was the traffic passing by his front window. His head was dropped and in the palms of his hands and his eyes were filling slowly with tears. He loved her. He loved her more than life itself. This time he would change. He knew he'd been taking her for granted, but wasn't that just what happened when you'd been with someone for so long? He just needed another chance to put things right, and he was going to do everything in his power to make it happen.

Larry's place was a bomb site. It was littered with enough empty beer cans to give the impression he'd been hosting a party, but it had just been himself and his telephone.

He began to ponder. It was time to get his head together and plan a strategy. Going over to her flat unannounced wasn't an option; she would think he was getting a little *too* desperate. He'd probably done enough damage in that area already with the crazy voicemails. If she was avoiding his calls there was no point in trying again from his house or mobile number. She had caller I.D and would likely just ignore him. He decided to get cleaned up and pay a visit to a public phone box.

Larry made his way down Cadzow Street towards the nearest call box. The more he thought about Becky the angrier he became and the stride from his long legs lengthened and quickened as he hastened to get to the phone box even faster. He was well known in the area and several of the locals said hello as he paraded past them, but Larry said nothing in return, oblivious to their greetings. He was focused on what he was going to say to her and how he could explain and neutralize the nasty comments from the night before.

Becky sat at home daydreaming. Originally she'd seen Stevie as a decent distraction to her troubled life with Larry and a bit of excitement that she'd been missing for so long, but he'd exceeded all expectations. He was definitely good looking and his sharp wit only added layers to the attraction, but she could tell he had a respect for her that she'd never encountered before. The fact she'd been willing to spread her legs for him the night before and he'd declined, stating he didn't want her to be a one night stand not only surprised her, but made her believe that he could be the one for her. It was crazy that they'd only been out on one date, but he turned her on in ways that Larry could only dream of. During their flirtatious conversation at the Italian restaurant, her panties had been soaked through and he hadn't even put a hand on her. She had wanted him so badly at the dinner table. Had it just been the two of them having a meal at her place she would've probably swiped the plates and cutlery off the table, climbed on top and screamed "take me now." She couldn't wait until he called her later and hoped tonight would be sexually productive.

Her mobile phone rang and she looked at the caller I.D. She didn't recognize the number, but was relieved to see it wasn't Larry. Perhaps he'd realized the break-up had been for the best.

"Hello."

"It's Larry; please don't hang up, I just want to talk to you. I'm sorry about some of the things I said on the messages I left."

Becky let out a sigh. It seemed like he hadn't realized the break-up was a good idea after all. Just then she perked up.

"What messages Larry? And what do you mean you're sorry about some of the things you said?"

She was sitting in her black and white polka-dot pajamas and was on her home phone. She quickly reached into her brown leather purse at the side of the couch and pulled out her mobile.

It was still switched off. She'd turned it off after arriving at Stevie's place the night before as she envisioned that Larry *might* call while she was on her date and felt it would've been an inappropriate distraction and dull the mood.

"Well I tried calling you a few times last night. I'd been drinking and might have said a few things that I didn't mean. I guess I was just missing you and realized I don't want to lose you. Becky, I don't want to give up on the last two years of our lives and I want you back. I want to give it a proper go this time and be everything you want me to be."

"Larry it's over. It's time for us to move on; I thought I made that perfectly clear yesterday. You're like a broken record. It's the same story with you every time. You say you're going to change and treat me right, but it's a bunch of bullshit. You change for about a week, but always slip back into your old uncaring ways and take everything for granted."

"Where were you last night anyway?"

"Larry, that's none of your business."

"Were you out with another guy?" he said, his tone changing from caring back to irritated.

"As I said, that's none of your business."

"You were weren't you? You were out with another fucking guy!"

"Larry, we're not together anymore. What I do in my free time isn't a concern of yours, and I really don't appreciate your tone right now."

"I'll be watching you," said Larry, slamming down the phone receiver.

Becky was almost in shock. Had Larry lost his mind completely? What did he mean by watching her? She contemplated calling the cops, but realized that wasn't the brightest of ideas.

Her phone rang again; it was the same number, so she ignored it. It rang and rang and rang, so she disconnected the cable from the wall rather than putting up with any more of his crap. She was slightly relieved though. He was probably calling to apologize for his crazy behavior, but she was still a little concerned by his stalker-like comment.

Larry repeatedly slammed down the phone in the call box. He pushed his way out of the door, almost knocking over a young teenage boy who'd been waiting outside patiently. The kid gave Larry a horrified stare.

"What the fuck are you looking at?" said Larry.

The boy said nothing.

Becky swallowed hard on her coffee before tentatively switching on her mobile phone. It connected to the network and repeatedly beeped indicating messages waiting; six to be precise.

The first two were fairly mellow, just Larry saying he was thinking about her and wanted to talk. There was a slight slur to his words, so she could tell he'd been drinking. The third had more irritation to the tone, telling her to call him, asking if she was ignoring him. The fourth was building up towards rage, asking her where she was and who she was with. The fifth was littered with expletives. "Where the fuck are you Becky?" was the classy opening line, which was followed up with "you better not be fucking another guy." The sixth just appalled her. "Fuck you then you stupid slut," was just plain out of order, and a labeling she didn't deserve.

She closed the flip on her phone and took a gulp from her mug, her hand trembling as she removed it away from her mouth.

It was apparent Larry was going to go down fighting, and that it wouldn't be the last she heard from him. Her concern turned to Stevie and she began to worry about his safety.

Stevie was on cloud nine as he cracked two eggs into the frying pan. He whistled the tune to the Beatles classic "She Loves You" as he flipped over the yolks and loaded two slices of brown bread into the toaster. The date had been one of the best nights of his life and he was proud that he'd resisted his urges to sleep with her. He was confident she admired the move and saw it as a breath of fresh air as well as ensuring her he was there for more than a quick poke in the whiskers.

He scooped his eggs onto a plate he'd been warming up under the grill, added the toast, and spread on a thick covering of *I Can't Believe It's Not Butter* to each. He sat down in his armchair and flicked on the omnibus edition of *Eastenders* on the TV before getting tucked into his breakfast.

Just then his mobile phone rang and his eyes lit up with joy as he saw who was calling.

"Good morning sweetheart. Guess you couldn't wait for me to call you this afternoon."

"Hi Stevie," said Becky in a somber voice.

"What's up? You sound a little down."

"It's nothing really. I just wanted you to cheer me up. Larry called me this morning and was giving me a lot of grief. Turns out he left me a bunch of messages while we were out last night and a few of them weren't very nice."

"Would you like me to have a word with him?" said Stevie abruptly; the hairs on the back of his neck now rigid.

"That wouldn't be a good idea Stevie. He knows *a lot* of people who could make your life a living hell, so it's probably best I take care of things."

"Well the offer stands if you change your mind."

"Thanks Stevie, I know you mean well."

"You still sound down so I'm obviously not doing a very good job cheering you up. Listen, I just made myself some breakfast. Why don't you pop over here and I'll make you some. It'll get you out of the house and away from things."

"That might be nice. Give me twenty minutes to get ready, so I should be there in just over half an hour."

"Great, see you then," replied Stevie, more than a little surprised she'd agreed to his idea.

He abandoned his toast and eggs and sprinted for the bedroom, ripping the crusty sheets off the mattress and removing the pillow cases as well. The bare white pillows were speckled with stains; an accumulation of months worth of drooling. He had no back-up sheets either, but figured nothing was better than the festering set that had been on there. He chucked them in the washer, hastily shook in some powder, and switched the dial to the ultra clean setting as he figured the regular wash might not get the job done.

He was getting a little ahead of himself, but like his days back in the boy scouts, be prepared was the motto of the day. This would technically be their second date so he was up for anything if it happened now.

There was no way the sheets would be washed and dried before she arrived but that was the least of his concerns. He hadn't even brushed his teeth yet and it felt like each and every one of them was wearing a tiny woolen cardigan. His general body hygiene wasn't in much better shape and he badly needed a shower, so there were many more pressing issues than drying of sheets.

Stevie sat all fresh and clean in his armchair, becoming more and more excited as the seconds ticked by. It wasn't necessarily the prospect of making love to her, just the fact he was going to see her again.

Right on the half hour mark the intercom sounded. He answered it cheerfully and buzzed her up. He'd thought about putting on some jeans and a smart t-shirt but had opted for a black pair of knee-length surfer shorts and a plain white v-neck t-shirt instead in order to create the appearance of not trying too hard.

He stood with the front door open waiting for her to appear at the top of the stairs. Suddenly he questioned his choice of attire. She was like a heavenly vision and more smartly dressed than she had been for their first date. Stevie closed his mouth tightly to avoid his tongue from hanging out and drool cascading onto his chin. Virtually painted around her lower half was a tight fitting black mini-skirt. As she walked towards him he could see her toned thigh muscles working with every step. On top was a matching black t-shirt with fake diamonds stitched into the front and spelling out the word "JUICY." Juicy was a description as accurate as any could be. Her chest looked soft yet perked and was locked in firmly to the confines of the shirt. She leaned in for a kiss as he greeted her and Stevie didn't have to bend over at all as a result of her six inch stiletto heels that looked about as comfortable as walking around with a bunch of gravel in your shoes.

"Well hello there," said Becky, slowly pulling away from his lips.

Stevie was still speechless but managed to maintain his composure.

"How do you like your eggs Becky?"

"Preferably unfertilized," she said laughing.

"No need to worry about that, I always pull out in time," replied Stevie, hoping his rather crude remark wasn't taking things a little too far, and also wouldn't give out the impression he was partial to participating in unprotected sex.

"No chance of that with me buddy, I'm a safety girl, protection used or nothing at all."

"I know, I was joking. I'm the same way myself. Anyway, come on in. What would you like for breakfast?"

"Nothing, I've already eaten this morning."

"What, I thought we'd made plans for me to cook?"

"I know Stevie, but I was really just looking for an excuse to come over and see you," said Becky a little embarrassed.

Gazing deep into Stevie's eyes she dropped her black handbag onto the carpet. Stevie took the hint and began kissing her soft lips. Her embrace became tighter and tighter as she pushed her tongue hard into his mouth and then moved both hands into his hair and ruffled it around. Stevie's hands wandered from her back and down onto her firm buttocks. Their lips unlocked and she moved her attention to his neck, groaning as he squeezed firmly on her arse cheeks, pulling her in tightly towards his ever-growing groin. He then lifted her up, Becky hanging around his neck like a Koala, and she interlocked her legs behind his back; her black mini-skirt riding up even further and now resembling more of a belt than a piece of clothing.

Becky was becoming more and more vocal and Stevie wasn't far behind her. Her groans were pleasure noises, but Stevie's were those of pain. All the rubbing and grinding had caused some of the material from his shorts to become trapped in his foreskin, and the constant movement was making him a little raw, but he was reluctant to put a halt to the proceedings. Thinking fast he dropped Becky back to her feet and swiftly removed her t-shirt. Staring back at him were two perfectly formed C-cup breasts. He was delighted there was no bra to deal with.

Within thirty seconds they were both sporting only their birthday suits and were frolicking with even more enthusiasm on his sofa. He moved his head south; cunnilingus was a breakfast substitute he would take every time, and Becky's sweetness was everything he'd envisioned it would be. She was completely shaved, and that only seemed to enhance the overall freshness.

Becky switched positions. She was on top now as they simultaneously dished out the oral pleasure. Stevie could hardly believe how the morning was turning out. He certainly hadn't expected sex, but was as delighted with the outcome as any young teenage boy getting laid for the very first time.

He reached with his free hand onto the floor and grabbed his shorts. Fortunately they were close by as he could see nothing other than Becky's inner thighs from his current vantage point. He slipped his wallet out of the right hand pocket and removed a condom. He delicately removed Becky from on top of him and sat up on the couch and instantly rolled on the rubber. Becky climbed on top and gently slipped him inside her. In their cowgirl position, Stevie attempted to start slowly by limiting Becky's hip movement, but she was in control and quickly picked up the pace and began bucking around like a rodeo rider on an angry bull. Stevie was thankful he'd masturbated that morning otherwise he'd be victim of an early arrival at the finish line.

Their frantic love making continued on at warp speed; Stevie keeping one eye on the clock and was pleasantly surprised he'd managed to reach the fifteen minute mark. He was more than impressed by the stamina that Becky was showing and even more delighted when she slumped on top of him after a huge orgasmic scream. He was close himself so flipped her onto her back and finished off missionary-style.

"Oh my God Stevie, that was incredible," she said, still panting with exhaustion.

"I know, it was fantastic, unbelievable, but fantastic," said Stevie, sweat running down his forehead.

"Why unbelievable, do you not usually last as long?"

"No I didn't mean it like that. I meant unbelievable as in unexpected. Having sex with you this morning wasn't something I was taking for granted."

"Well if I'm being honest Stevie, I was expecting it. As you probably know, it was running through my head last night. I figured if I dressed sexily this morning I might have more success."

"Well that went according to plan then."

"And I'm glad it did. Stevie, I was fantasizing about this ever since you left my office the day I removed your stitches."

"Really?"

"Yes, really."

"Wish I'd known that back then. I tell you, it would make our jobs a hell of a lot easier if we knew what you guys were thinking."

They kissed again, this time with a softness that had been missing from their wild session. It was true love. He loved her and she loved him. They might've only been together for an extremely short span, but it was hard to argue with love at first sight.

Too Much Drama

It had been two weeks to the day since their first date and Stevie was completely smitten, but he was feeling extremely uneasy. Becky had assured him that her future was with him and that Larry was no more than a distant memory, but he seemed to be hanging around like a bad smell. He could understand it in a way as she *was* the catch of a lifetime, but wished Larry would just take the hint and take a hike. It was becoming more and more annoying hearing virtually daily about the calls he was making to her as well as the love letters he'd sent, begging for forgiveness and a fresh start. Stevie didn't need the drama and wasn't in the mood for any confrontation. His holiday stabbing had mellowed out that side of him and he just wanted to get on with life without further complications, but Larry's constant presence was becoming overbearing.

It was Saturday night and Stevie called Becky at home but the phone was engaged. He contemplated calling her mobile but figured there was no point if she was on the other line. He tried again fifteen minutes later but it was still engaged. They were supposed to be going out together for a couple of drinks around 7:30 pm and it was already 7:20 pm. He took a quick shower and put on some clothes and tried her number again, but it was *still* busy. Stevie was mildly agitated she hadn't got in touch by now, so rather than sitting wondering in his living room, he headed out to The Crown for a couple of pints, figuring he would call again from there.

The bar had a fine scattering of people, but mainly regular male customers who'd ventured out on their own, probably as a brief reprieve from their home lives to relax with a few drinks and some chit-chat with familiar faces.

Stevie's usual seat at the bar was open which was no surprise. The regular drinkers were creatures of habit and seating arrangements during quieter times at the bar were not too distinct from the old sitcom Cheers. The boys often joked with Stevie that his parents should've had the foresight to christen him Norm.

He ordered up a Guinness from Sandra and called Becky from his mobile. Again it was engaged and he was becoming very impatient. He gulped down half his pint and sparked up a Marlboro, inhaling deeply, attempting to settle down his wandering mind. Perhaps it was an important call she was on. As sick as it was he even hoped someone had died or something and that Becky was taking time to sooth and comfort a friend or family member. Anything, regardless how severe, was a preference to Larry being the culprit.

He guzzled down the second half of his beer and ordered up another, which ended up empty even quicker than the first. He called again. The line was *still* busy. He decided to call her mobile anyway but it went to voicemail after four rings.

"Hey sweetheart it's Stevie. Just calling to see what's going on tonight. Give me a call as soon as you can."

His tone was pleasant. He wanted to give her a piece of his mind but refrained in case his earlier thought of someone dying was indeed the truth.

It was now 9:05 pm and he'd just signaled to Sandra to pour his sixth pint when his phone rang.

"Hey," he said in a downhearted voice.

"Hi Stevie, I'm *so* sorry for calling so late."

"I was beginning to get worried about you. I've been trying to get a hold of you since around seven o'clock."

"Again I'm really sorry. I've been on the phone for the entire time."

"Let me guess, fucking Larry."

There was a brief pause from Becky before she finally answered,

"Yeah, it was," replied Becky solemnly.

"Becky, this is getting out of hand and *really* starting to piss me off."

Stevie's voice was becoming more and more raised, and enough to prompt some attention from his fellow bar-side drinkers. Even Sandra's ears had perked up. He decided to take his troubles outside.

"Stevie, I don't know what to tell you. It wasn't like I called him."

"That's irrelevant Becky. We were supposed to be getting together around seven thirty tonight and you never even called. However, you found the time to spend two fucking hours on the phone with your loser ex-boyfriend who's supposed to be history.

I'll tell you what, this is *way* too much drama for me and I don't think I can do it any longer. This relationship is beginning to feel like a fucking threesome and there are way too many cocks involved for it to work for me."

'That's out of order Stevie. I've told you it's you I want to be with."

"Well be with me Becky. Sever all ties with this prick once and for all or I'm gone. I've *really* had enough of it."

Stevie loved her but meant every word.

"I know, and I've told him it has to stop."

"It took you two fucking hours to tell him that!"

"He was upset Stevie. I'm not trying to make excuses, but I was trying to convince him to move on. I told him he had to get on with his life as I was with you now, but for some reason he knew about you already. I guess word spreads fast or something. I do love you Stevie and don't want this thing with us to end. I really think we have something special going here and have a long-term future ahead of us."

There was such conviction to her words that they effectively calmed him down.

"I feel the same way, but understand, it's hard for me with him sniffing around you constantly. Put yourself in my shoes for a second. How would you feel if some crazy ex-girlfriend of mine was carrying on the same way?"

"It would drive me crazy."

"Exactly."

"Listen, I think he finally got the message. Anyway, I'm changing my mobile and home phone numbers first thing on Monday morning. That will prevent any more unwanted calls."

"OK Becky. Listen, I just want everything to work out without all these hassles."

"That's what I want as well. Can I still see you tonight?"

"I'm sure that can be arranged," said Stevie, his mood beginning to perk up. "I'm at The Crown right now if you want to come over and meet me?"

"I'm not really in the mood for drinking now. Would you be up for coming over to my place? I feel like just curling up on the couch with you and watching a DVD or something."

"I can do that, as long as you promise not to take any more calls from Larry while I'm there."

"Don't worry about that, he went out to work. He's nightshift tonight."

"Just as well for you," replied Stevie, a smile on his face that could be deciphered from his tone of voice. "Let me finish up my pint and I'll jump in a taxi."

"Perfect. I'm looking forward to seeing you."

"I am too sweetheart. Talk to you soon."

Stevie went back happily to his barstool and took a huge slug of his Guinness.

"You seem a lot cheerier than you were before you went outside," said Sandra.

"Yeah, woman trouble."

"Some things never change with you Stevie," said Sandra shaking her head, before heading off to serve a customer.

Stevie hastily polished off the remainder of his pint and headed down the main street to Village Taxi Cabs.

He let out a huge grunt as the taxi office came into view. The place was packed with young people waiting outside the rectangular Portakabin. Most of the folks – including Stevie – had a nice alcohol buzz going and were no doubt heading over to Hamilton to continue their evening adventures at the bars and clubs of the busier town. There were around thirty people in total and most of them no older than twenty one, with the exception of an elderly couple who looked disgusted at being caught up in such juvenile drink-infused rowdiness.

Deciding to take a chance anyway, Stevie pushed open the hickory old entrance door and was greeted by the balding middle-aged dispatcher with less than zero enthusiasm.

"How long for a taxi mate?"

"Forty five minutes to an hour," said the dispatcher smugly, almost smirking as he dished out the doom and gloom, likely happy for someone else to share the fun he was having.

"Fan-fucking-tastic. I'll take a rain check," replied Stevie, storming his way back out the door.

He squeezed his way carefully past four young women, being extra tentative as one of them was attempting the throw-up right there in the street. He was amazed how some of these kids insisted on making a night of things when it was clear they were hammered after two or three drinks. No wonder they probably woke-up in weird places at times, confused where they were, why there was a used condom on the floor beside the bed, and why their arse was causing them some discomfort. He chuckled though. Who was he to judge? That had been grossly similar to his care free modus operandi for many months, and had it not been for the timely intervention of Becky and Gordon's beer goggles to some extent, it may have been him again tonight.

He was a little tipsy as he headed back to his flat, but nothing compared to his usual over the top state. He passed by the side of the Tunnock's factory, taking the usual inhale of the caramel and chocolate fumes into his lungs. The smell was making him hungry as he hadn't eaten dinner yet.

The street as he neared his flat was verging on desolate; the only interruption to the quietness was the barks from a couple of neighborhood dogs. He felt as though his head was clearing a little as he neared the car park, making the mistake of eye-balling his little blue Citroen Saxo. He stopped dead in his tracks. Did he really want to head upstairs, find another taxi number, dial them and find out the wait was as long with their firm? The decision was made. He *didn't* want to go through the rigmarole of heading up to call as he knew it was going to result in certain disappointment, and didn't want to bother Becky with the hassle of coming over to pick him up either, so stupidly decided on driving himself.

Poor Peter Whiskers

Peter sat miserably at his computer desk, the bedroom bleak and dark even though there was a glimmer of daylight remaining outside. His dark blue curtains were drawn tightly and he'd even made the effort to overlap them slightly in order to filter out the long, fine, strip of light that was visible where the material met in the middle. His mood was darker than dark, and his plan had to be carried out with a level of secrecy usually reserved for a President being blown in his office by a chubby intern.

Tears filled his sad eyes; the bottom lashes battling to hold them back as effectively as a cardboard dam. A steady stream made its way down each cheek, meandering lethargically along and providing little relief to his warm and aching face. A few of the salty droplets splashed firmly onto the paper as he began composing his letter.

To Whoever Finds This,

I should never have been around long enough to write this. It should've been me hit and smashed to pieces exactly one year ago to this very day. It was my selfishness and disrespect that led to my father's death and I cannot take the guilt any further. My current life is a sack of depressing shit anyway and that's even when I put aside the emotional beating I give myself everyday.

My dad was a great man. He was tough on me, but now I see it was for my own good. If only I had realized this over a year ago. Compared to the hell my mother's new boyfriend puts me through he was nothing less than a saint. How could my mother move that sick bastard in so soon after my father's passing? She is a complete slut and I hate her and hope she suffers in the future.

I shouldn't have pushed him in the chest and I don't blame him for pushing me back much harder. He didn't know it would cause me to stumble into the road as that car was coming. He should've just let it hit me, but being the man he was he got there in time to push me out of the way before it crushed him.

It should have been me, and I cannot go on. I deserved to die, so that is what will happen today. PLEASE, PLEASE, PLEASE, take mercy on the random driver who hits me. IT IS NOT THEIR FAULT. THEY WILL HAVE NO TIME TO AVOID THE ACCIDENT. Take this note as evidence of my guilt and not theirs in any way. Maybe this is a selfish act, but I wanted to give the full story so that perhaps whoever finds this will understand and make the news public.

This will also be payback to my bitch of a mother who is ignoring the sexual abuse her boyfriend has been inflicting on me. I know she knows. He knows I will never tell the police due to the sheer embarrassment and humiliation of it all. When I am dead though I will not care who knows.

Again, be fair to the driver of the car who hits me. They are just a random victim, and should be made aware of these words so they can continue with a normal life without feelings of guilt and have a clear conscience for the rest of their days on this awful planet.

I just hope that if there is a God out there he will forgive me for my sins.

Bye,
Peter

PS - If there are any doubts about my claims of sexual abuse, check under the floorboards of my mother's bedroom cupboard. That dirty disgusting bastard of a boyfriend has been filming some of the stuff, and I'm not the only kid he has on tape. Please stop this sick wanker.

And with that, Peter folded the note and tucked it into his back pocket and nervously waited for nightfall before venturing out to the location of his father's death to reconstruct the events of that awful day.

Officer Jackson

What a night it had been for Officer Jackson; first on the scene of the horrific death of fourteen year old Peter Whiskers. He'd only been on the force for a couple of years, and although he'd seen dead bodies before, he'd never seen one so young so pulverized. At first he wasn't sure if it had been a young boy or girl. The face was bludgeoned red, dissected shockingly by the thick front bumper of Stevie's car. The blood was so fresh it was flaming red and just beginning to congeal.

Jackson hated drunk drivers with a passion. He hated drunk people in general. They were a constant pain in his arse and made up over eighty percent of the calls he responded to on the weekends. He hated how alcohol turned many average Joe's into complete pricks. He was no angel himself though, and a complete pot-head when not on duty, and there were a few limited occasions on slow midweek nights when he violated his "not on duty" policy, choosing to find a quiet and dark parking spot in the public park, puffing away and jerking off to the rhythm of the nearby cars filled with frisky young couples.

In his mind though, marijuana was a justifiable recreational activity and should've been legal anyway. He'd never been called to a violent scene as a result of two stoners beating the crap out of each other. It was a mellowing drug for him as well as every other user. The only damage he'd ever carried out on it was to destroy the contents of his entire fridge.

Jackson's mother was also a user. She was severely hampered by the effects of rheumatoid arthritis; her warped fingers appearing more like a couple of claws belonging to a horror film character. She was a kind woman and Jackson loved her dearly. He'd almost forced her to give it a try and was delighted by the rejuvenating impact on her pain as well as the positive spiritual affect it had on her fragile mind. It maddened him that the government was so dead against it and even considering moving it back to a class B category.

He was essentially above the law though and it was a cheap habit for him as well, never paying for any of the "gear," instead opting for depleting the supply held at the station from confiscations at rowdy parties or random street searches. All the officers helped themselves to this private stash, even the Chief Inspector was at it.

Peter Whiskers naked body had already been transported to the morgue for autopsy. As the first officer on the scene of the accident, Jackson had been put in charge of going through and documenting Peter's belongings. There wasn't much to speak of: clothes, wallet, cell phone, and an interestingly folded piece of paper in the back pocket of the jeans.

Stevie sat motionless in the cold and empty police cell. He stared at the dreary walls in disbelief. The only thing keeping him company was the eerie sound from a dripping water pipe. He may have been over the legal limit at the time of the accident, but he was certainly sober now, and the reality of the situation was beginning to sink in.

His eyes quickly filled with tears as he again pictured the battered and bloodied face of the poor young man lying on the road. He composed himself and wiped his eyes with the cuff of his now sweat-stained shirt. If only he'd been wearing his beer goggles. The kid had come out of nowhere, but Stevie was convinced the boy had smiled at him just prior to the haunting impact. It was as though he'd done it on purpose, but there was no way of proving it. His glasses would've given him the only outlet to possibly proving his innocence, but even then he was beginning to wonder if he had indeed imagined the kid's smile. Who would smile before piling head first into an oncoming car?

It was no random event that Larry Jackson happened to be first on the scene of the crime. He hated Stevie McDonald with a passion, and had been tailing him meticulously ever since Becky, the love of his life, had abandoned and replaced him with this drunken bum. Who the fuck did this loser think he was? Just stepping in and destroying his life together with Becky. Larry had been hoping to pin something on Stevie, but the events of the evening were way better than he could've imagined. He figured he may have got him on a drunk driving charge or perhaps something drug related that could've put him in jail for a short period of time or at least give him some ammunition to take back to Becky, to *really* show her he was a waste of space and that she should give it another chance with him. No excuses were needed now though. Stevie had just killed a boy and had blown over the legal limit. He was going down for manslaughter in addition to the drunk driving and was now going to be out of the picture for a long time.

Larry smiled to himself sadistically. He felt no sorrow for the young kid that Stevie had mowed down. He was glad. He didn't know the boy. He figured he was probably a loser anyway. All that he cared about was that Becky and he looked like they were going to have a future together after all.

Larry and the desk sergeant talked about the accident as Peter's belongings were recorded on paper by the older fat officer.

"Fucking drunk drivers, they really piss me off. Some poor young kid killed for nothing. I couldn't even imagine being the parents. Not sure I could handle coming here to identify a body and pick-up my kid's stuff," said the desk sergeant, shaking his head and fighting back his emotions.

"I know sergeant, it's unbelievable. My heart really goes out to the poor kid. He probably never saw it coming. By the looks of the body though I think he didn't know much about it. It's not much consolation, but I think he was dead on impact so at least he didn't have to suffer," said Larry, shaking his head and closing his eyes.

His distress appeared extremely convincing, but he'd closed his eyes to hide any signs of glee.

"Listen Larry, it's been a rough night for you kid. Let's get these belongings logged and you get yourself home and relax for the night."

"Good idea sergeant."

"OK, one pair of jeans, one t-shirt, one pair of shoes," rambled the sergeant to himself, noting them down on his checklist as Larry handed him the items one by one.

"One wallet, one photo ID," said the sergeant, again to himself.

The phone rang and he gave a huge sigh.

"Excuse me for a second Larry."

Larry was left holding the piece of paper from the back pocket of the jeans. He unfolded it and began to read. His previous joy quickly turned to horror. Stevie was innocent. It had been a suicide. He could still get him on drink driving charges, but so what. He might lose his license for a long time and have a hefty fine, but it was unlikely he would do any jail time. If he had a good lawyer he could play the trauma card anyway, asking the judge for leniency, stating Stevie was suffering enough due to having recurring dreams of the impact on his car, as well as pushing the issue that Stevie was indeed a victim himself. This was not good. Larry had to think fast. Stevie would just be going straight back to the arms of Becky. That could not happen. Larry loved her and had to have her back.

Larry read the remainder of the note as the desk sergeant was still on his phone call. He looked at the note, back at the sergeant, back at the note, then back at the sergeant again.

"OK chief, I'll take care of it," said the sergeant, before putting down the phone receiver.

Larry thought fast. What to do? He crumpled up the piece of paper like a shiny silver chewing gum wrapper and slipped it into his back pocket.

∾

Stevie sat behind the thick bars of his cell, his thoughts interchanging between the sound of the kid's head smashing against his front bumper, and Becky's beautiful face. There was a pungent smell of urine in the cold and grey room, but he was too preoccupied to notice. The tiny cell may have been chilly, but he was warm, sweating from every pore, flooding the alcohol from his system. It was too late for that though as the cop had already nailed him with the breathalyzer. He wanted Becky. He wanted her with him. He wanted her to tell him she was there for him through thick and thin. He sat upright momentarily but quickly slouched over, his head falling into his waiting moist palms. Why was this happening to him? For once in his life he'd found the path he was meant to take, the path to lead him to salvation, his yellow brick road, the junction leading away from the nightmares of his father's presence, the trail to a happy life. The detached house, the white picket fence, the two hyperactive cute kids screaming "daddy daddy," the SUV to transport them to daycare, and all the other shit with it that would complete his life. He'd learned so much from the beer goggles, but had still managed to ruin everything as a direct result of his drinking. He sobbed, but nobody was listening.

"I think everything is accounted for sergeant."

"No problem Larry. Listen, take yourself home, I'll get it from here. Go home and have a nice night with Becky and try to forget all the shit you've seen tonight. You'll feel a lot better in the morning."

Larry shed a crocodile tear, wiping his eyes with his white shirtsleeve as the desk sergeant gave him a sympathetic nod and he made his way out of the door. He smirked as he walked away; nobody knew Becky had broken things off with him and perhaps they never needed to know now.

"You take it easy," said the sergeant, seemingly feeling the pain Larry was apparently going through.

"I'll try sir," replied Larry, turning back to his senior with a put on smile on his face.

Larry made his way out of the station, debating with himself as to what he should do. He hit the cold open air of the street, heart pounding. He stared up at the full moon and took a packet of cigarettes from his trouser pocket and threw one of the Regal's into his mouth before reaching for his lighter. He paused for a second before sparking up and then reached for the crumpled up suicide note in his back pocket. He sucked heavily on his cigarette and opened up the creased note; using both hands to smooth it out as best he could. He began reading it one more time, looking occasionally over his shoulder to make sure nobody was around. He pictured Becky and Stevie being intimate together and it made his skin crawl. He visualized poor Peter Whiskers lying there in the road, soaked in blood and barely recognizable as a human being. The poor kid must've been going through so much in order to take such a radical course of action.

Larry looked over his shoulder again as he finished reading. The coast was clear. He flicked on his lighter and edged the flame over to the bottom right corner of the note. It started to burn, the fire furiously eating its way towards the top, dissolving Peter's words and all of Stevie's hopes at the same time. Larry let out a yelp as the traveling flame reached his thumb and index finger holding the top left corner, and he dropped the remains on the pavement, stomping frantically on them. The evidence was gone other than a small pile of smoldering ashes. He turned and made his way to his parked car in the station lot with a smirk on his face. He could hardly wait to call Becky with the tragic news that Stevie would be spending many years behind bars. Tomorrow though, he would be heading round to Peter Whiskers house to bust his mother's boyfriend on pedophile and child abuse charges. In his mind one good turn neutralized a bad turn and his conscience was clear.